_Lisa, Murray and +
Thank you.
Character n..... ....
for a bad guy. Your life-long friend,
Christi Corbett_

TAINTED
DREAMS

by

Christi Corbett

Clean Reads

GREAT STORIES. NO GUILT.

www.cleanreads.com

Tainted Dreams
by Christi Corbett
Published by Clean Reads
www.cleanreads.com

To My Mom

ACKNOWLEDGEMENTS

My Sincere Thanks to...

My family and friends, for your encouragement and support.

Kevin Hatfield, Adjunct Assistant Professor for the Department of History, University of Oregon, for taking the time to educate me on the countless challenges women faced when settling in Oregon Territory. Your advice and information allowed me to understand the real "legal loophole" in the Land Claims Law.

Douglas Card, for your insight into early Oregon.

My critique partners, Margo Kelly and Artemis Grey, for taking time away from your own writing to dig deep into my early drafts, for offering your in-depth analysis on character motivations, and for being there from the very first page of Kate and Jake's journey west. Mere words cannot express how grateful I am to have you both in my writing life.

My Content Editor, Nia Shay, for slogging through every page, and uncovering a ridiculous amount of errors and commas. Your attention to detail is phenomenal, and much appreciated!

My Beta Readers: Tracy Smith, Jenny Bloom, Michelle Naquin, Brenda Basham Newsome and Heather Trenk. For giving your opinions and suggestions to help make the book better.

The Ridge Writers, for providing insight and guidance with a smile, and for talking me down when I get frantic about word choice.

Jackie L. Meadows and Christie Nicholas, for lending me informative books that helped me portray Oregon with greater depth.

The staff at Mazama Sporting Goods, for sharing your knowledge about guns of the 1840's.

Scott Curry, Peter Bergin, and Megan Full, for helping me

figure out French.

"TV" Jeff, for keeping my virus-addicted computer limping along.

And finally, Stephanie Taylor, for making my writing dreams come true.

CHAPTER ONE
Oregon City

Wednesday, November 8, 1843

JAKE FITZPATRICK CLENCHED REINS AND SLAPPED flank as his horse thundered down the hillside overlooking Oregon City. His lovely Kate rode alongside him, her smile jubilant as she stood in her stirrups to take in the long-awaited sight of buildings and homes lining the banks of the Willamette River.

Together they'd survived and conquered the Oregon Trail. Six months and two shallow graves lay behind them, and now Oregon Territory and all its possibilities spread out before them.

Trail life was over.

Jake caught sight of the trampled grass path that led to the town's entrance and slowed his horse. Kate did the same. William and Margaret, a married couple who'd joined them during the last leg of the trail—rafting the dreaded Columbia River—gathered close behind with two packhorses in tow.

"We're about half a mile from a town that's neither settled, nor civilized," said Jake. "We'll ride in four across,

William and I on the outside."

"Why?" Margaret asked.

"Darkness tempts men who spend their day against a rail, tipping back false courage by the glass. Women are rare out here, and the rowdier men might approach for a closer look."

Jake's jaw tightened at the mere thought of someone hurting his precious Katie. Though she was only twenty-two years old, she'd already suffered a lifetime of sorrows. He was determined to protect her from any more unhappiness.

After they'd repositioned themselves four wide, William looked to Kate with a wistful frown. "I almost wish Margaret was dressed like you, Kate. No ruffian will give you a second glance."

Jake's eyes narrowed at the veiled insult, but Kate was quicker. "Impressive," she said.

"What?" William asked.

"How with one statement you've declared your value of propriety over safety, and insulted me—the woman who helped save your life not two weeks ago."

Jake chuckled softly as William stammered through a clumsy retraction. Kate had a fiery temper when riled, a fact he knew firsthand since he'd been on the receiving end of her ire a time or two. Judging by the set of her jaw, the next few minutes wouldn't bode well for William. However, instead of another biting retort, Kate merely looked to Jake with a sly smile.

"It seems my choice for comfort has yet another advantage." She patted her trouser-clad leg. "A disguise."

Jake knew different. Though she'd abandoned dresses and bonnets midway through their journey in favor of men's clothes, the sturdy attire couldn't hide her curves, and her father's hat did nothing to conceal the auburn curls trailing down her back.

While Kate graciously accepted William's apology, Jake

shifted in his saddle to check his rifle and pistol once again. The distraction helped tamp down the urge to pull her onto his saddle, to keep her where his arms or his gun could shield her from the hard days to come. She'd refuse, of course. After overcoming everything the trail had thrown her way, she'd fight him like a wildcat if he dared to suggest she cling to him instead of relying on her own abilities. Her stubborn strength made him love her all the more.

Jake forced a reassuring smile for the group. "Ready?"

They murmured their agreement and he started them off, keeping a slow, steady pace. A quarter-mile later William broke the silence. "I hadn't thought to ask before now, but do you two have a place to stay tonight?"

Kate turned to face Jake, her wide eyes betraying her trepidation. "I figured once I reached town I'd take up residence in the store my father purchased, but he never told me where it's located and the deed doesn't have a map."

William smiled sympathetically. "My uncle owns the town's hotel. He has a room waiting for me and Margaret. I'm sure two more won't be a problem."

Margaret snorted her disgust. "William, I refuse to live in a hotel for any longer than I must. We have to claim our land and build a home right away."

"My dear wife," William said, "right now we don't even have a blanket to our name. There's a bath and a bed waiting for us, and I'm not too eager to leave them for a frigid river or a bedroll anytime soon."

Jake pulled off his hat and eyed the brim, now stained with the sweat of hard miles and brutal decisions. He ran dirt-caked fingers through his stiff, shaggy hair, neglected of a proper washing for nearly a month and scissors for three. A hot bath certainly sounded appealing—it'd be his first in six months. Fresh clothes sounded even better. All but one of his shirts had been left trailside as tourniquets and bandages, his threadbare overcoat held more patches than a quilt, and he'd lost a boot heel rafting the Columbia. Any reputable cobbler would take one look at his boots and recommend the nearest burn pile. His hat and rank clothes should probably follow.

"A hotel would be much appreciated." Kate's saddle creaked as she twisted toward William. "Are you sure it won't be any trouble?"

"Given all you two have done for us, it's the least I can do," William said. "Well, that and settling up on the sixty dollars I owe for the raft fare. No need to worry; my uncle should be able to repay you tonight."

"Two rooms, then," Jake relented, taking note of smoke curling from chimneys and drifting across the darkening sky. While he'd intended on them camping outside of the city that night, Kate needed the protection and warmth of a hotel room, and he couldn't risk the money and deeds she carried in her pocket. "Kate and I will get cleaned up, and tomorrow after I collect what I'm owed we'll be on our way."

Once he recouped the money he'd lent William, he and Kate could leave town and start searching for the house her father had purchased before they'd left Virginia. He was eager to begin their new life together, starting with a proper proposal—something he should have done days ago.

Oregon City was just a momentary interruption to his well-laid plans. Plans for a future he hadn't had a chance to explain. A future with a woman who now sat stiff in her saddle, eyes forward and narrow, likely mulling over how he'd just answered for her.

"Of course, that's if she agrees," he amended.

Before she had a chance to forgive him, a man stumbled from the shadows of a building about twenty yards ahead.

Jake slid his rifle from its scabbard and laid it across his thighs, his finger waiting alongside the trigger. Given the man's staggering, he likely had only one thing on his mind—finding a place to sober up—but if trouble loomed, Jake intended to be ready.

All were silent as the stranger lurched across the road and then steadied himself against a lone pine tree on the left. With a gurgling groan, the man bent at the waist.

Jake's tension, and finger, eased. Any man content with splattering a day's wages onto the dirt posed no threat, except to himself.

He urged the group on and led them directly into Oregon City. On their left ran the Willamette River. A set of falls—small in size but powerful enough to support several mills—spanned a gentle curve in its course. The main street through town ran parallel to the river and consisted of mud and hoof-print-sized puddles of standing water. Boardwalks on either side provided relief to townsfolk who opted for traveling by foot instead of horse or wagon. Businesses and houses crowded together in a refreshing glimpse of progress and stability.

Jake's senses were overloaded with the massive changes that had taken place after the last time he'd left—in spring of 1841. While the smells and sounds were the same as his first two trips in, this time there was so much more to see.

More buildings. More two-story clapboard houses on the hillside across the river, their boards already weathered from exposure to endless misty rain. More horses lined up at hitching posts, their hooves shifting between pungent piles. And further down the street, there'd be more men milling through the saloon's swinging doors.

Jake leaned to Kate and spoke low. "Well, what do you think?"

She let out a shaky laugh. "It certainly is different."

Different indeed. They'd traveled across barren country for six months with only forts scattered along the way. The crudeness of a settlement striving toward civilization had to be a shock.

Beside him, Kate rode with tight lips, a straight spine, and her chin up. A stranger might peg her as steady and brave, but he knew her well. Very well. He saw her uncertainty as she took in darkened alleys and men lingering against building corners, tapping their pipes into barrels of musty, standing water. He saw her disgust as she stared at horse troughs, their outsides slick with mold, and kitchen gardens rife with weeds and neglect. However, most important to him was what he *didn't* see in her eyes.

Regret.

Angry shouts rang out from the alley near the blacksmith's building and Kate urged Nina, her prized mare, closer to him. Jake patted her hand, eager to reassure her of his protection, both now and for the rest of his life.

Men appeared from the shadows to stare openly at Kate and Margaret, but Jake detected only low, appreciative murmurs or indifferent shakes of their heads. Things changed a block later when they rode by a crowd of drunken men. Upon seeing the women, they lost interest in singing their loud, raucous songs in favor of catcalling.

Glares from Jake shut them up and he led his group past the leering, but now silent, men.

At the end of the block a man burst from the saloon and stumbled into the street, stopping mere inches from Jake's horse, Plug. Instead of backing away, the man lurched forward and reached for Jake's saddle horn.

"Hey there!" Jake said. Raising his left leg, he ignored the resulting twinge of pain and shoved the stranger aside with his boot heel. "Watch it!"

The man drew back and stared at him, his eyes bloodshot and unfocused. He raised an unsteady finger, slurred an unintelligible response, and then fell face-first into a patch of mud.

"Drunken fool," Jake muttered, then faced the others. "Let's keep moving."

High-pitched squealing foiled his plan.

On the upper deck of the saloon a horde of harlots stood

clustered together, giggling and shrieking as they pointed toward him. Clenching his jaw, he focused on the street ahead, all the while hoping Kate didn't notice one woman in particular who'd separated herself from the others and was now hanging over the railing, calling him by name.

Jake pressed his boot heels into Plug's side, urging him to a steady trot. Thankfully the others followed and they quickly left the saloon behind.

Minutes later, Kate motioned to the end of the street. "William, we're running out of road and I still don't see a hotel."

William pulled a rumpled paper from his pocket. He studied it briefly and then eyed the surrounding buildings. "My uncle sent me a rough sketch of where it's located, but there are so many new buildings, it's useless. Jake, do you know where it's at?"

Jake shook his head. "There wasn't a hotel the last time I was here."

"Perhaps one of those men sitting in front of the apothecary would know?" Margaret suggested.

"We'll find it ourselves," Jake replied. He led the group around the corner and onto the next street.

Buildings, so new their fresh pine scent still hung in the air, lined one side of the street while the other side held only two—an enormous livery and a two-story building with the word Hotel prominently displayed on a white sign with black lettering. A matching sign beside a light-rimmed window read Rooms Available by the Day or Week.

They dismounted, secured their horses to the empty hitching posts in front of the hotel, and headed for the door. William reached for the glass knob, then turned to the others with a worried frown.

"I haven't seen my uncle in over seven years, so I don't know what to expect. Though from what I've observed so far, living out west doesn't seem to improve manners." He stepped inside and ushered Margaret and Kate through the doorway. Jake followed them, then stopped cold.

Behind the hotel's front desk sat Theodore Martin—the one man Jake never wanted to see again as long as he lived.

CHAPTER TWO
Buried Memories

KATE ENTERED THE HOTEL LOBBY AND stood behind William and Margaret. While she waited for Jake to join her, she gazed around the spacious room.

Rag rugs dotted the gleaming pine board floor and a marble-topped oak desk sat in the back left corner. Navy plaid curtains on both windows—one overlooking the front steps and the other facing the alley—were pulled closed, yet the room was well lit by three oil lamps and warmed by flames flickering in the stone fireplace at the back wall.

Behind her, Jake shut the door and then stepped so close she felt the brim of her hat brush against his chest.

Jake—the man who'd hired on as her family's guide across the Oregon Trail.

Jake—the man who'd supported her through the darkest time of her life.

Jake—the man she loved.

"William! You're finally here!" The man Kate assumed to be William's uncle rose to his feet and hurried around the desk and across the room. Though by the creases around his eyes he looked to be in his early forties, he had hair the color of coal, broad shoulders, and a trim waist. His clothing, while outdated by nearly a decade, was impeccable, and a brown silk cravat perfectly arranged at his neck and embellished with a gold pin completed the outfit.

This man was a welcome change from the other men she'd seen so far in the town.

"I've been waiting for you to walk through that door for weeks." He grabbed William into a fierce hug, then pulled back to look at him again. "I was worried you'd run into trouble."

"We did," William replied.

"We?" William's uncle finally took note of the others lingering at his door. His eyes scanned the ragged group, narrowed briefly when they reached Jake, and then returned to his nephew.

William removed his hat and beckoned Margaret a few steps forward to join him. "Uncle Theodore, I'm proud to introduce you to my wife, Margaret. We married the day before departing from Independence."

Theodore took Margaret's hand and bowed with a grace and confidence Kate hadn't seen since the ballrooms of Virginia. "Please pardon my initial shock. My nephew is a lucky man to have a bride as lovely as you."

"Thank you," Margaret murmured, absently running her free hand along the curve of her waist.

"You're welcome." Theodore released her hand. "I consider it a privilege to have you as a member of our family." He straightened and eyed the lobby doorway, where Kate still waited with Jake at her back. His smile faded. "William, you mentioned trouble earlier, a fact that doesn't surprise me now that I see who you kept company with on the trail."

Kate's mouth dropped open. What had she or Jake done to offend this man?

"The return to civilization can be a tough adjustment."

Theodore motioned to William's bare head, then to his hat clutched against his leg. "I'm pleased to see you haven't forgotten the formalities of polite society."

Kate's cheeks flamed. Propriety had been ingrained in her since birth, but she'd only been wearing a man's hat since July—her father's hat, willed to her on his deathbed. While she had no intention of replacing it with a bonnet any time soon, she did intend to do her best to act according to society's conventions. She quickly pulled off the hat and ran her free hand from her forehead to her collar several times in a futile attempt to tame her wild curls.

Sighting Theodore's slack-jawed astonishment, Kate bit her tongue to stifle a laugh. He likely regretted his pointed words; she didn't need to further add to his embarrassment.

"Seems your companion has better manners than you." Theodore nodded toward Jake, who, to Kate's surprise, still hadn't removed his hat.

"Seems so," Jake replied, slowly pushing up the brim with one finger.

Kate kept quiet, but wondered what would possess Jake to purposely be so rude to someone he'd just met. Especially a prominent business owner, one that could potentially serve as an ally if she ran into trouble with her future plans.

"William," Theodore said, smoothly turning to address his nephew again, "who is this beautiful creature hiding beneath those ill-fitting clothes?"

William glanced at Jake and gave a nearly imperceptible shrug of apology, then focused again on his uncle. "I'm pleased to introduce Katherine Davis—"

"And the infamous trail guide, Jake Fitzpatrick," Theodore finished.

"You know each other?" William asked, his tone mirroring Kate's own surprise.

Jake gave a curt nod. "We've met."

"And then some." Theodore's laugh seemed more smug

than jovial. "We came across the trail together a few years ago."

Margaret clapped her hands together in delight. "Isn't that something? Two friends meet again after all this time."

"Friend isn't a word I'd use to describe him," Jake said, removing his hat and stepping beside Kate in one fluid move.

Kate wasn't fooled by Jake's bland expression. His white-knuckled hold on his hat brim and the vein throbbing in his ruddy neck told of his anger. Theodore's bright smile didn't fool her either. She'd seen the same one at dinner parties back home in Virginia. The smile one wore just before insulting an enemy—in a refined, witty manner, and usually in public. Granted the two men weren't suited for friendship, with Jake being a man of the land and Theodore a man of more refined tastes, but what had led to such an intense hatred of the other?

Theodore stepped before Kate and waited for her to present her hand. She complied, more from habit than desire.

"It's a pleasure to meet you, Katherine Davis." He lifted her hand and pressed the back to his lips. His warm breath against her bare skin startled her and she fought the impulse to yank her hand away.

But why? Countless men had kissed her hand at dinner parties and costume balls over the years, and this was no different. His actions were flawlessly executed and appropriate—he didn't linger, nor tickle her palm with a wandering finger.

The reality was she wanted no one to touch her but Jake.

Theodore lowered her hand, but instead of releasing the hold, he covered it with his other hand. "My dear, you are simply breathtaking. What a treasure it will be to have a woman like you-"

"You'll never have her." Jake punctuated the muttered warning by shifting his weight, allowing the full length of his body to press against Kate's side.

Predictably, like the gentleman he'd been bred and

trained to be, Theodore continued as if nothing were amiss. "—in my town."

CHAPTER THREE
Whispered Warnings

LONG AGO, JAKE'S FATHER TAUGHT HIM many things:

Words have power so use them wisely—especially when angry.

A man's reputation is all he's got in this world.

Avoid trouble, and those who seek it.

And when the last one proved impossible, he'd also taught Jake how to bust both the nose and cheekbone of an opponent with one smash of the fist.

"We need to see about the horses," he said, eyeing a mole on Theo's face, just above his left nostril.

"How many?" Theo asked William, who to Jake's surprise had done his best to blend into the wall during the past few minutes. Jake wouldn't have pegged him as timid, especially given the man's bravery on the trail. Time would tell which impression was correct.

"Six," William replied. "Four mounts and two packhorses."

Theo nodded. "I own the livery next door. You can leave them there as long as you need. There's a pump out back, plenty of fresh hay in the loft, and brushes and blankets in each stall. While I'm low on feed right now due to a late shipment, there should be enough for them to get their fill." Theo smiled and clapped his nephew on the back. "William, I'm pleased to see you're doing so well for yourself. Six horses are a fine asset, and that kind of money makes for a good start to a new marriage."

William shook his head. "We were on foot until we met Jake and Kate. The horses are theirs."

"Well then," —Theo's jovial smile faded as he faced Jake— "that's a different matter entirely. From what I recall of your financial standing I assume you'll need credit, which I don't extend. Really is too bad, especially since I own the sole livery in town."

Jake slipped his hand inside his coat pocket and fingered his wages earned from acting as Kate's trail guide—a thick stack of bills and a leather bag heavy with coins. "Any payment owed will be made on time, and in full."

"Of course," Theo said, smoothly abandoning his challenge. "Since the sun is about to take leave of the sky, I recommend you and William allow these young ladies to stay here with me while you tend to the animals. Can't be too careful, especially with all the ruffians roaming about town."

"Oh, I agree!" Margaret waved her hands in the air and began an animated retelling of the leering men they'd already encountered on the way in.

Two subtle, yet sharp pokes to his ribcage were quickly followed by Kate's whispered refusal of Theo's plan. And while the jealous side of him was overjoyed at her preference of tending to the horses with him over making small talk with Theo, Jake knew he couldn't allow it. She'd be safer indoors. Even with a snake in the grass like Theo.

With a polite smile and a demure shake of her head, Kate declined Margaret's invitation to assist with her story. Unfazed, Margaret blathered on again.

"Jake," Kate whispered, louder this time. "I know you

heard me. I'm going with you."

"No," he whispered in return. "It's not a good idea."

Kate pinched his arm. Hard.

He bit back a grin. What she lacked in patience, she certainly made up for in passion. Just thinking of the kiss they'd shared less than an hour before on the hilltop overlooking Oregon City had him shifting his stance to avoid embarrassment.

As Margaret continued her tale of woe, her descriptions and details growing more elaborate by the minute, Jake found a tempting distraction. One look at the woman he loved and for a few brief, glorious moments Jake forgot all his troubles and allowed his eyes to linger. To admire. To imagine.

"Jake, you haven't changed," Theo said, then pursed his lips in disgust. "Still willing to focus on a woman than the task at hand."

Kate stiffened, but remained silent.

"Perhaps you need a reminder of what can go wrong when your attention is waylaid by a pretty face?" Theo walked to his desk, lifted an oil lamp covering the front right corner, and traced a three-inch groove in the marble with his fingertip. "The damage done that day was permanent."

Jake knew the groove well. The moment it had happened was etched forever in his memory as the moment Theo had proven himself to be the type of man who valued property above all else, no matter the burden to his oxen or the danger to a fellow traveler.

One traveler in particular.

"I'm not here to relive the past," Jake said. "Though you'll do well to remember that the damage done that day to Collette's leg was permanent, too." He placed his hat on his head, tugged the brim into place, and lowered his lips to Kate's ear. "This time of night you're safer in this hotel than outdoors, but watch out. He's got the tongue of the devil and bite of a rattler."

Buttoning his coat tight against the raindrops he heard pelting against the window, Jake turned to William. "Coming?" he asked, not particularly caring about the answer.

William nodded.

"Take your time with the horses and don't worry about us three back here," Theo said, offering his elbows to Kate and Margaret, then grinning as they obligingly twined their hands around his forearms. "We'll be on the other side of those curtains," —he nodded toward a doorway covered by brown curtains— "in the parlor, getting to know each other."

As Jake watched the woman he loved walk away on the arm of the man he hated most in the world, he couldn't help but wonder if just once he should ignore his father's advice.

After all, there were few things Jake longed to hear more than the satisfying crunch of Theo's bone and cartilage giving way under his fist.

CHAPTER FOUR
Parlor Tricks

KATE CLOSED HER EYES AND INHALED deeply. The long-ago familiar smells of wood polish and cigars enveloped her in memories.

Virginia.

Father's study.

Family, and all she'd lost on the trail.

While Theodore fussed over Margaret, Kate stood quietly and allowed her gaze to roam around a room decorated in a simple yet elegant manner, with furnishings rivaling her own parlor back home in Virginia.

A patterned rug, likely imported from overseas, covered half the floor. On the opposite wall from the doorway, a bookshelf with over two-dozen titles stood to the right of a window, and a flat-topped canvas trunk trimmed with iron bands sat to the left. Centered in the room an oval mahogany table surrounded by three matching chairs. Scrollwork carved into the arms and legs begged for a fingertip to trace the intricate designs, though given the amount of dirt caked beneath Kate's fingernails and deep within the whorls of her fingertips, she didn't dare.

"Please, make yourselves comfortable." Theodore extended an arm in a practiced gesture toward the chairs. "I suspect you're exhausted from your recent weeks in the mountains and rafting down the Columbia."

Spoken like someone who'd made the journey by trail instead of ship. Kate wondered what had brought a cultured man like him across the trail to settle in a land that was neither owned nor governed by the United States of America.

More importantly, why Jake despised him so.

Kate eyed the three chairs Theodore urged them toward, taking special note of the upholstered seats. The cream-and-teal velvet didn't stand a chance against her rough, pungent clothes. Judging by the shrug of indecision Margaret gave Kate, she had similar thoughts.

Theodore noticed their hesitation and motioned to a pine bench against the wall. "Perhaps this would be better suited to your current attire?"

"I agree," Kate said, fighting the urge to tug the ragged ends of her coat sleeves over her hands and fasten the two remaining buttons over her dirt-streaked sweater, bought at Fort Boise over a month prior and worn every day since.

While Margaret took a seat on one end of the bench, Theodore picked up a thick stack of newspapers from the other end.

"Oregon City has a newspaper office?" Kate asked, excited at the thought. Back home in Virginia, she'd loved to curl up in a fireside chair and peruse the papers her father had shipped down from New York every week. Politics were her favorite subject, followed closely by business management and growth.

Theodore shook his head. "No, though Charlie Pickett has talked about doing one longhand until we can get a printing press out here." He set the papers on a nearby table, taking care to align their corners with a series of gentle, repetitive taps. "I brought these out from Boston."

Kate settled herself beside Margaret on the bench. Theodore turned one of the chairs to face them, sat, and then looked to Margaret. "How did you and William meet?"

In a voice breathy with newlywed excitement, Margaret prattled on about the first time she'd laid eyes on William and their subsequent wedding a few weeks later. When she launched into the complexities they'd faced buying supplies in Independence, Kate grew bored with the one-sided conversation and began looking around at her surroundings.

A table matching the one centered in the room sat against the left wall, with a tall china vase and two silver candlestick holders on top. A glance at the opposite wall revealed the source of the soft, rhythmic clicks she'd heard since stepping in the room—a wall clock, its gold pendulum swinging with rhythmic perfection, hung beside the bookshelf. Polished pine frames, hung by silk cords from the picture rails, held paintings of sweeping mountain ranges and stern men.

Getting everything in this parlor—and the lobby's marble-topped desk—across the trail in such pristine condition must have been a nightmare.

What a change in perspective she'd undergone since leaving Virginia! Six months ago such items had meant prosperity and luxury, now they represented the sacrifices undoubtedly made in the form of hunger, labor, and time. She'd learned that lesson the hard way on the bank of the Wabash River.

"And then when we reached Fort Laramie I was so relieved that I cried," Margaret said, showing no sign of concluding her animated chatter about her love for her husband and their plans for the future. To Kate's chagrin, Theodore caught her eye at the precise moment she raised the back of her hand to her lips to stifle a yawn.

Instead of acting affronted at her obvious distraction, he grinned.

"Margaret, my dear," he said, leaning forward to pat her hand, "I must interrupt your fascinating tale for a moment to ask if either of you would care for some tea?"

"Yes, please," Kate replied quickly.

"Very well," Theodore said, slipping his hand into his vest pocket. He removed a silver bell, held it aloft, and shook it three times. "I apologize for not thinking of it sooner."

Moments later a woman appeared through the brown curtains covering the doorway between the lobby and the parlor. Judging by the amount of grey in her hair and thickness at her waist, Kate pegged her age at early fifties, and the deep creases around her eyes and mouth hinted at a life lived with lots of laughter.

"They'd like some tea," Theodore said. "None for me, thank you."

She nodded, then stepped back through the curtain.

"Clara's is a sad story with a happy ending." Theodore slid the bell into his pocket, patted it twice, then leaned back in his chair. "She lost her husband during their journey and arrived here with nothing. I'm a widower myself, so once I heard of her misfortune I offered to provide her room and board in exchange for her taking on all the cooking and cleaning for my hotel."

As Kate wondered if Clara agreed with Theodore's earlier assertion of his goodwill, or if she viewed him as a man who'd taken advantage, a stunning realization hit hard. Without her father's foresight and planning, she would have faced a plight similar to Clara's. He'd seen to every last detail of starting a new life in Oregon City, including the advance purchase of a building on the main street and a house built on two acres outside of town.

Kate's hand drifted to her trouser pocket. Inside was her entire future, in the form of two deeds and a pocketbook with enough money to ensure she'd want for nothing for the next five years. Long enough to get her father's mercantile up and running, allowing her to turn the profits over to his ultimate dream for their lives in Oregon—starting a horse ranch.

He'd died in pursuit of his dream. A dream now up to her to fulfill.

"Ladies, your tea has arrived," Theodore said as Clara entered the parlor, tray in hand. Without a word, she crossed the room, placed the tray on the side table, then left again.

Theodore rose. "How do you take your tea?"

"A dash of cream and two sugars, please," Margaret answered.

"I'll have the same, thank you," Kate said, eager to enjoy tea again after months of surviving on river water or fire-scalded coffee.

Theodore went to the tray, and though his movements were partially hidden by his body, Kate could see he took his tea preparation seriously—precise pours of the cream, centering the sugar cubes over their cups before dropping them into the steaming liquid, and replacing the silver spoon in exactly the same position when he was done stirring. After an inordinate amount of time he finally returned to the bench, handed over two china cups with matching saucers, and then took his seat.

"How is it you two know Jake?" he asked, crossing one leg over the other and draping a hand upon his knee.

"My father hired him as our trail guide out here," Kate replied.

Theodore frowned. "Where is your father now?"

"He died along the way. As did my brother."

"I'm so sorry to hear of your misfortune." Theodore leaned a fraction too close to pat her hand a time too many. "You have my deepest sympathies, for I too know what it's like to be alone."

He was wrong. Kate had the support of a man who'd seen her through the worst times in her life. A man who'd held her as she cried over two graves, and then kept his word and guided her safely into Oregon City, and ultimately captured her heart.

"I'm not alone," she corrected with a tight smile. "I have Jake."

Theodore uncrossed his legs, rested his elbows on his knees, steepled his fingers together, and gave her a long, calculating look.

"Perhaps life in Oregon City will reveal other options besides a skirt-chasing cowhand. If I recall correctly, my last memory of Jake was watching him hightailing it out of town with two saloon girls hot on his tail."

After seeing the cluster of women pointing at Jake as he passed the town's saloon, she didn't doubt Theodore's revelation, but she also recalled Jake's warning about Theodore before leaving for the livery. *He's got the tongue of the devil and bite of a rattler.*

There'd been a time she hadn't trusted Jake's instincts, and her actions had put both their lives in danger. Ultimately he'd saved her from a horrific fate at the hands of a vile mountain man. Jake had earned her loyalty that day, and while she wouldn't defend him against something that had taken place years before they'd met, she refused to stand idly by while this man smeared his reputation into the dirt.

"Margaret, why don't you continue telling Mr. Martin about your journey?" She leveled a cool gaze at the man, ready to prove he wasn't the only one proficient in steering a conversation for personal benefit. "Be sure to include what Jake did less than ten minutes after meeting you and William."

Margaret nodded, eager to oblige Kate's request. "I really have Kate to thank. She's the one who saw me tumbling down the hillside, heading right for the Columbia River. And convinced those horrible men to land the raft."

"Horrible indeed," Kate agreed. "They wanted to charge William and Margaret triple the normal fare."

"Shame on them!" Theodore slapped his knee. "I detest

those who take advantage of the less fortunate. Though I would have gladly paid ten times the amount to ensure the safety of you and William."

Margaret continued. "Jake convinced the men to accept the regular fee. Then, when I told him we'd been robbed and left with nothing, he paid our way with a loan." Margaret laid her hand upon Kate's and gave it a gentle squeeze. "If it weren't for Kate and Jake, we wouldn't be here now."

"Yes, of course." Theodore nodded his agreement, then faced Kate with an expression she recognized as more calculating than sincere. "As you've probably gathered, Jake and I don't get along, mainly because I can't condone his past behavior. However, in this instance, I'm thankful he was willing to set aside our differences to help ensure the safe arrival of my dear family."

"I appreciate your candor, Mr. Martin," Kate said. He was a smooth talker indeed, given that Jake hadn't known of their relationship to Theodore before tonight. Jake had simply done what was right.

"Please, call me Theodore. While we're on the subject, William introduced you as Katherine, but I've heard Margaret call you Kate several times. Which do you prefer?"

Kate considered her answer. She'd been raised around men of his ilk and wasn't fooled by his brow, furrowed with feigned concern, nor his eyes that begged her to believe his words. However, she was about to be a business owner in a town where this man obviously carried a big influence, so it would behoove her to keep him an asset, not an enemy.

She forced a smile. "Kate is fine."

CHAPTER FIVE
A Chink in the Armor

FIVE WEEKS.

It had taken Jake five weeks, and saving Kate's family and all their possessions after their overloaded wagon sank in the Wabash River, before she'd allowed him to use the familiar address of Kate instead of Katherine.

She'd bestowed the same honor upon Theo in less than an hour.

Jake pulled the room-dividing curtains aside and stepped into the parlor, determined not to let his expression betray his unease.

Seeing her didn't help. Though she wore trail clothes and a week's worth of dirt, Kate seemed perfectly at ease in this parlor crammed with everything he'd fought Theo on bringing along. She even held a china cup full of tea on her lap!

His unease deepened.

She'd come from a life of luxury, and had left it all trailside. At his demand. Now she was again surrounded by items he could never provide, talking with a man who belittled anything or anyone that didn't benefit his self-serving interests.

"How disappointing to see the two of you back so soon," Theo said.

Jake took petty pleasure in noticing the man's hair, now cut short in an effort to disguise the thinning on top. At least there were some things money couldn't buy.

"These charming ladies and I were having such an enjoyable time getting acquainted," Theo said. "In fact, Margaret was just filling me in on your interesting adventures on the trail. Jake, it seems you've learned some shrewd negotiation skills since our last meeting."

Given Theo's tendency to twist the words and actions of others to suit himself, and never let an opportunity to slander a rival go to waste, Jake cast a glance to Kate.

She rewarded him with a smile that left no question her affections lay with him.

Doubt fled as fast as it had taken hold.

Theo rose from his chair and crossed the room to stand with Jake and William. After casting a discreet, sidelong glance at the women to make certain they were watching, he made a grand show of removing a white handkerchief from his pocket and blotting his eyes.

"Jake, my nephew and his bride are the only family I have left, and I…"

As he trailed off, seemingly overcome with grief or fright, Margaret cooed sympathetic nonsense from the bench and William slid a comforting arm around his uncle's shoulders. Seconds later, Theo put up a hand to show he'd collected himself enough to continue.

"Jake, I've already let Kate know how grateful I am to her for saving their lives, and now I must offer you the same."

Jake stayed silent and kept still. This man was a proficient gambler, capable of keeping a face of stone for hours should the need arise. His display of emotion had a reason, and it wasn't gratitude.

Theo folded the dry handkerchief, returned it to his pocket, and focused on Jake. "Please, let me know if there is ever anything I can do for you."

"It was an honor to do it and I expect nothing in return," Jake said.

"On the contrary, I hear you *do* expect something in return," Theo said, then turned and faced William. "We have a financial matter to discuss?"

Margaret hopped to her feet, her brow creased with worry. "William, perhaps it wasn't my place to do so, but I mentioned our debt we owe to Jake."

William sighed. "I'm sorry, Uncle Theodore, but if we didn't get on that raft I would have died, leaving Margaret alone and unprotected in the wilderness."

"What are the terms?" asked Theo, ever the businessman.

"The fare was sixty dollars. Jake expects repayment tonight."

Jake's eyes narrowed at the use of the word "expects," especially since William had been the one who'd suggested the timeframe. He opened his mouth, prepared to correct William's view on the matter, but Theo spoke first.

"Jake, you and Kate shall dine as my guests tomorrow morning for breakfast. I'll have the money for you then. In the meantime, have you considered where you'll stay for the night?"

As much as Jake hated to be under the man's roof, he wanted Kate to have the protection it provided. "We'll take two rooms."

"Two rooms?" Theo's eyebrows rose in surprise, and then his lips curled into a wolfish grin. "I will check with Clara right away." He slipped through the curtains and disappeared into the lobby.

Guilt hit Jake. He'd allowed himself to doubt Kate's affections when she'd given him no reason to do so. In fact, given Theo's reaction to his request for separate rooms, Kate must have implied they were married, or at least courting. He'd been so caught up in his own issues with Theo that he'd lost sight of what was most important—starting a life with Kate.

Theo returned. "I have one room available."

Kate eyed him with a worried frown. "One?"

"I'm sorry," Theo said, raising a shoulder in an apologetic shrug. "We're booked through the rest of the month. There's such a rush of people coming in that I can't keep a room empty for more than a few hours, except for the one I've saved for William's arrival. I have this one because the man occupying it was killed in a gunfight this afternoon. Kate, after Clara clears out his things, the room is yours for the rest of the week."

Kate's eyes were like windows into the battle raging within—stay in the comfort of a hotel without him, or camp outside of town with only him?

While they'd spent nearly every waking moment together on the trail and slept beside each other every night, their time in town would be a different matter. Jake had no intention of inviting speculation as to Kate's reputation.

Before she could utter a word, he saved her from herself. "I'll see you to your room, and then I'll be back in the morning."

"But it's raining, and cold, and I want..." Kate's voiced faded as she likely realized the futility of protesting. Even out west, there was still an expectation for a single woman to maintain a certain level of propriety.

Never one to miss an opportunity to impress, Theo tapped a finger against his pursed lips a few times, then snapped his fingers as if brilliance had suddenly struck. "I don't know why I didn't think of it earlier. There's a space at the end of the upstairs hallway. I typically keep extra supplies there, but you're welcome to it."

Jake had an idea of what kind of space Theo was offering

him—likely a cramped closet that held bedpans awaiting an emptying—but it was late, he was exhausted, and at least he'd be out of the weather and close to Kate.

Tomorrow he'd find a more suitable arrangement. And a preacher.

"Margaret, are you all right?" William crossed the room to the bench and kneeled before his wife, whose cheeks had paled considerably.

"I'm just overwhelmed with everything," she replied, her tone wavering between desperation and fear. "Especially hearing there's a man who's just been killed that was staying in this hotel!"

She bent at the waist and hid her face in her hands. As the first of many muffled sobs filled the air, Kate rose from the bench and motioned for William to take her place. He slid beside his wife and began murmuring comforts and reassurances.

"Forgive me," Theo said after she'd regained her composure. "I wasn't trying to upset or scare you. But now that the topic has been raised, you'd all do well to understand Oregon Territory is a wild place, filled with wild men. Until we are accepted for statehood—which brings with it the strength and enforcement of federal laws—mayhem and murder are a way of life out here."

Theo pulled a gold pocket watch from his vest pocket, flicked it open, and then checked the time against the wall clock.

"It's getting late and I still have a few things I need to get done before I retire for the evening, so I'll show you to your rooms now," he said, closing the watch and returning it to his pocket. "I'm sure you want to get settled in after your trip. Baths are taken in a room off the kitchen. Clara handles heating the water—" he paused to again check the time, then shook his head, "—but she's done for the day, so you'll need to wait until tomorrow."

While he returned his watch to his pocket, Jake and the others gathered their belongings. With Theo leading the way and Jake bringing up the rear, the group headed back into the lobby and then through another doorway at the back of the room. They walked past a kitchen on the left and the dining room on the right, then several closed doors on either side of the narrow hallway.

Theo stopped at the last door on the right.

"William and Margaret, I've had quite a time keeping this empty for you." He unlocked the door and pushed it open, revealing a wallpapered room with a brass bed, plump pillows, a colorful quilt, a three-paneled dressing screen in the corner, a washstand with a basin and pitcher, a dried flower arrangement sitting on the dresser, and two cozy chairs positioned near the window.

"It's perfect," Margaret said, stepping inside. "Thank you so much."

"Breakfast is served promptly at seven-thirty in the morning. I'll see you then." Theo handed the key to William as he slipped through the doorway to join his wife. He shut the door behind them and then eyed Kate's saddlebags she'd hoisted over her shoulders.

"Where are my manners? I'll take those for you." He reached to retrieve them, but she sidled beyond his grasp.

"I prefer to carry them myself, thank you."

"Suit yourself." His tone was pleasant, but his expression told of his irritation at the snub. As did his stomping up the staircase.

Jake grinned all the way to the second floor. Kate was stubborn to a fault when it came to carrying her own saddlebags, a lesson he'd learned long ago.

Theo led them down the dimly lit hallway, then stopped at the last door on the left.

"The lock's broken," Theo said, opening the door with a quick twist of the glass knob. "It's nothing fancy, but it's clean."

"Thank you," replied Kate.

Jake looked over her shoulder and saw a room that was sparsely furnished, yet contained the basic necessities—thick mattress on a sturdy pine frame, chair, a bi-fold screen to wash and dress behind, and a table with an oil lamp. A cracked mirror hung on the wall above a washstand that held a floral patterned basin with matching pitcher and a stack of thick white towels. Though the bed was bare, folded linens and two pillows sat at the end.

When Theo stepped inside to light the lamp, Jake leaned to her ear. "I'll miss you tonight," he whispered.

She smiled, but Theo's return prevented any response.

"There's fresh water in the pitcher," he said, sweeping his arm over the room and then settling his hand on the knob. "Clara will bring you more tomorrow at first light."

Kate slipped past Theo and into the room. Once inside, she turned. Her eyes sought Jake's and betrayed her uncertainty at leaving him.

"Goodnight, Jake."

"Goodnight," Theo said, then shut the door before Jake could reply.

Jake clenched, then restrained his fists, settling instead on adding this latest action to the growing list of reasons— starting with breaking Collette's leg—why he'd have no qualms about one day giving Theo the thrashing he deserved.

Theo let go of the knob and then stepped into a small alcove across the hall. Ignoring Jake, he rummaged through items on a shelf until he found a basket of stubby candles destined to be melted down during the next candle-making session. He lit one and placed it carefully in a holder, scorching his finger in the process, much to Jake's amusement.

That amusement faded when the flickering flame revealed his earlier prediction as correct—the space was little more than a cluttered supply closet. The floor was littered with piles of used linens, and dirty towels were heaped upon the sole piece of furniture—a dilapidated wooden chair that looked more suited for a burn pile than a hotel.

"As I see it, you've got two options," Theo said, turning to him. "You can bed down for the night in here. Or, since you probably prefer the company of animals, you're welcome to make yourself comfortable in my livery."

Jake briefly considered the wisdom of letting at least one punch fly right then, but ultimately decided Kate would open her door and question the ruckus. On the day he and Theo finally settled their long-running feud, he wanted no chance of interruption.

"Here will do," he said.

"I figured," Theo said. "Since no guests come to the end of this hallway, no one will be the wiser should Kate desire your—" he tilted his head as if unable to think of the correct word, then continued with a smirk, "—assistance."

Jake stepped forward until Theo's nose was less than an inch from his chest, forcing the man to look up to meet his glare.

"Don't question her honor, or her innocence. Ever."

Theo backed away, mumbling under his breath about Jake being too simple-minded to understand what he'd meant. After a few steps he executed a quick turn. His fast and firm footsteps echoed down the hall as he headed toward the staircase. Then he was gone.

Jake grabbed the back of the chair and tipped it forward until the stained towels cascaded to the floor. He spun it on one leg until it faced Kate's door, then sat in stages, gingerly testing if the wood would hold his full weight.

It promised to be a long night.

CHAPTER SIX
Propriety's Influence

KATE TUCKED THE BACK OF THE WOODEN chair under the doorknob, then stood in the middle of the room, saddlebags in hand, willing her mind to let go of all this moment could have been. Should have been.

Her father in the next room going over his extensive lists, checking and rechecking every detail, no matter how minor, of each step of his grand plan to open a mercantile in Oregon City. Her dear brother Ben traipsing between their doorways, babbling excitedly about all they'd seen that day and what was next to come.

As she'd done countless times since their horrific deaths, Kate closed her eyes and thought again of Jake's words of encouragement and comfort he'd spoken to her on a moonlit night months ago.

The night she'd finally overcome the mind-numbing pain and shock that had threatened to pull her down forever. The night she'd realized moving on wasn't a betrayal to her family, but instead the best way to honor their memory. The night she'd chosen to ride away from all she'd ever known, and head toward everything she'd ever wanted.

A long, slow creak from a floorboard in the hall set her nerves on edge, especially when a glimpse between the door and threshold revealed shadows. Her eyes never left the doorknob as she slowly crouched and lowered her saddlebags to the floor. Slipping her hand beneath the flap covering one of the bags, she fumbled inside until she felt the familiar leather sheath. After palming the handle of her knife, she straightened.

First priority tomorrow morning would be retrieving her father's rifle from Jake.

Another creak of the floorboard.

Kate crept to the door, her left hand extended toward the glass knob, intent on holding fast should it begin to turn. Her right hand hung at her side, concealing the blade within the loose folds of her trousers.

"Who's there?" she bellowed, doing her best to keep her tone low and abrasive despite the fear closing her throat like a vise.

"Me," replied the voice she knew so well.

She let out her relief in one long breath, then pulled the chair out from under the knob. She opened the door and smiled at the man standing there, as always, steadfast in his silent support and protection.

"Jake, is everything all right?"

"Yes," he said, eyeing the knife in her trembling hand. "Is everything all right with you?"

Knowing Jake would see through any false bravado, she spoke honestly. "I got scared. I can't stop thinking about Theodore's speech earlier about wild men, especially given the debauchery I saw firsthand as we arrived."

She crossed the room to put the knife back in its sheath. Returning to the doorway, she motioned to the chair. "The lock is indeed broken, and this won't hold up against drunken persistence."

Jake eyed the glass knob and keyhole. "Town's got a blacksmith so there's no good reason why Theo won't be getting this fixed tomorrow. Until then, you've got no need to worry. I can see your door from where I'll be, and I have no intention of making the same mistake I did the night that degenerate cut the barge ropes."

Bile rose in Kate's throat and she swallowed hard, recalling Henrick's breath, rank and warm against her cheek, and his brutal strength that yielded only to Jake's gun.

In truth, the mistake had been hers. One she'd almost paid dearly for.

She raised her eyes to meet Jake's, striving for bravery but at the same time thinking of the town's men stumbling toward her, brazen with curiosity and drink.

"I'll protect you, Kate." Jake gently captured her hands in his and pulled her close. "Tonight, and for always."

"I know," she whispered.

Silence reigned between them until Jake shifted his weight and focused over her shoulder at the room. "I better let you unpack and get settled in for the night. I'll be by in the morning to escort you to breakfast."

She frowned, then looked from one end of the hallway to other. "Where are you sleeping?"

"Don't worry about me," Jake said, brushing off her question with a smile and a shake of his head. "Do *you* have everything you need?"

Kate wasn't fooled by his attempted distraction and leaned to peer around him. Shock grew to anger as she spotted Jake's saddlebags in an alcove across the hall, dumped in a dusty heap beside a rickety chair.

"Is that the 'space' Theodore provided for you?" she demanded.

Jake stayed silent, but his flaring nostrils and ruddy cheeks hinted at his resentment.

She shook her head, stunned at Theodore's gall to be so

blatantly rude and disrespectful. And at Jake's willingness to tolerate it.

"You certainly can't sleep on that," she said, pointing to the chair in disgust. "Grab your things. You'll share my room."

"I can't," he said.

"You deserve a good night's sleep just the same as I."

"Your reputation is far more important than my comfort."

"My reputation?" she scoffed. "Here, where saloon women holler their bedroom talents to men on the street?"

"Kate, there are good people in this town," Jake replied, his tone betraying his exasperation and exhaustion. "You need to consider them, and the impression my staying in your room would give."

"We've been together every night for the past six months," she said, frustration warming her cheeks. "Why is tonight any different?"

"Because what happened on the trail left us alone, with no choice. This is different and we both know it."

The harsh reminder hit hard. She still hadn't escaped the confining customs of Virginia; they persevered here in Oregon Territory. Perhaps not as diligently followed, but those who dared to demand respite were apparently still shunned.

The realization infuriated, and then empowered.

"Jake, I'm a grown woman, fully capable of making my own decisions on what constitutes a lifelong mistake, and inviting you into my room certainly isn't one. You've proven yourself to be a man of honor on countless occasions and you don't need a hotel door between us to continue."

She crossed her arms and raised her brows.

"I didn't travel thousands of miles only to again allow the opinions of others to dictate my life, so let's be practical. You can't sleep on a chair, and given the amount of shouting—and possibly gunshots—I've heard since stepping foot in this room, neither one of us will get much sleep. We can spend this time unpacking and sorting through our supplies."

Without another word, Jake walked across the hall, shouldered his saddlebags and rifle, and then stepped back into her room.

CHAPTER SEVEN
Tethers Deferred

JAKE CLOSED THE DOOR BEHIND HIM, wedged the chair beneath the knob, and settled his saddlebags and rifle against the nearest corner. Kate stood at the end of the bed, her hands fisted so tight at her sides her knuckles gleamed white, her expression both one of triumph and trepidation. Perhaps wavering in her choice of invitation?

If so, she wasn't the only one.

Yes, he could twist words and intentions. Pretend his presence was the only way to relieve the terror he'd seen in her eyes when she'd first opened the door, knife clutched in hand. Convince himself that tonight was no different than those last few months on the trail.

However, one simple fact remained. He'd promised Elijah he'd watch over his daughter, and at the first opportunity he'd made a choice that risked Kate ridicule—or worse—should Theo or anyone else learn of their sleeping arrangements.

"I'll bed down on the floor tonight, and leave before Clara brings you more water at dawn," Jake said.

In the morning he'd make certain the door lock would be fixed and then sleep elsewhere—hopefully in the house her father had purchased before they'd left Virginia. She could remain at the hotel while he concentrated on any repairs the house might need. The situation wasn't ideal, but until they were married, they had no other viable option.

Theo was the only thing stopping him from bending a knee right then. No way did Jake want to associate the moment he declared his lifelong intentions to Kate with having taken place under that man's roof.

Tomorrow. Tomorrow he'd propose.

They began unpacking and sorting the contents of their saddlebags, an arduous and at times sobering task given all the memories uncovered. Though most of the keepsakes she'd brought along had survived intact, she was especially disheartened to discover the two dresses she'd wrapped tight and placed in the bottom of one bag were spotted with mold and smelled of wet leather.

"I believe a visit to the town's dressmaker will be in order, sooner rather than later I'm afraid," Kate said, inspecting the calico dress she'd worn during their time with the wagon train. With a sigh, she crumpled the shredded, stained fabric and tossed it into the corner without ceremony. "It doesn't look much like a hotel room now, does it?"

Jake nodded his agreement. Supplies and airing bedrolls littered every surface, be it tabletop or floor, and their clothes were draped over a line he'd strung between the bedposts along the length of the bed.

He walked to the window and peered outside. "It's late. Are you tired?"

"Yes," she answered, then reached for the stack of neatly folded linens on the end of the mattress and began making up the bed. As she smoothed a sheet over the mattress, Jake grabbed the other sheet and watched in dismay as the two pillows and quilt tumbled to the floor.

"Seems I'm better suited to a bedroll beside a fire," he said, then chuckled at his clumsiness.

Together they finished making up the bed, then discovered yet another challenge—changing into their nightclothes. On the trail they'd been able to walk away from the fire to dress under the cover of darkness, but here there was only a rickety screen.

They looked at each other and laughed.

"We could put the lamp out and change in the dark," Kate ventured. "Or you can wait in the hallway while I freshen up, and I'll do the same for you."

"I'll give you the room, but when it's my turn I'd prefer you stay while I use the screen. No sense in you standing alone in the hallway."

She quickly agreed and Jake stepped into the hall.

Minutes later she called for his return, and then sat on the bed with her back to the dressing screen. He entered, washed and redressed quickly, then leaned over and blew out the lamp. They fumbled their way into their respective beds—his being blankets on the floor—and prepared for sleep.

****

Kate lay in the bed, listening. All the noise in town was quite a change from what she had become accustomed to over the past six months. Piano music complimented with boisterous, out-of-tune singing and the occasional outburst of harsh words made sleep impossible. Things were obviously different here, including the idea of being quiet at night. She dozed fitfully for a few hours, then gave up entirely after a fierce argument took place on the street below their window.

"Can't sleep?" Jake's whisper carried easily through the wall of airing clothes hanging between her bed and his space on the floor.

"How did you know?"

"I've listened to you toss and turn since I blew out the lamp." Jake chuckled. "I can't sleep either. I keep thinking I need to feed the fire and check on the horses."

"It's impossible with all that noise. The howling of wolves isn't nearly as scary as what I'm hearing on the street."

"I forgot how rowdy it gets come nightfall," Jake said.

"What time is it?"

Jake rose from his blankets, picked up her father's pocket watch from the washstand, and headed to the window above her bed. Pulling the curtain aside, he tipped the watch face into the moonlight.

"A few minutes after two. Those men should calm down in the next hour or so. It takes hard work to get through even one day here, and the tension and worry can bring out the worst in some men."

He dropped the window curtain into place and Kate heard the soft clink of him returning the pocket watch to the washstand, then the rustling of him sliding beneath his blankets.

"Kate, you'll find that most of the time arguments are all bluster and no bite."

She seized the opportunity to finally ask the question that had plagued her since they'd stepped foot in the hotel's lobby. "What about you and Theodore?"

"What are you implying?"

"You two obviously don't get along, and I get the feeling it goes deeper than simple blustering between two men. What happened?"

"A story for another day," Jake replied, his easy words at odds with his cold, unyielding tone.

She didn't pursue it, choosing instead to move to something else on her mind. "Jake, earlier today when we were standing on the hillside overlooking the city, I didn't have a chance to finish telling you what I wanted to say."

She hadn't finished because she'd been interrupted—by

his kiss.

Her first true kiss, if she didn't count the one Crandall had stolen after a church social when she'd been twenty-one. And she certainly would never compare a quick peck on her cheek with the kiss she and Jake had shared only hours ago.

"What's on your mind?" he asked quietly.

She sat up in the bed and opened the window curtain, allowing moonlight to spill into the room. But seeing the room wasn't enough. She wanted to see his face, so she slipped her hands between two shirts hanging on the line between them and eased them aside.

Jake lay facing her, his head propped against his hand.

"These past few months haven't been easy," she said. "It turned out to be quite a different trip than you signed up for."

"That it has," he said simply.

"We've both changed since those first days on the trail."

"I agree."

"You were mean when I first met you."

He chuckled softly. "I suppose, but what about now?"

"Now you're...not." This wasn't going at all like she'd planned.

"What do you really want to tell me, Kate?"

So many things. She wanted to tell him how she was trying to envision a future without her family—a future her father had planned to the smallest detail, but had died before sharing any of his arrangements with her. She wanted to tell him her unease of how the success, or failure, of her father's plan lay squarely on her inept shoulders.

Most of all, she wanted to tell him how she'd been waiting for something since their kiss. Actually, if she were being honest with herself, she'd waited for it since the Columbia River as they'd lain together on the raft, soaking wet and trembling with fear for the life that had almost been lost that day.

How could she tell him she was waiting for his proposal

of marriage? After all, that was the next logical step, wasn't it? She thought so, especially given his words to her just before he'd pressed his lips to hers.

I'd love nothing more than to be by your side and share a life together with you.

Silence reigned between them, and eventually her nervousness subsided into an overwhelming urge to slide her hands around Jake's waist and kiss him again. As she leaned closer to where he lay, her eyes locked with his and then fluttered closed.

To her chagrin, aside from an awkward clearing of his throat, Jake remained still.

She opened her eyes.

"I wanted to tell you…" She faltered, and ultimately lost her courage. "I wanted to tell you I have an extra pillow, and you're welcome to it," she said, blinking back her rising frustration, and humiliation.

Jake took the offered pillow, then reached up to the clothesline and slid the shirts together again.

"Goodnight, Katie," he said softly.

Silence again settled over the room.

Kate slumped against her pillow, more confused than ever. After all, it wasn't as if she'd asked him to share her bed. Yet. She'd just wanted another kiss.

Hours ago she'd been certain of Jake's feelings, and now she couldn't stop thinking of the raven-haired beauty calling him by name as they'd passed the saloon.

CHAPTER EIGHT

Plans and a Promise

Thursday, November 9, 1843

Kate woke to a long forgotten sound—someone knocking at her door. A peek through the shirts on the clothesline by the bed revealed Jake was gone. His blankets were folded and stacked neatly in the corner.

"Who is it?" she called, scrambling from beneath the quilt and running across the room to the dressing screen.

"Clara."

"I'll be there in just a moment," Kate answered, pulling on her trousers. After slipping into her shirt, she fumbled the important buttons into place and then opened the door.

Clara stood in the hallway with a pitcher of steaming water in one hand and fresh towels and a small bar of soap in the other. "Sorry to wake you, but Theodore insisted you have these before I serve breakfast."

"Please, come in," Kate said, reaching to relieve her of the pitcher. The woman's smile was friendly, but judging by her tired eyes she'd already been working for hours.

Clara stepped into the room and settled her offerings on

the washbasin table. Turning, she eyed Jake's saddlebags against the wall and then his folded blankets, but thankfully made no comment.

"I appreciate you bringing these by." Kate plucked the soap from the towels and held it to her nose. The lavender scent brought back memories of her nightly baths back home in Virginia. "I didn't get a chance to do much more than wash my face and hands last night."

Clara scooped up the towels she and Jake had used, then continued. "Of course, sponge baths aren't any kind of substitute for the real thing. Which brings me to what else I came here for—Theodore wanted me to remind you of our bathing room downstairs off the kitchen. There's a tin tub, heated water, and I can help rinse your hair if you'd like. You interested?"

"Yes, of course," Kate said eagerly. "Except..." She sighed as she recalled the state of her wardrobe. "The only thing I have that isn't filthy rags is my nightgown. I hate to waste such a luxury like bathing by dressing again in my trail clothes immediately after."

Clara frowned. "You didn't bring anything?"

"A simple calico dress and two fancy ones, but before they're presentable they'll need to be washed. I learned how on the trail, but I don't know how practical doing so would be given that I'm in a hotel. Is there a woman who takes in laundry in town? Or a dressmaker?"

"Neither." Clara shifted the dirty towels to her other arm. "I'll let you use the kitchen to wash what you need, but you've got to clean up after yourself. I've got enough to do already; can't take on more messes."

"Oh, thank you so much for your kindness!"

"I need to get downstairs. Theodore expects breakfast promptly at seven-thirty, and doesn't take kindly to late arrivals."

Clara picked up Kate's empty water pitcher from the

previous night and headed for the doorway, where Jake now lingered. "Young man, the floor in here gets cold in winter. There's more blankets downstairs if you need them."

Jake grinned and tipped his hat as she passed. "Ma'am."

"She's a lively one," Kate said, uncertain whether to laugh or cringe at Clara's obvious knowledge of her and Jake's secret.

"I'll say," Jake said, removing his hat altogether and running his hand over his hair in an effort to smooth his stiff, shaggy waves. Kate wondered if Theodore had made him the same offer to use the bathing room.

"I've checked on the horses and they're doing fine," he added. "Ready for breakfast?"

"Yes," she replied, beckoning him inside with a wave of her hand, "but I want to show you something before we go."

****

Jake stepped into the room and shut the door. No sense risking another guest wandering by and hearing their conversation. Or Theo.

"I don't want to keep the deeds, or father's money, in my saddlebags or hidden in this room. I can't chance losing them."

"Smart thinking," he said, still wondering why she'd called him into the room.

"I want to get the store up and running as soon as possible," she said, pulling from her pants pocket the familiar butter-yellow envelope with the red wax seal— the one Jake had taken from her father minutes before his death.

He nodded. "I agree."

"I'm thinking by the end of the week. There won't be anything on the shelves, but I can at least introduce myself to fellow business owners and potential customers."

Leave it to Kate to have a plan in place.

"As for getting supplies to sell, my father didn't tell me much about his plans, but I know contracts are already in place with some of his most trusted suppliers, and next spring he'd arranged for two wagons to deliver supplies. An additional three wagons are expected a few months later."

Jake nodded again, impressed with her control of the situation. Where exactly in these well-laid plans did he fit in?

"Trouble is," she continued, "I don't know where the store is located. Or the house." She reached inside the envelope and brought out two official-looking documents. "I think one is the deed and bill of sale to the store, and the other one is the deed to the house and land. I can't decipher the codes at the top of either, or where the small map on the top corner of the house deed leads to. Can you help me understand?"

Jake took the offered papers, unfolded both, and laid them flat on the bed. After a brief inspection, he was as confused as Kate. This was far beyond his realm of experience.

"My best guess is we walk around town and find the empty store. Logically, that will be the one you own. Same goes for the house, but I'd prefer to first ask around as to the location of one or more of these landmarks on the map so we're not riding over random hillsides and trespassing on settled claims. Your father never discussed these with you?"

"The first time I even knew the deeds existed was after we'd rafted the Columbia, when you gave me the envelope. Did he say anything when he gave them to you?"

"Nothing specific. His main concern was making me promise to get you and Ben safely to Oregon, and watch out for you both after we arrived."

A promise Jake had failed to keep—Ben had died less than a month later.

The excitement faded from Kate's eyes and she quietly gathered the papers, refolded them, and slid both back into the envelope.

Jake swallowed hard to clear the rising lump in his throat. "So, breakfast and then a walk around town?"

With a curt nod, Kate tucked the envelope into her pocket and headed downstairs.

Jake followed.

CHAPTER NINE
Battle of Knowledge

JAKE ENTERED THE DINING ROOM WITH Kate at his side. Theo, William, and Margaret were already seated at the long, rectangular table—a table now loaded with platters of pancakes, bacon, and scrambled eggs. A cloth-lined metal tray featured an array of biscuits and frosted pastries, and a dish of butter sat near an urn of syrup. A large glass bowl of cinnamon-sprinkled applesauce sat in the center of the table.

"Glad you two could make it," Theo said, rising to his feet and placing his napkin beside his empty plate.

"Sorry to be so late." Kate crossed the room and sat in the chair Theo pulled out for her. After murmuring her thanks, she allowed him to unfold her napkin and place it over her lap.

"Think nothing of it." Theo said, taking his seat again at the head of the table. "You've had a long journey and rest is the best recovery."

Jake shifted his weight and stared at the empty chair next to Kate's, debating whether dining with Theo was wise.

Theo tolerated the indecision only a few moments before

he let out an exaggerated sigh and motioned to the clock on the wall. "Jake, I have a busy day ahead and can't hold breakfast any longer. Are you joining us or not?"

He sat, telling himself Clara had obviously gone to a lot of trouble to create such an extravagant meal and he didn't want to be rude. Though niggling at the back of his mind was the real reason he'd capitulated—if he left, Theo would use the time alone with Kate to his advantage and further insinuate his own importance.

After a quick prayer, water glasses and coffee mugs were filled, platters were passed and emptied, and the clinking of silverware filled the air as everyone began eating. Except for Margaret. Her gaze roamed the table, but she only sipped water and shook her head at William's repeated attempts to fill her plate. Eventually she accepted a small spoonful of applesauce and all seemed fine until William waved a slice of glistening bacon below her nose.

"I've missed this smell, haven't you?"

Margaret's face went as bone-white as the china plate before her, and she scooted her chair from the table with an urgency bordering on frantic.

"Excuse me," she whispered, then fled the room with one hand covering her mouth. Within seconds a new sound filled the air —violent retching.

Unfazed, William turned to Theo and soon they were engaged in a lively conversation about their family back east.

Kate's fork hung in the air mid-way between her plate and her mouth as she stared at them, obviously aghast at their indifference. "Should I go check on her?"

William declined the offer with a shake of his head. "She'll be fine in a few minutes."

Eyes narrowed, Kate rose from her chair, dropped her napkin onto the table, and left the room without a word.

William sat back in his chair and let out a long sigh. "Margaret is fine. She's just..." His frustration quickly gave way to a sheepish grin. "She's in a delicate condition right now, and prefers to be alone during these moments."

"Congratulations!" Theo said, leaning from his chair to clap his nephew on the back. "I'm thrilled, and you can count on me to be the best great-uncle to your little one."

"I appreciate everything you're doing for Margaret and me." William's expression changed to regret. "Mother spoke often about your stance on a man making his own way in the world, and I want to say again how sorry I am at needing you to handle my debt to Jake."

"Ah, yes," Theo said. "I'd almost forgotten." He reached into his pants pocket and brought out a navy-colored cloth bag. After a few shakes to show it was heavy with coins, he tossed it across the table.

Jake caught it one-handed.

"William, thankfully the loss of that money won't hamper my ability to help you and Margaret get settled." Theo gave Jake a pointed look. "However, it's too bad when men decide to take advantage of a situation."

William needed to provide for his growing family, so Jake could almost forgive his silence when opportunities arose to correct Theo's interpretations regarding the debt owed.

Almost.

On the other hand, Theo was in a newfound position of power in the community, and to an extent, with Jake. A petty man in his element.

Jake had nothing to prove to either of these men, so he remained seated and said nothing.

****

Kate held back Margaret's hair as Margaret bent over a pail Clara had hastily offered after they'd rushed from the hallway into the hotel kitchen.

"I'm so sorry." Margaret raised her head and focused her

worried, watery gaze on Kate. "You and Jake have been nothing but kind, and I've been so worried about my own troubles, and the new life William and I are bringing into this world, that I'm afraid I've been a bit petulant towards you. Can you ever forgive me?"

Kate smiled, sympathetic to the woman's plight. "Consider it done."

Margaret let out a long sigh of relief, then glanced across the room where Clara stood, silently waiting. "Thank you as well, Clara. You put out quite a meal this morning, and I'm certain William is enjoying it."

"No trouble at all, my dear." Clara crossed the kitchen with a damp cloth in one hand and a glass of water in the other. "Since I keep a small herb garden year round in the kitchen window, I was able to add a sprig of mint to your water. It should help settle your stomach. You take a few slow sips while Kate and I run a comb through your hair and you'll be freshened up in no time." She bent and patted Margaret's shoulder several times before handing over the cloth and heading back across the room.

"What a wonderful woman," Margaret murmured, and Kate nodded her agreement.

Eventually, after a few minutes of assisted primping, Margaret agreed to return to breakfast. Kate followed her across the hall and back into the dining room. Taking her cue from Margaret in pretending nothing was amiss, she sat, replaced her napkin on her lap, and took up her fork again. Theodore and William followed suit.

Meanwhile, Jake's brooding silence indicated trouble at the table during her absence.

"William," Theodore said. "Before you get started with whatever you've got planned today, I need to ask you a serious question."

Though all in the room waited for his next words, he took a pancake from the stack and took his time at buttering the entire circle, including the edges. He then proceeded to make four precise cuts, separating it into eight equal wedge-shaped pieces. After placing his silverware on the rim of his plate, he finally continued speaking.

"Given all the opportunities in town to open your own business, are you certain you want to pursue a life of guaranteed hardship as a farmer?"

"I've never been more certain of anything in my life, aside from the love I share with my beautiful wife," William said, covering Margaret's hand with his own. "No need to worry about us. Soon we'll be safe and warm in our own cabin, and the trail will be just a memory."

Margaret placed her free hand over her stomach and managed a weak smile.

"Uncle Theodore, as you've obviously discovered, Oregon Territory is the land of unbelievable opportunity. It's the land of milk and honey, the land with cows so fat they roll down the road, and the land where the bugs do your work for you."

Kate couldn't hold back her laughter. "Where did you hear such things?"

"You don't believe me? I have the flyer right here." William pulled a well-worn paper from his shirt pocket and passed it across the table to Kate.

"I've seen this before," Kate said. "My father had this same flyer posted on the store wall behind the counter."

It had hung on many walls in towns back east. But like most people, her father had taken the information given in the many posters and booklets with a grain of salt. William didn't seem to have the same consideration; not only had he believed everything he'd read, he'd committed it to memory. As Jake would say, he was a tenderfoot of the worst kind. Misinformed and willing to spread incorrect information around with unbridled enthusiasm, an enthusiasm now evidenced by his wide grin.

"William, you certainly didn't see the elephant on your way here, did you?" Theodore asked, then gave a good-natured chuckle.

Kate noted the confused expression of the others, and realized she wasn't the only one uncertain of what he meant. "What does 'see the elephant' mean?" she asked.

"It refers to how most travelers start out with the greatest of expectations and loftiest of goals," Theodore said. "They leave their homes bright-eyed with wonder for all they'll see on the trail, and twitching with anticipation for the riches they'll find out west. However, most suffer so much during the crossing that by the end of their journey they feel defrauded." Ignoring William, Theodore focused on the rest of his guests, his brows furrowed in sympathy. "I'd say it's fair to assume you three saw the elephant?"

Margaret nodded solemnly and William swallowed hard before he broke the awkward silence of the room. "To answer your earlier question, Uncle Theodore, yes, we do plan on farming. In fact, after we finish up here we're going to start scouting the land for our claim."

"You'll need mounts," Theodore said.

"Jake was kind enough to lend us his horses, proving yet again how that flyer is right—in the Oregon Territory, whatever you need is at your feet as soon as you speak."

Theodore focused his attention on Jake. "I paid a visit to my livery this morning. Are all those horses yours?"

"Two are mine," Jake replied. "The other four are Kate's."

"Really?" Theodore said, eyeing Kate with appreciative surprise. "I know horseflesh and you've got good ones in there."

"Thank you," Kate replied, all the while hiding a smirk at the man's admiration. Not only didn't Theodore know which four were hers, but Plug was a runner if given any opportunity, and Old Dan was a pile of bones, shied at sharp noises, and was stubborn to boot.

Undaunted, Theodore continued. "While I don't typically allow my guests to dine with me, I'm always willing to make an exception when circumstances warrant. Kate, should I tell Clara to expect you for dinner this evening?"

"Jake and I plan to explore the area today, and we might be back late," Kate replied. "Is there a restaurant in town we might try?" She'd prefer to dine with Jake, alone, instead of in the company of this lout of a man.

"Yes, but it's not appropriate for a genteel woman like yourself. I've been a few times, but honestly it caters to a rougher crowd. You'll feel much more comfortable, and safe, here in my dining room."

"I don't want to impose," Kate replied, "or take advantage of your generosity." She'd hoped by now Jake would have asserted his desire to spend time with her, but since he seemed more interested in twisting his linen napkin into a knot than making eye contact, she wasn't certain of his intentions.

"Nonsense." Theodore waved her words away. "You've got to eat anyway—might as well be among your own kind. Dinner starts promptly at six o'clock. Jake, you're welcome too, but if you prefer the saloon I understand."

Kate's confidence waned. Could that be the reason for Jake's silence? She had no desire to keep him from reconnecting with old friends and understood, albeit begrudgingly, there were places in town she wouldn't be welcomed. Still, the realization made her ponder their compatibility for the first time.

Jake's belated reassurance—his hand sliding onto her knee and giving it a light squeeze before pulling away—filled her with both relief and unease.

"Well, Theo," he said, tossing his napkin beside his plate and leaning back in his chair, "I enjoyed this morning's meal, if not your company, so yes, I will dine here tonight."

"Very well," Theodore replied, and then adeptly changed

the subject.

When food and conversations began to dwindle, Theodore withdrew the silver bell from his vest pocket and shook it three times. Moments later, Clara appeared and began collecting their plates. When she reached Margaret, she patted her shoulder before quickly moving on.

Once the table had been cleared and a final round of coffee filled everyone's cups, Theodore reached into a wooden box on a nearby buffet table and extracted a cigar and a silver ashtray. "Mind if I smoke?"

When none claimed an issue, he proceeded to clip and light it with a practiced efficiency Kate hadn't seen since her father. Jake's wistful expression indicated he'd caught the similarity as well. Theodore was oblivious to anything but his own concerns as he tipped his head back and blew a series of smoky circles into the air.

"Jake and Kate, I realized something late last night," Theodore said. "In all the confusion of getting everyone settled, I neglected to mention how room payments are handled. Typically it's up front and by the day, but in certain cases I've been willing to consider a weekly rate."

He rested his cigar in the ashtray, propped his elbows on the table, and steepled his fingers together, pointing them first at Kate, then Jake. "Do you two know how long you'll be staying in my hotel?"

Jake fixed a steady, hard gaze on Theodore. "As long as you'll promptly see to getting the lock fixed on Kate's door, last night was my last."

"Very well," Theodore replied. "Kate, how about you? Will you be taking advantage of my earlier offer of your room for the week?"

Kate glanced at Jake for guidance, but when he gave none, she shrugged. "I'm not certain. I have some legal documents I need to sort out the meaning of first before I can give you an answer."

"Oh?" Theodore perked up. "Perhaps I can be of assistance?"

"My father purchased a building in town. I'd like to see it, but I don't know where it's located. Might you know of any stores that went vacant about a year ago?"

Theodore thought for a moment, then slowly shook his head. "This is a thriving town, and new buildings are sprouting up every day. Two men that might have some insight, given they own a mercantile, are Albert Wilson and George LeBreton. I'm scheduled for an evening of dinner, cigars, and brandy with them and a few others next week to discuss pending land claims along the river, so I'll be able to inquire as to your situation."

"Thank you for the offer, but there's no need. Jake suggested he and I take a stroll through the town until we figure out which one is empty. Likely it will be my father's."

Theodore scoffed. "Wandering the streets aimlessly and peering into random windows is a preposterous plan."

Only the memory of her aunt's firm insistence on the need to act polite and respectful toward those with political or social influence, even if they didn't always deserve it, kept Kate from giving Theodore the vicious tongue lashing he deserved.

"What you need is to check in with the land claims office," Theodore said, tapping the ash from his cigar into a shallow metal tray. "Plans are in the works to open one in Oregon City sometime in the next few weeks."

"Weeks?" Kate shook her head. "I couldn't possibly wait that long."

"Then you'll need to go to Champoeg," Theodore said. "There's a land claims office out there—or rather the beginnings of one. Regardless, it's a good place to find answers to your questions since right now there is no governing body in Oregon City."

"Is it far?" she asked.

"Champoeg's about two days travel from here, and since danger lurks in the woods as well as the streets, I would like to formally offer my services as your escort."

Tension blanketed the room as Kate struggled for a way to graciously decline Theodore's offer—though she'd much rather slap him across the cheek for treating Jake in such a derogatory manner throughout breakfast—and signal Jake of her desire to leave town right away. With him.

"The only one escorting her will be me," he said, his response saving Kate from her temper swirling within and threatening to burst loose.

"Of course." Theodore focused solely on her with the smarmy smile of a man who'd just lost a battle, but had every intention of winning the war.

She rose from her chair. "I'm heading upstairs to pack."

"Give me about twenty minutes to straighten out some things here," Jake said, shifting in his chair to face Theodore, "and I'll have our horses ready and waiting out front."

CHAPTER TEN
Setting Limits

JAKE REMAINED SEATED AT THE TABLE, silently watching Kate rush from the room. Theo, William, and Margaret excused themselves and left shortly after, leaving Jake alone with his thoughts.

While a lesser man would have resented how Theo had ultimately been the one to give Kate the information she'd needed regarding the deeds, Jake didn't begrudge him for his knowledge. After all, America was settled by wise men who spent more time with pen and paper in hand than an ax or a gun. However, he detested Theo's attitude—on full display from their first meeting on the trail coming out west—that Jake and men of his ilk were beneath him.

What Theo hadn't yet realized was that America, and now the Oregon Territory, was also settled by men like Jake, and he too deserved respect. During breakfast Theo had let far too many cheap shots fly, but since Kate and the others had been present, Jake had been unwilling to retaliate. Not so now. After all, there was a limit to how long he could hold back his tongue, and fists, against Theo's insults.

He left the dining room and went into the lobby. Theo stood behind the marble-topped desk Jake had detested upon first sight, in Theo's wagon years before.

"Kate and I won't be needing dinner tonight," Jake said while opening the navy bag Theo had thrown across the breakfast table. "Furthermore, I'm here to pay in advance for the next week on Kate's room, and space in the livery for four horses."

"Where's Kate?" Theo asked.

"Upstairs packing," Jake said evenly. "Now, back to something you should actually be concerned with—will you hold Kate's room while she's gone?"

"Of course," Theo said, punctuating the disparaging remark with a withering glare.

Jake withdrew a handful of coins into his palm, eyed them briefly, then tossed a few onto the desk.

Theo cupped his hand around the payment, slid them into his other hand, and slipped it all into his pants pocket. "I won't bother counting this now, since you've always made such a spectacle of doing the right thing."

Jake shook the bag in his hand, raising his eyebrows as the remaining coins clinked against each other. "I won't bother counting this now, since I know where you sleep."

He took simple pleasure in seeing Theo's hand quiver as he needlessly smoothed back his hair.

"I've already sent word to the blacksmith, and the door lock on Kate's room will be repaired by the end of the day," Theo said.

Jake gave a simple, quick nod at the news. Once again, he was grateful that he'd opted to publicly eliminate any chance at sharing her room again. Sliding those shirts in front of her pleading eyes and willing lips had taken every ounce of control he'd been able to muster, and removing himself from temptation seemed like the best option. Though he wasn't positive he could resist a similar invitation again.

"I might have a room available for you upon your return," Theo said, a smirk playing across his lips. "Though, given how I saw you sneaking out of Kate's room early this morning, I doubt you're interested."

Jake attempted a nonchalant shrug at Theo's revelation, but was furious with himself at getting caught. He never should have agreed to stay in her room, no matter the reason.

"I'd rather sleep in a rainstorm than under your roof for another night," he replied, his tone leaving no mistake about his rising anger.

"What about Kate? I'm surprised at how a woman of her social stature is willing to abandon the comforts of civilization again so soon after leaving the trail. Perhaps she'd like to instead send a messenger out to Champoeg and remain here in my hotel, surrounded by the luxury she undoubtedly was born and raised into."

"Kate handles her own business affairs, and unlike you, she understands transporting useless luxury often comes with too high of a price." Jake thumped his knuckles against the top of Theo's desk, and then pointed to the groove near the corner. "Or have you already forgotten the day that happened?"

"I'll never forget the day your incompetence led to my property sliding around the back of my wagon."

"How fortunate for your desk that Collette's leg broke its fall. I'm certain her life-long limp and empty arms won't ever let her forget about that day—the day you chose your property over the wellbeing of a fellow traveler."

Years ago, on Jake's first trek across the trail, an *enceinte* woman had grown so tired from the constant walking that she couldn't keep up with the others and risked being left behind. Given that her wagon was overflowing with needed supplies, Jake had insisted she be allowed to ride in the back of Theo's wagon, and his beloved desk be left behind trailside. Theo had fought hard against Jake's order, arguing that Collette could either squeeze into a small space beside the desk, or ride with someone else.

Eventually Jake had relented—a decision he'd regretted ever since.

Later that same day Theo had ignored Jake's orders to slow his oxen, and ultimately driven his wagon too fast around a sharp curve. One of the front wheels had slipped from the path, the load had shifted, and the desk had slammed into Collette's leg.

Jake closed his eyes, remembering the woman's guttural screams as he and two other men—neither of them Theo—had frantically worked to free her.

She'd lost the baby three days later.

"I'm not heartless," Theo said, crossing his arms over his chest. "I tried to give her and her husband something to make up for what happened, but nothing was good enough. Not a platter made of the finest silver, not a brass headboard, or a mahogany chair with a seat cushion of the finest silk. However, they refused everything I generously suggested. Except money, of course. They took the money I finally thought to offer."

"Seems more like a payoff to guarantee their silence."

"You're wrong, as usual," Theo said, stepping from behind the desk. "Now, if you'll excuse me, I have something pressing I need to attend to."

"Where are you going?" Jake asked.

"To ask your lady friend, Kate, to have dinner with me upon her return to town. I intend to impress upon her all I can provide, including a wagon and driver, should she choose my companionship the next time she needs to travel again."

"She'd never choose a man like you."

Theo scoffed. "Who she spends her time with is her own choice. And, since I've confirmed she's not otherwise engaged, I figure her time is fair game."

Blood pounded in Jake's ears and he had to fight to keep his voice under control. "Stay away from her."

Theo placed a hand over his heart as his lips turned downward into an exaggerated frown. Someone who didn't know this man would believe him consumed by grief, especially once his chin began to quiver.

Jake knew better.

"You don't have to worry about me," Theo said, his eyes wide with feigned innocence. "I'm just a harmless man who lost his wife and decided to start his life over in Oregon Territory."

"As I recall, 'decided' is a stretch." Jake's eyes narrowed. "You can go on twisting the tales of why you left Boston, but you and I know the truth. Remember, I was there the day you pleaded your case to join the wagon train." Theo had fled his hometown of Boston in the middle of the night, his reputation in shambles due to losing his wife's family fortune at the card tables. "Theo, right now you still appear honorable to the influential men of this town. Wouldn't want to have John McLoughlin or anyone else knowing what you're really like, would you?"

Theo's nostrils flared, but he stayed silent.

Jake leaned down until he was eye to eye with the man. "Kate is off limits to you. Find another pretty woman to impress with your lies."

To Jake's surprise, rather than fleeing from the room, Theo's expression turned from fearful to triumphant. "Speaking of a pretty woman, Emily Bird stopped in here late last night."

Jake held back a grimace. Likely Theo had invited Emily—the saloon girl who'd called him by name as he'd ridden by on the street below—to act as his bedroom companion for the evening. Even more likely, it had been a prearranged meeting, set up long before Jake's return to town. Neither of which bothered him in the slightest. The woman was trouble, always had been, and he wanted nothing to do with her.

"What you do on your own time is not my concern," Jake replied.

"Oh, but it is your concern." Theo's lips stretched from a smirk to a wide grin. "Emily came by specifically to see you. Perhaps I'll mention to Kate your—" he paused, savoring his victory for a moment before continuing, "—familiarity with Emily, so she can know what *you're* really like."

This time it was Jake's turn to stay silent.

"Seems Emily knows you're back in town and was checking if you were staying in my hotel. Of course, I happily confirmed her assumption. Though I didn't mention how you'd slept in another woman's room. I figured the poor dear suffered enough the last time you snuck out of town, leaving her to realize you'd been giving her and her kind nothing but coins and empty promises."

Jake struggled for control, to remain steady and not reveal even a glimmer of the fear now running rampant through his mind. Fear of what Emily's interference, no doubt guided by Theo, could do to the life he had planned with Kate.

Theo continued. "From the moment we met you were demanding and demeaning. However, we're not on the trail anymore. So it goes without saying—almost—how thrilled I am to find myself as the one with power and knowledge."

An eerie calm took hold of Jake, allowing him to clearly consider the familiar footsteps he heard coming down the stairs. Kate had seen him fight a man once, and though it had been for a good reason, he had no intention of subjecting her to such physical violence again.

Instead, he opted to lean close and speak low. "You're a spineless coward, and always will be. You might think you have power now, but I'm confident one day your true colors will be revealed to this town. One way or another."

Kate entered the room, her saddlebags slung over her shoulder and Elijah's hat clutched in her hand.

"Ready?" she asked, her shining eyes and shifting feet

betraying her impatience.

Jake nodded, then turned to Theo. "We'll finish our discussion later."

He held out a bent elbow to Kate, who took it with practiced ease, and he led her out of the hotel.

CHAPTER ELEVEN
A Crushing Blow

Saturday, November 11, 1843

KATE RODE INTO THE SETTLEMENT OF Champoeg with Jake at her side and the familiar butter-yellow envelope hidden deep within her pocket. At the end of the main street sat the land office, a weathered building that held the details of all claims made in Oregon City and the surrounding area.

Though the trail had taken nearly everything from her, two shining glimmers of hope had survived. Deeds that were the key to her new life—a life that would begin the moment she learned the locations signified by the strings of numbers scrawled across the top of both papers.

They secured the horses at the hitching post and then headed for the door. Jake knocked twice to announce their arrival and then pushed it open, revealing a room with a sagging cot on one side and a freshly polished stove on the other. A wrinkled man with a trim white beard stood up from his desk, walked over, and clapped a hand on Jake's shoulder.

"Jake! What a surprise!"

"Kate, I'd like you to meet a friend of mine, Jim."

"It's a pleasure to meet you, ma'am." Jim nodded to her and then motioned to two scratched but sturdy oak chairs opposite his desk. "Please, make yourselves comfortable."

Jake pulled out her chair and waited until she was settled before sitting beside her. After they'd exchanged a few rounds of inane chatter about the weather, Jim rested his elbows on the desk and laced his fingers together.

"What can I do for you today?"

Kate dried her palms on her trousers and took a deep, calming breath before speaking the words she'd waited over four months to say.

"My father purchased a building in Oregon City and a house two miles outside of town. I'm here to learn their locations."

"I don't understand," Jim said. "Why didn't he get this information when the claims were first made?"

"He bought the deeds in Virginia, from a man who'd changed his mind about living in Oregon Territory." She slid a trembling hand into her pocket and withdrew the butter-yellow envelope with the red wax seal. Tucked inside were the two pieces of parchment paper that represented her father's dream for the rest of his life.

And now his unfulfilled dream was hers.

Her house. Her land. Her future.

"I see you've got something there," Jim said. "Let me take a look."

She set the first paper—the one she surmised was the deed to the store—into Jim's extended hand.

He pulled the oil lamp closer and leaned over the desk, peering at the paper with a deepening frown. After a long moment he pressed and slid his thumb over the numbers written at the top, grimacing at the smear of ink left behind.

"Jim, is there a problem?" Jake asked.

"The plot numbers don't match anything I've ever seen and the wording is all wrong. Give me a minute." With the paper in hand, Jim crossed the room to inspect three plot maps nailed to the wall.

While they waited, Jake placed a calming hand upon her bouncing knee and gave her a reassuring grin—a grin that slowly faded when Jim resumed his seat with a heavy sigh.

"I'm sorry, ma'am, but this deed is forged. It's worthless."

"Forged?" She stared at him in horror. "Are you certain?"

"Without a doubt." Jim emphasized the point with a slow, sympathetic shake of his head. "Article Four of the Law of Land Claims clearly states that no person is entitled to hold a claim upon city or town sites. Looks like someone took your father for a fool."

"How is this even possible?" asked Jake, who looked as stunned as she felt.

"Ruthless men will take advantage of every loophole out here, and then some, until there's a solid system of land laws and government in place. Unfortunately, I fully expect to see a lot more people in your situation." Jim shrugged as if already resigned to future deceit. "I wish I could offer more than my apologies, but unless you know who sold it to your father there's nothing I, nor anyone else, can do." He slid the paper back across the desk and waited patiently while she refolded and returned it to the envelope.

Blinking back tears, she held out the second deed. "And this one?"

Jim took the parchment from her and inspected it closely before again rising to stand before the maps. Flattening the paper against the wall with his left hand, he traced a thin, wandering line on a map with his right index finger.

"Now this one seems legitimate." He glanced between the deed and the line several times before shaking his head. "However, I can't say for certain since I don't have the corresponding map." Deed in hand, Jim returned to his seat. "Where are you two staying?"

"Oregon City," Jake replied. "We just got in a few days ago, and headed out here after someone advised us this office could determine the locations represented by the deeds."

"We've got a man up there opening an office near the mercantile in about a week. Actually—" he paused, shuffled papers around on his desk until he found what he wanted, then nodded, "—he's opening next Saturday. He'll have information I don't have. Metes and bounds maps of the area with notes on specific landmarks, registration information, things of that nature."

"I still don't understand how one deed could be fake and the other one real," Kate said, grasping to comprehend.

"Remember, I'm still not certain it's real," Jim cautioned. "Though, if I were a betting man I'd say you've got yourself a valid claim. As for how it happened, I'd guess whoever sold those to your father probably realized more deeds meant more money, and drew himself up a convincing forgery, using the real one as a guide. Selling them back east was an especially brilliant aspect of the scheme—it's improbable your father, or any other victims, will ever risk the return trip for a confrontation."

Jim's eyes narrowed and he focused a probing gaze on Kate. "Why isn't your father here asking these questions? I'd prefer to discuss these issues with him."

"He died on the trail." She didn't yet know whether to take comfort or feel shame that those words no longer brought on an immediate rush of sadness.

"Well, that changes things," Jim said, dismissing Kate with a curt nod and turning to Jake. "If her father's deed is valid—and again, I suspect it is—the land claim should transfer over to you with minimal trouble."

"Why would it go to Jake?" she asked.

"Well, it was your father's and now it will go to you and your husband," Jim said.

The hair on the back of Kate's neck stood on end and she

had to force herself not to soothe away the goose bumps rising on her arms. "He's not my husband."

"I apologize for the incorrect assumption," Jim said, raising placating palms in the air. "Are you married?"

"Why are you asking me this?" Kate's voice was little more than a whisper as she fought back rising dread, and the realization that even thousands of miles from home, in an unsettled land, gender still took precedence over the willingness to work hard.

"Because if your father is dead and you don't have a husband, your claim is worthless." Jim paused, his brows furrowed in confused concentration. "At least, I think that will be the case. Right now we're only a territory and not officially part of the United States and their laws, but the precedent has already been set so it's a solid assumption."

As fury overtook dread, Kate's fingernails pounded an angry rhythm on the desktop, inches from the deed. "So your conclusion—even though there is no law in place confirming it, *and* I have a deed in hand that you assert will be valid—is I have no right to this land because I'm a single woman."

Jim let out a frustrated sigh. "Unfortunately, yes."

Kate clasped her hands so tightly her fingers went white in places and red in others. Memories of time spent in her aunt's parlor back home in Virginia rushed through her mind. The parlor where she'd been reminded weekly of society's expectations for a woman of her standing. The parlor she'd spent her youth wishing to escape.

And now that she had escaped, sacrificing nearly everything along the way, she was again ruled by stifling laws and obligations. Jake hadn't asked for her hand—and showed no intention of doing so—which meant her future would entail a life similar to Clara's, forced to work toward the dream of another instead of her own.

Aunt Victoria had been right after all.

Two years ago, Kate had engaged in a rousing discussion

with her aunt regarding the theories behind Machiavelli's treatise, *The Prince*. At the time Kate had been vehement in declaring her disgust at many of the ideas, but now one concept in particular made perfect sense. Sometimes, the end justified the means.

Pushing aside the memory of her mother's admonition to never act coy to impress or cajole a man, Kate began creatively claiming what was rightfully hers. After all, lying was the only option she had left.

"It seems I misspoke earlier," she said, then smothered a feigned giggle with practiced fingertips. "I am married. The name on the deed, Elijah, belongs to my husband."

The set of Jim's brow went from confused to disbelieving. "Why isn't he here?"

Doing her best to ignore the man at her side, his mouth now agape, she continued. "He had some final business to attend to back home and sent me out early. I expect him next spring, but in the meantime I'd love to explore the water on our land." She flashed Jim a knowing smile. "That is what you were tracing on that map? A river or creek?"

Eyes wide, Jim simply nodded.

"Do you happen to know the name of it?" she asked.

"Yes, but I'll again refer back to what I said earlier," he replied in a tone that left little doubt of his rising irritation. "After your *husband* arrives, send him into the Oregon City office. Once the claim is confirmed, they'll share the specific location."

Kate disguised her despair with a flurry of useless motions—smoothing a wrinkle from her trousers, brushing at a smudge of dirt on her wrist, and finally rolling the brim of her father's hat between her fingers. Then, fearing the loss of what she had left should Jim insist on holding onto the deed until her husband arrived, she eased the parchment off the desk and onto her lap. After refolding and tucking it into the envelope, she slid it deep into her pocket.

"You two going back right away, or do you have time to join me for dinner?"

Kate's hopes soared, envisioning an evening of seemingly innocent questions and observations, all crafted with the goal of Jim ultimately letting the name of the creek slip, giving her a vital clue to where to begin her search.

"How kind of you to ask, and of course we'd love to—"

"No." Jake sprang from his chair, then brought her up beside him with an insistent pull of her upper arm. "We need to get back to Oregon City immediately. Seems we've got some things to sort out."

"I understand," Jim said, rising to his feet. "It was good to see you again, Jake. Don't be a stranger."

"I'm almost certain I'll be seeing you around again soon." Jake's grim tone matched his eyes.

Kate stayed silent as Jake's hand, unrelenting and unforgiving, settled on the small of her back, spun her around, and firmly propelled her toward the door.

CHAPTER TWELVE
Justifications

RIDING AWAY FROM THE LAND CLAIMS office, Jake contemplated which was worse—watching the woman he loved tell blatant lies, about her father no less, to a future government official, or to then watch her resort to acting like a simpering fool to gain information.

An hour ago he would have sworn Kate had changed from the spoiled, demanding woman he'd met the first day on the trail, but after seeing what she was capable of and comfortable doing, he wasn't so confident.

Old habits died hard. Or in her case, perhaps not at all.

"You certainly are full of surprises," Jake said, struggling to keep both his tone and his irritation under control.

"What's that supposed to mean?"

"Most women would have collected their tears in a scented lace handkerchief after hearing Jim's assessment. Not you. You set your jaw and spout lies."

Kate straightened in her saddle and gave him a sidelong look. Her expression—one of unbridled determination to get what she wanted, no matter the cost—startled him.

"One thing I learned on the trail—crying and hysterics accomplish nothing. So yes, I lied." She paused, her eyes daring him to challenge her next words. "I won't allow clueless men to stand in the way of what is rightfully mine."

Jake shook his head in disbelief at what he was hearing and seeing. Instead of showing concern or regret, she sat calmly in her saddle, an elbow draped across the horn and the reins in hand. As if she hadn't a care in the world.

"Kate, you have no idea what you've brought upon yourself with your lies! Jim is a petty man who thrives on gathering information, then twisting it for his own benefit. Once he figures out a way to profit from the fact you're in possession of a fake deed, he'll eagerly share that knowledge with the first person who offers to increase his pocketbook or political influence."

He glared at her, still disgusted with how easily she'd resorted to deception. "Jim's smart, too," he continued. "Don't think for one minute you've convinced him you're simply biding your time, waiting to be reunited with your dear *husband,* Elijah."

She stared at him, incredulous. "You think I'm proud of how I acted like a helpless simpleton back there? You think my father would be proud to see his daughter grovel for scraps of information?" Her eyes narrowed. "I'll never know if he'd have approved or scorned my actions today, but I'm certain he'd want me to go after what is rightfully mine."

She halted her rant, took a deep breath, then studied him thoughtfully. "I'm curious; how would you have handled it?"

The unexpected question took Jake off guard. Admittedly he'd never considered land ownership laws from a woman's perspective, and he knew little about the intricate details of starting a business, much less what it took to successfully run one. After spending more than a minute weighing various ideas, the truth hit him hard—he had nothing to add, nothing to offer, and no way to help.

"Don't insult how I handle my affairs." Nostrils flaring, she pointed an accusing index finger directly at his chest. "Especially since you're unwilling to propose anything better."

Opting for forced silence over blurting out something he didn't—or did—mean, Jake set his jaw and urged his horse to a trot. As he led the way across the well-trodden trail back to Oregon City, he finally figured out what had bothered him the most about watching Kate lie.

He'd kept quiet, which made him a liar too.

CHAPTER THIRTEEN
Clarifications

THEY RODE FOR HOURS. SILENTLY.

The day remained uneventful, allowing Kate the time she needed to consider her next move. Back home in Virginia, chess had been a favorite pastime and she'd often battled her father or his friends long past twilight. While she appreciated outright daring in a player, her strongest plays had always been ones she'd carefully plotted and then swiftly executed. Usually within a few vicious moves.

Acquiring her land would be no different.

For starters, Theodore's business knowledge and contacts would be a valuable asset to mine if she did want to pursue opening a mercantile, which appeared to be the next logical step. Especially given the five supply wagons already due into Oregon City next year, paid for and arranged by her father.

If she spent the coming winter planning and plotting— hopefully with Jake by her side—she could potentially flip an open sign in a window next spring. Eventually she'd be able to move onto the second part of her father's plan—the entire reason she'd agreed to settle out west—a horse ranch.

Then there was Jake and their future.

He'd seemed certain of his love as they stood on the hilltop overlooking Oregon City.

He'd seemed certain as he'd proclaimed his desire to share a life together with her.

He'd seemed more than certain as he wrapped his arms around her waist, pulled her into his chest, and thoroughly kissed her.

Now, three days later and still without a proposal, Kate couldn't help but wonder if he'd simply been caught up in the emotion of finally crossing the trail. Admittedly things had been tense since they'd arrived into Oregon City, but she hadn't once wavered in her feelings. She admired him, respected him, and wanted him as her husband. Figuring out what he wanted was proving to be a challenge she hadn't anticipated.

When daylight waned, the temperature hovered near freezing and a drizzle covered everything with frigid dampness. An uncomfortable night loomed.

Months of making camp together allowed for brevity in their discussions of where to tie off the horses, place the fire, and what they'd eat for dinner. Within an hour of stopping, all needs were tended to, including the horses, which left nothing to do but keep warm by the fire.

Kate sat as near the flames as her cheeks and chin could tolerate, huddled beneath a well-worn quilt. Even her wool coat, leather gloves, and father's hat couldn't fully dissuade the chill. Across the fire, Jake lay with his left leg positioned closest to the meager warmth offered by the hissing flames. Judging by the low groans he'd failed to hide every time he shifted, he was sore and in want of a bed that wasn't a tattered bedroll on damp ground.

Though their last few hours had been marred by tension, she couldn't bear watching the man she loved grimace in pain. She tossed a handful of pinecones on the fire, and then added a log.

"If you're cold, I can add another," she said, her hand hovering over the dwindling pile of branches.

"I'm fine."

Silence reigned until she again broke the quiet in the hopes a conversation might distract from his discomfort. "I'm eager to return to the hotel. How about you? A hot bath should do wonders for your leg." *And your attitude.*

Jake's eyes locked with hers as he slowly shook his head. "I'd rather wash from a horse's water trough than spend one more night under Theo's roof."

Maybe Jake didn't realize professional relationships were often forged atop a mutual hatred between men, yet respect for the usefulness they each possessed. In her interactions with Theodore he'd more than proven himself to be mercurial, but business was another thing entirely. If Jake would put his personal feelings aside instead of being stubborn to a fault, he'd see a working relationship with Theodore had immense benefits.

"I recall you don't care for him. However, he has extensive knowledge of treaties and pending laws. His relationships with business owners and upcoming politicians will be a valuable asset if we open a mercantile."

And perhaps Jake would realize that by her use of the word "we" that she was considering their future. A future together.

"Kate, why are we here?"

"What do you mean?" she replied, looking around in confusion. "You know we prefer to camp next to water, and a creek is right over the hill."

"I mean, you need to question why Theo sent us to Champoeg. You insist he's a smart man who knows the law; he could have told you both deeds were worthless. He could have mentioned an office opening up next week in Oregon City."

"He did mention it. If you'll recall, I insisted I couldn't wait. Why are you so intent on berating a man who was simply trying to help?"

"Why are you so intent on defending him?"

"I'm not defending. I'm clarifying." Kate let out a groan of frustration. "Theodore said a land office would open in Oregon City 'within a few weeks'. And I never mentioned I held actual deeds. Based on the information I gave, his advice was appropriate and correct." She paused to give him an appraising glare. "Besides, you could have spoken up."

"Something you'd like to say?"

She raised her eyebrows and took his challenge. "You should have told me months ago women couldn't own land in the territory."

"I didn't know! I never had reason to pay attention to the laws about women. I thought if you had the deeds, you had the right to the land. Never occurred to me you'd need a husband to make a proper claim."

Kate let out a heavy sigh instead of another snappy retort. Fighting wasn't helping.

"You don't know him like I do." Jake's features softened and he raised his palms in defeat. "He's got one thing on his mind: how to turn any situation around to benefit himself."

She recalled Jake's similar declaration about Jim. Did he have a problem with men of influence? No, that wasn't true, since he'd spoken so highly of Captain Payette when they'd stopped at Fort Boise on the trail.

"Trust me, Kate. He's got an ulterior motive for everything he does, including sending us on this waste of time trip." Jake waved his hand across the treed darkness. "He'll feel no guilt, either; he's a proponent of Machiavelli."

The revelation proved yet again that not only was Theodore cultured and well read, but also shrewd. Perhaps one day Jake would understand what it took to operate a thriving mercantile. And trust in her judgment when it came to doing so.

She eased her blanket aside and rose from her bedroll. "I'm going to check on the horses."

Without a backward glance, she crossed camp to where they'd tied out their horses, Nina and Nickel. She reached Nina first. After a thorough check of her shoes and legs, Kate took a brush from her saddlebag and settled in for a much-needed removal of several knots from Nina's forelock.

About the only thing she had left to be confident in was her ability to nurture and train horses. She certainly had nothing else. She'd been cheated out of a mercantile, had no right to her land, and now she couldn't help but wonder if Jake even saw her as his potential wife. Given what she'd heard from the woman leaning over the saloon's upper balcony railing as they'd entered town, Theodore's warning of Jake's womanizing ways wasn't unreasonable.

What was she going to do?

As if sensing her owner's trepidation, Nina lowered her head and pushed her nose against Kate's shoulder in search of a scratch and nuzzle. For the first time that evening, she smiled. Nina was a fine horse, her father's prized mare in fact. He'd chosen her as one of the two horses Jake had allowed her family to bring across the trail. He'd picked her specifically to breed, which would have been the start of a strong line on their horse ranch.

Kate recalled her father's words when he'd confessed his desire to leave Virginia, cross the trail, and start over.

We'll start with a general store. We already have the knowledge and the contacts, and with the way people are talking, the next ten years will see more people going west than ever before. After a year or two of certain profits we'll pick out a spread large enough to support a full-scale ranch. Then we'll round up mustang stallions and start a new line with the mares we'll bring with us.

He'd been so eager, so prepared, so confident of future success.

New settlers will need supplies. Horses too. Horses from a ranch I can build with my own hands.

And now Kate faced the real possibility of stabling Nina, Old Dan, and her two packhorses for the winter. Possibly longer. It seemed such a shame to waste precious months, or even years of their lives in a stall. Though even if she could figure out a way to open a mercantile, Kate would feel just as trapped as her caged horses.

While she'd always enjoyed certain aspects of working in her father's store—bookkeeping and displaying the various wares in an organized, yet pleasing manner—she'd never fully embraced dealing with customers, enforcing deals with vendors, and overseeing deliveries. Or tolerating impudent elites like Theodore. If only she could skip opening the mercantile and move right to ranching!

No. If it would be possible, her father would have suggested it. He'd been a brilliant businessman who'd meticulously planned everything to the last detail, so it *must* be a vital step.

Or was it? Ranching first would mean she'd have to start on a much smaller scale, but eventually, if she worked hard enough, she'd see her father's dream to fruition.

As she pondered her options, reality sunk in. Passing over the mercantile in favor of building a ranch was an intriguing idea, but right now her most pressing concern was surviving the winter in an unknown land. Without a home. Without squandering her father's money on a hotel room for months, or years, to come.

Half an hour later, after a needlessly thorough evaluation of both horses, she returned to her bedroll, her shoulders slumped in resignation over how little control she had over her future.

"All good with the horses?" Jake asked as he tossed a fresh log onto the fire, sending a plume of sparks and smoke into the air.

She gave a quick, unconvincing nod, thankful the crackle of the rising flames hid her face. She had no desire for Jake to see her trembling chin and looming tears.

As always, he noticed something was wrong. Within seconds, he'd stepped around the fire and was crouched at her side.

"Tell me."

His simple, whispered request made her long to bury her head against his chest and admit her concerns and fears. She settled for a weak smile and a reluctant shrug.

"I've survived the ordeal of crossing the trail only to find no schools, no library, and no churches. Sometimes I can't help but wonder, what was my father thinking?"

"He was giving you his dream," Jake replied.

"Some dream. A forged deed and land I can't claim."

She made an elaborate process of removing her father's hat and smoothing back her hair. After the fifth time she tucked loose curls behind her ears, Jake placed his hand upon hers and gave a small squeeze. The tender gesture reminded her of how gentle he'd been on the trail when she'd been so mired in despair. Oh, how she missed her father and brother!

"Jake, I feel so inept. I wish my father were here to tell me how to fix this. To tell me what to do next." She swiped the tears from her eyes. "I have nothing left but his dreams, and so far I haven't been doing well with them."

Judging by the vein throbbing in his ruddy throat, he was waging a battle over his next words. Finally, he spoke. "What makes you so certain he'd want you to pursue his dreams instead of your own?"

The question brought on a fresh rush of emotions that made her blink fast. Even considering abandoning half the plan her father had sacrificed his life for felt like the ultimate betrayal. How could she say the words aloud?

CHAPTER FOURTEEN
Unflattering Words from a Floundering Fool

"KATIE," JAKE WHISPERED, ALL WHILE FIGHTING the urge to kneel forward and pull her into his arms. "You don't have to be strong all the time. I can help you. Let me help shoulder the burden you're under."

Instead of confessing her worries, she remained motionless before him, contemplating an inner battle where only she knew the terms.

Meanwhile, Jake waited and wondered. Why wasn't she telling him the truth? Did she think he wouldn't understand or sympathize with the rotten hand she'd been dealt? Or did her hesitation stem from not knowing what he'd planned for his own future?

Granted he'd never gone into detail about his own dreams; he'd simply supported her in hers. Rather her father's. His plan had always been simple—raise cattle and crops. And though his dream wasn't as grand as hers, it was solid, realistic and, given his past experience, entirely possible.

He recalled the exact moment he'd known he'd wanted to travel west again, this time to lay down solid roots—April 26,

1843.

In the spring of 1842 he'd grown tired of life as an ambling saddle tramp—a life that had grown tougher since breaking his leg the previous year—and decided to try living as a settled man. He'd bought thirty acres outside of Charlottesville, Virginia. The first month he'd put in corn and potatoes and planted a kitchen garden. Over the next few weeks he'd built a small, yet sturdy log cabin. The day he'd cut the hole for the front door had been bittersweet—the itch to move on already niggled.

Summer passed. He sold his crops with moderate success. Farming his plot grew increasingly tedious knowing thousands of acres were available for the taking out west.

Then he'd met Valerie.

While on a rare trip into town that fall, he'd happened upon the willowy blond. Her flawless appearance had drawn him to her at first; costly dresses and jewels were her daily attire and she took great care to maintain a flawless appearance. It had taken months of courting and more than a few baubles, but finally he'd seen a glimpse of warmth beneath her icy shell.

With their future life together in mind, he'd spent the end of winter trying to convince her of the opportunities available in Oregon Territory. Valerie typically listened to his reasoning without comment.

On April 26, 1843, he'd ridden out to her home, intending to discuss the matter again. Instead he'd found a note addressed to him pinned to her door. With a sinking heart, he'd broken the wax seal.

Jake,

Traveling across a barren land to spend a lifetime in a shoddy cabin is barbaric, and I want no part of such nonsense. It is obvious I want more from my life than you can give me.

You needn't bother calling again.

Valerie

Furious with himself for pursuing such a worthless woman, Jake had returned home, stood on his front porch and surveyed his land; he couldn't leave fast enough. He'd hired on as Elijah's trail guide across the Oregon Trail two days later.

Now he had enough money to cultivate and manage all the acres the territory would grant. He could make a profit on crops next fall and then put it all toward a herd of fat cattle. Within three years, he'd be prosperous.

However, he couldn't imagine any of it without Kate by his side. As his wife.

He should have asked her already. He'd had plenty of opportunities. He could have asked after she'd saved his life by pulling him from the frigid Columbia River. He could have asked when he'd stood on the hillside over Oregon City, his mouth exploring the soft curves of her neck and then moving to linger over her lips, which had parted so seductively.

No, even after sharing a passionate kiss he'd found reasons not to ask.

The timing wasn't right. Asking her while in Theo's hotel would render the scoundrel a permanent reminder of the special day. He didn't have flowers. He didn't have a ring. He didn't have a finished doorway to carry her through after their wedding.

No more excuses. No more waiting. He loved her. He wanted to marry her. He was going to ask her. Right now.

"Kate, I wanted to ask…" He pulled his hat from his head and subtly shifted so his right knee rested on the ground. "Kate, I think that we…" He grimaced as he faltered again.

She studied him thoughtfully. "Jake, what's wrong?"

"Nothing. I've had something on my mind for a few

weeks, and after what happened in the land claims office it's all the more important that I say this now."

His mouth had gone unexpectedly dry and he wished his canteen wasn't across the camp. Maybe he should start with letting Kate know her father had approved of him enough to ask that he take care of her after his death.

"Oregon Territory is an unsettled and dangerous land, and will be for the next few years. Or longer. Even after civilization takes a firm hold, there is no guarantee of your safety."

He forged ahead, wishing he'd planned this moment better. Why were his hands so sweaty?

"Your father knew of this, which is why moments before he died he asked for my word that I'd watch over you. He worried how you'd fare if you were alone, and so I promised to care for and protect you like he would have done."

Kate's unblinking stare made it difficult to gauge her feelings.

This wasn't going well. At this rate, he'd be better off just blurting out a proposal. After all, he had the rest of his life to tell her how he felt.

"Katherine Davis, will you ma—"

Kate held up her hand. "Wait."

CHAPTER FIFTEEN
Released

"DON'T SAY ANOTHER WORD." KATE FOCUSED on her trembling hand raised in the air between them. She had to look at something, anything, besides the man who'd just broken her heart. The man who, instead of professing his love for her, was only concerned with honoring her father's dying wish.

Certain conversations made sense now. And angered.

"Jake, the other night in the hotel room you said something that bothered me, but I couldn't figure out why. Until now. Until you tried to propose—not out of love, but out of loyalty to my father."

"That's not what—"

"Stop," she commanded. "Let me finish."

Muscles in Jake's neck stood out in cords and a vein in his temple throbbed, but he stayed silent and motioned for her to continue.

"In the hotel room, you said as my father lay dying his biggest concern was securing a promise from you to watch over me and Ben." She drew in a ragged breath in an attempt to calm herself, but the harsh and inevitable truth remained.

"You're not asking me to be your wife out of love. You're asking out of duty."

Jake slowly shook his head. "Not true."

"It is true! Otherwise you wouldn't have waited so long." She stared at him as a sickening realization took hold. "Now that everything is going wrong, you want to swoop in on your white horse and play the part of valiant rescuer to helpless princess."

She'd been such a naive simpleton. Not only had she invited him to share her room in the hotel, she'd nearly thrown herself at him that same night. No wonder he'd rebuffed her attempt at a goodnight kiss. After all, why would he want her when there were so many other women available?

"Your father wouldn't want you to be alone, and neither do I. Kate, I want you in my life. Forever."

She crossed her arms across her chest. "No, what you mean is now that my deeds are problematic, you're *stuck* with me. Forever."

Eyes wide, he placed a steadying hand on the ground and shifted from bended knee back to a crouch. "What was agreed upon between your father and I has nothing to do with today."

"How flattering," she replied, her tone dripping in sarcasm. "You're sweeping me off my feet with your romantic words."

"I shouldn't need romantic words to convince you your ideas are pure foolishness." He snatched up his hat and set it in place with a firm tug. "I know what you're thinking with that deed; you'll ride around until you find an empty house and fallow land. However, even if the deed is real and you manage to settle in, there's no guarantee someone won't try to take the place from you—lawfully or by force. Face it, Kate. I'm your best option."

"What you're offering isn't a marriage I could ever consider." She couldn't, and wouldn't, have a marriage built on a misplaced obligation to her dead father. "I'd rather be alone."

"I just thought maybe one day you would..." He trailed off and bowed his head.

They both fell silent.

As Kate listened to the whispers of the fire's hot coals and the rhythmic clicks of their horses enjoying their grass dinner, she reconsidered her stance.

His proposal was a selfless act, and it wasn't his fault she fervently wished it had stemmed from love instead of honor. He'd tried to do the right thing, which was admirable and deserved her understanding, not her anger.

"Jake, I release you from the promise you made my father." Kate took a deep breath and slid her hand over his forearm. "As for your proposal? Thank you for asking, but my answer is no. All my life I've been dependent upon others. Now's my chance to make it on my own, and I'm going to take it."

As much as Jake—and apparently her father—viewed her as vulnerable and helpless, she didn't need a caretaker. Hard times were definitely ahead, but if she made smart decisions and worked hard, she could succeed.

Before he could say another word, she crawled into her bedroll and turned toward the darkness.

Jake was right. She was a convincing liar.

CHAPTER SIXTEEN
Returning Empty-Handed

Sunday, November 12, 1843

THEY WOKE EARLY, RODE HARD ALL day, and arrived into Oregon City just before midnight. Sunday and a steady rain kept the streets clear all the way to the livery, and exhaustion kept them quiet while they tended to the horses.

Gathering two of his saddlebags and one of Kate's, Jake led the way out of the livery and down the boardwalk. He stopped at the hotel's front door, tested the knob, then gave it a firm push.

After motioning Kate through the doorway, he followed her upstairs without a word. At her door, Kate removed a sealed envelope with her name that had been affixed to the wood just above the knob. Upon opening it, she produced a silver room key. Once inside they made short work of unpacking damp supplies and trading sodden clothes for dry ones.

Unbidden, Kate laid out blankets and a pillow on the floor, then collapsed across her bed. Jake, too weary to protest the invitation, blew out the lamp, then scooted across the wood planks until he felt the makeshift bedroll and fell promptly asleep.

****

Monday, November 13, 1843

Jake sat on a chair in the shadows of the hotel room, watching the morning sun spill in through the window and onto the bed where Kate still slept. Overnight her hair had worked free of its braided constraints, and now sprawled across the pillow in brown ribbons. Her blankets lay in a tangle around her waist, revealing a sleeveless cotton nightgown that strained against her full curves with each breath.

She was beautiful, even with tinges of blue below her eyelids. Obviously the trip had sapped her strength, and if it was up to him she'd spend the day in bed, relaxing.

But she'd made her choice, which left him with no say anymore.

He should leave. Now. After all he was ready, if not willing. He'd spent the last hour dressing and silently repacking his bags—bags now waiting by the door.

Kate, eyes shut tight, let out an alluring sigh, then rolled onto her side and tucked her hands, palms together, between the pillow and her cheek.

With a groan of pent-up longing, Jake shifted his position in the chair.

Stubborn woman.

He loved her still, yet hated the recent glimpses of what she'd been like the day they'd first met and their first few weeks on the trail. He also hated how she hadn't understood the intent behind his proposal. Yes, hindsight confirmed leading with the promise to her father hadn't been his shining moment, and yes, he'd phrased every part poorly, but his pride still stung at her refusal. A refusal which had unwittingly revealed her independent streak still ran deep.

However, since poking a bear had never been his idea of fun, he wasn't about to point out the countless flaws in her plan of making it on her own.

Five days.

Five days until the land office opened and Jake could make his own claim.

Five days of the town slowly flooding with men arriving from the outlying areas, eager to stake their name to a claim and seek trouble in the saloon while they waited.

"Good morning." She gave him a sleepy smile as she lifted her arms over her head, inadvertently distracting him as the thin cotton stretched taut across her chest.

"Good morning, Kate." He breathed a sigh of relief when she pulled her blanket up and around her shoulders.

"You're up early." Her brows furrowed in confusion as her gaze slowly traveled from his boot-clad feet up to his coat-clad chest, then moved to his saddlebags piled near the door. "You're leaving?"

He nodded, then rose.

"Oh," she murmured, slumping against the pine headboard.

"You made your choice. I have to go, Kate."

Swallowing back the emotions roiling within, Jake grabbed his saddlebags, slung them over his shoulder, and picked up his rifle. One glance at her sitting wide-eyed and forlorn made him seriously consider falling to his knees beside the bed and begging for her love.

Instead, he opened the door.

"When will I see you again?" she asked as he stepped into the hallway.

He turned, and for the first time that morning, he smiled. "Kate, I've never been a quitter, and I don't intend to start with you. You'll see me again soon. I guarantee it."

He winked just before pulling the door closed behind

him.

CHAPTER SEVENTEEN
A Hard Place to Fall

JAKE WALKED DOWN THE HALLWAY AND reached the top of the staircase just as Clara stepped onto the landing.

"Hello," she said, her smile pleasant as she moved aside to allow him passage.

Jake took quick note of the hefty stack of linens kept firmly in place by her chin, a fresh pillow tucked beneath her arm, and her other arm curled around an empty water pitcher and bowl.

"Let me help you," he said, ignoring her startled expression as he leaned his rifle against the wall, dropped his saddlebags to the floor, and relieved her of the pillow, pitcher, and bowl. Balancing everything neatly against his chest, he grinned. "Where you headed?"

Clara matched his grin and nodded toward the nearest door. "Not too far."

With a sheepish shrug, Jake leaned against the wall and waited while she produced a ring of keys from her apron pocket and unlocked the door.

"You and Kate got in late last night," she said, stepping

inside. "No wonder you both slept through breakfast."

Jake followed her into a room that matched the one he'd just left, minus any personal effects. He cringed in disgust at the boot heel marks on the rumpled bed sheets and dirtied towels strewn across the floor. Clara was a saint for tolerating such disrespect.

"This room unoccupied?" he asked, setting his borrowed burden on the nearest tabletop.

"As of this morning, yes." Clara eyed him, her expression both curious and wary. "Something wrong with the one you and Kate are sharing?"

"It seems I've overstayed my welcome in her room. I'd like this one, if it's available?"

Clara nodded. "Theodore handles payments, so you'll need to square it away with him first. I'll have it cleaned and ready by the time you return."

"Thank you, ma'am," Jake replied. After a friendly nod in her direction, he spun on his heel and went out the door. Once he'd retrieved his rifle and saddlebags, he headed down the stairs. He grimaced with each step, this time not from pain but at the thought of handing over his hard-earned money to Theo.

Unfortunately, he didn't have much choice. He could always buy a few supplies at the mercantile and hightail it out of town until the land office opened, but camping on someone else's land, even unintentionally, was inviting trouble. And not just from an irate landowner unwilling to bargain with a trespasser.

Two years ago he'd suffered a broken left leg and been plagued by pain ever since. Oregon winters were soggy, cold, and unpredictable. Sleeping outside on damp ground would only worsen his suffering. Until the land office opened and allowed him a claim, he was stuck in the hotel. And, given how his leg already ached, he'd likely remain until he'd built some sort of shelter, however primitive.

At least he'd be close to Kate.

He'd left her room, but had no intention of giving up on her completely. She'd cited his utter lack of romance when she'd declined his proposal; now was his chance to show her he was fully capable of sweeping her off her feet. And then some.

Even if she truly wasn't interested, one thing was certain—though Kate had set him free of the promise he'd made her father, he had no intention of honoring her somber declaration.

Jake entered the hotel's lobby and found Theo sitting at his desk, pen in hand, frowning at two identical parchment papers lying side by side before him. When he saw Jake he quickly stacked the papers and pushed them into a drawer.

"Clara informed me the room at the end of the upper hallway is vacant. I'll take it."

Theo raised an eyebrow. "Trouble in paradise?"

Jake glared at him, but said nothing.

Theo—oblivious as always to looming danger—leaned back in his chair, laced his fingers behind his head, and smirked. "I recall some tough talk from you only four days ago. Something about how you'd rather sleep in a rainstorm than spend another night under my roof. And yet here you stand, wanting what only I can provide."

Jake waited, and fought the urge to relocate his rifle to a more meaningful position.

Eventually Theo lost their impromptu stare-down and lowered his gaze to a nearby ledger. He flipped it open, traced a long list across two pages, and then looked to Jake again.

"Yes, the room is available. Question is, can you afford it?"

Jake snorted. Leave it to Theo to ask for money from a man, yet at the same time insinuate payment was impossible. Mentally calculating what he'd paid for Kate's room per night, Jake dug into his pocket.

"I'll take the room for two weeks," he replied, tossing the required amount of coins onto the desk. Though rationally he knew there wasn't another option, he still hated seeing his money disappear into Theo's wall safe instead of going toward supplies and seeds for the next spring's crops.

Meanwhile, Theo bent over the desk and, with painstaking attention to detail, slowly wrote Jake's name to the room ledger. He then opened a shallow cupboard on the wall and plucked out the sole key amidst several empty brass hooks. As he held out the key, his focus drifted to something just over Jake's right shoulder.

"Jake, I *almost* forgot to mention who stopped in to see you while you were away," Theo said, his expression one of innocence. "Emily Bird sends her regards and will call on you again. Soon."

A small cough behind Jake clarified Theo's taunting tone.

"Hello." Kate's voice drifted across the room like honey on warm bread. "I'm sorry to interrupt, but I had a question."

Theo pressed the key into Jake's hand and deftly sidestepped around his desk, raising a mocking eyebrow as he passed.

Jake swallowed hard and focused on sliding the key into his pocket, even as anger and dread left his hands shaking. Slowly, he turned. Theo stood in front of Kate—too close if Jake had any say—running his mouth.

"Good morning, Kate," Theo said. "I'm happy to hear of your safe return from your trip. Hopefully I'm not being too forward when I say how much I've missed your company these past few days. I do hope you'll be able to join us for dinner tonight."

"Us?" Kate asked, looking to Jake. To his surprise, he saw a flicker of interest in her eyes. "You'll be there?"

Though Jake knew full well Theo had been referring to William and Margaret, he also knew Theo would never dare to refuse his presence in front of Kate.

Jake nodded. "Of course."

"Then I accept," she replied.

"Kate, you said you had a question," Theo said, his tone bordering on annoyance. "Can I help you with something?"

"I'd like to take your suggestion I freshen up," she said, motioning first to her tangled hair, then to her trail clothes. "Can you tell me where I'll find Clara?"

"She's probably in the kitchen finishing up the breakfast dishes." Theo waved his hand toward the hallway in a grand gesture. "First doorway on your left."

"Thank you," she replied, then quickly left the room.

Theo spun to face Jake again. "As I see it, there's nothing you could have done."

"Meaning?" Jake asked, leery of the man's sudden confidence.

Theo leaned close and dropped his voice to a conspiratorial whisper. "You should have known a woman like Kate wouldn't be interested in a man like you for long. Especially now that she's seen what else is available."

Jake clenched his jaw so hard it burned, but refused to accept the bait. In a roundabout way he had a dinner date with Kate tonight, and he had no intention of showing up with skinned knuckles.

Without a backward glance, Jake headed out of the room and back up the stairs. Once inside his room, he made short work of shoving his saddlebags under the bed and propping his rifle in the corner nearest the door. Within a minute his boots were thumping down the stairs and out the hotel's front door.

The land office opened in five days, and he planned to spend the day scouting available sections. He headed for the livery, then abruptly changed direction when his protesting stomach reminded him the town's restaurant was the perfect place to learn the latest news.

As he stood before a glass-paneled door, his reflection

reminded him Kate wasn't the only one who needed freshening up.

CHAPTER EIGHTEEN
What Could Have Been

KATE STOOD IN THE KITCHEN DOORWAY with her calico dress, camisole, and nightgown draped over one arm and her mother's sewing kit tucked under the other. Moments ago she'd caught a glimpse of Clara slipping through the outside door into the alley, but since she was unwilling to invade the older woman's domain until invited, Kate waited for her return.

She'd grown up in a house teeming with servants, maids, and cooks, all paid to anticipate her whims and to do her bidding, so she'd never taken more than a cursory glance at the inner workings of a kitchen. Until now.

The design was simple, yet efficient. Three wide pine shelves spanned the far left wall, showcasing a myriad of items. Dishes—plain and china—were stacked beside rows of crystal goblets, baskets of silverware, and sturdy metal mugs. Wooden bowls and serving dishes sat beside metal pots and pans. The lowest shelf had hooks along the entire outer edge, displaying various spoons, spatulas, and rolling pins. Burlap bags marked as flour, sugar, and coffee leaned against the wall beneath the shelves. A cook stove sat against the far right wall, and a table adapted to hold a dry sink and water pump was located below a window overlooking the alleyway.

Centered in the room was a massive butcher-block table, showcasing Clara's assembly line of organization. A cutting board heaped with carrots and squash and a nearby roasting pan of raw meat smothered in seasonings hinted a stew might be on the evening's menu.

Eight hours until dinner.

She had eight hours to wash, dry, and press the ragged dress that had been buried inside her saddlebag since she'd parted ways with the wagon train over two months before. The fabric smelled of wet leather and mold, and most of the seams were hanging on, quite literally, by only a few threads.

If she worked all day to get the dress presentable, then she could wear it while washing and repairing her trail clothes, and to dinner that night at six o'clock. The next day she could buy cloth at the mercantile, and using the calico as a pattern, she'd attempt to cut out properly sized pieces and sew a new dress. And, if all went well, petticoats and underclothes. A lofty, if not entirely realistic, goal in light of her sewing skills. Jake had taught her well, but only to patch and darn. Never to create.

A year ago Kate would have scoffed at the idea of enduring such effort and planning all to be able to wear a threadbare dress to dinner in a hotel dining room. And now here she stood, trying valiantly to repair what most would consider rags. The old adage was certainly true—necessity was the mother of invention. Though fear could easily replace necessity.

The outer kitchen door swung open and Clara hustled inside, carrying a wicker basket heaped with potatoes. After swiping a hand across her forehead to clear droopy gray curls, she dropped the basket onto the dry sink table.

"Clara?" Kate asked, still waiting in the doorway.

"Oh!" The woman stumbled, nearly upending a half-filled pan of biscuits warming on the stovetop.

Aghast, Kate hurried to her side. "I apologize for startling you."

Smiling broadly, Clara waved off her concern. "No trouble at all. I was just dropping the breakfast scraps into the compost pile and tending to what's left of the garden. What brings you to this part of the hotel? You hungry?"

Kate hesitated, then shook her head. She was about to cause enough disruption; she could wait until lunch to eat. "I'm wondering if I could trouble you for the use of your pump, and a spot on your stove to heat water."

Clara frowned. "What do you need the water for, my dear?"

"To wash these," she said, hoisting the dirty fabrics into the air. "Then, if my presence doesn't cause you too much trouble, after they're dry I'd like to wash what I'm wearing now." Kate gave her a hopeful smile even as she gestured to her pants and shirt, taking care to showcase the worst smears of grime.

Clara clucked her tongue. "By the looks of things, you'll be in here for the rest of the day."

"Yes, ma'am," Kate replied, wishing yet again she had anything else fit for wear and wasn't dependant upon a stranger's generosity.

She'd left trunks of clothes trailside, saving only the calico, two dresses, a nightgown, and the camisole she'd twisted into a silken rope to bind it all into a manageable square. The two dresses were elaborate, impractical, and perfect for attending dinner. However, both were musty and wrinkled from months in a saddlebag. They needed to be expertly cleaned and pressed to restore them to their former glory, and Kate knew nothing of washing velvet or satin, nor how to protect the intricate lace and ribbons adorning the hems and bust.

"Board's over there." Clara pointed toward a washboard hanging on the wall behind the hallway door. "Wash tub and soap are under the sink."

"Thank you," Kate murmured.

"Of course." Clara smiled brightly. "There's an empty kettle on the floor near the stove, and an open space on the stovetop. Start your water, then we'll have a nice chat while I make you toast and a scrambled egg to tide you over until lunch."

"Thank you," Kate repeated, grateful for the woman's sudden kindness.

She moved about the room, doing as instructed. Once the water was heating and the washtub stood at the ready, she seated herself at the center table on the stool opposite the sink, thinking it to be the farthest from Clara's path.

She opened the cloth bag containing her mother's sewing kit and began comparing her rolls of thread against the calico, trying to pick the best color match for the coming repairs. After selecting a roll of navy thread, she placed it on the table beside her loaded pincushion and a scrap of velvet with a line of ten needles.

Clara peered across the table and gave a low whistle. "You've got some nice supplies there. You're especially fortunate to have scissors and all those needles. They're valuable out here, so much so that women are known to share one between them." She stopped peeling the carrots and stared at Kate, her eyes showing her curiosity.

"Are you planning to open a dressmaking or millinery shop? Is that why you asked me if there was one here already?" Oblivious to Kate's attempts at answering, Clara rambled on. "It's a good idea, since it's the only profession other than teaching that a respectable woman would be interested in. And seeing how there's not many kids out here yet, you can't be here to teach."

Kate chuckled. "As you'll soon see, my sewing skills are

passable at best. In fact, I'll be making my first dress this week, and I expect many setbacks and bloodied fingertips."

Lips pursed, Clara waggled her knife in the air. "Hopefully you're not planning on working in the rooms over the saloon?"

"No!" Kate's cheeks flamed at the mere thought.

"Good." Clara punctuated the word with a firm nod. "This town don't need any more soiled doves. Got enough as it is. Seems every time I walk down the boardwalk there's another one of them harlots strolling along, their head held high and no shame in their step." She gave Kate a curious look. "You're not married, so what are you going to do out here?"

"I hold a deed to land and a house just outside of town. I intend to claim it, work it, and make it mine. However, I've run into a snag with the location, so I'll be staying in the hotel for the foreseeable future."

Kate did her best to portray confidence, but uncertainty was quickly turning to fear. What would she do if she couldn't locate her property? Or, even worse, if Jim's hunch was incorrect and the deed turned out to be a fake?

"Water's boiling!" Clara exclaimed, rushing with a gingham cloth stretched between her hands to lift the kettle off the stove. After dumping the water into the washtub, she set the kettle under the pump spigot. "You'd better even that out with an equal amount of cold. Don't want to burn yourself."

Kate obliged, then knelt on the floor and plunged her dress into the warm water. Meanwhile, Clara fetched a drying rack made of thin wooden dowels and set it up near the stove.

For the next few minutes, Kate soaped and scrubbed against the washboard, eventually turning the water a deep shade of brown. After lugging the tub to the kitchen garden in the back and emptying the putrid water, she returned and rinsed the fabric well, this time with cold water. She wrung it out and hung it on the drying rack, then repeated the process for her camisole and nightgown. While they dried, a lively conversation ensued with Clara. An hour later, when the dress was barely damp, Kate pulled an arm's length of thread from the roll, threaded a needle, and got to work. She spent the next two hours stitching each rip and worn seam, then held the dress up for inspection.

Clara took note. "Looks to me as though you'll be needing an iron."

Kate sighed. "Yes, I'm afraid I do. I'm sorry to keep bothering you."

"No trouble at all." She waved off Kate's attempted protest as she disappeared into the hallway. Several minutes later she returned with an iron in her hand, a twinkle in her eye, and a grin on her lips. After placing the iron on the stove to warm, she ran testing fingers over Kate's greasy curls. "How about you finally take that bath I've been offering?"

Kate had spent the last six months rife with dirt in nearly every crevice; of course she wanted a bath! But guilt—and memories of being shooed from the kitchen by impatient cooks who'd declared her presence as bothersome—took hold and she shook her head.

"You've been so helpful and you're working so hard; I can't bear to ask you for anything else."

"Kate," Clara said, her tone openly chiding. "When's the last time you've managed more than a few swipes with a dampened cloth, or worse yet, a spit-soaked handkerchief?"

"You're right." She shrugged, knowing she'd been deservedly cornered. "Last time water went up to my chin was three weeks ago on the bank of the Columbia River. A bath would be much appreciated."

Clara's brow furrowed as she reached a comforting hand to pat Kate's shoulder. "We've all been there, my dear. Trail life is brutal."

Kate swallowed hard and nodded enthusiastically, thrilled to find another woman who understood. She was sorely in need of a friend and glad to find one in Clara.

"Well then," Clara said. "I'll have it ready in less than half an hour."

She began bustling about, filling and heating kettles of water, then carrying them through a small door to the right of the stove that led into the bathing room. Though Kate made repeated offers to help, Clara insisted she stay put and finish the difficult task of pressing wrinkle after wrinkle out of her dress.

True to her word, half an hour later, Clara stood in the doorway of the bathing room and motioned for Kate. "You've fussed over that dress long enough. Come on." She ran an appraising gaze over Kate's camisole and nightgown, still draped over the rack. "Leave everything. I'll hang your dress on a nice scented hanger and bring it and your other clothes to your room when they're fully dry. Your sewing bag too."

"What will I wear after my bath?"

Clara winked, then walked through the doorway. Kate hopped off her stool and followed her into a small, wood-paneled room with no windows and three metal tubs.

"It isn't fancy," Clara declared, "but it gets the job done. Aside from Theodore, the only ones in here are rough men whose biggest concern is if I'll allow them to smoke and drink while they bathe." Clara shook her head in disgust, then smiled. "It's been a nice change getting this ready for a woman of refined tastes. I took the liberty of setting out a bar of soap for you since I suspect you might be in need. I make them myself every year, scented with lavender from my garden. Also, make sure to help yourself to a towel from the shelf."

Kate murmured her thanks, truly appreciating Clara's small, feminine touches like adding dried flowers to the bathwater and providing a pitcher to aid in rinsing the soap from her hair.

"As for what you'll wear afterward..." Clara pointed to a robe hanging on the wall beside the sole steaming tub and a pair of slippers lined up neatly against the wall. "No other guests are inside the hotel right now, so when you're done you can slip upstairs without being seen." Clara gave a friendly tug on Kate's shirtsleeve. "Leave behind what you're wearing now. I'll put it all in the washtub to soak overnight. You can tackle them in the morning."

"I look forward to it." Kate bit her lip and blinked back tears, overwhelmed at Clara's thoughtfulness.

"Come visit anytime," Clara said, smiling wistfully. "Water and coffee are always on."

She returned to the kitchen, pulling the door closed behind her as she left. Once Kate heard the soft click of the latch settling in place, she made short work of dropping her trousers and shirt to the floor. She eased into the tub and sank down, sighing as the glorious liquid heat surrounded and soothed her dry, rough skin.

It seemed so long ago since bathing had been a nightly ritual, drawn by her personal maid and finished off with treating herself with the finest of powders, softening creams, and perfumes. Then, after maids combed and arranged her hair, she'd lounge in a satin nightgown and matching slippers and finish the daily accounting and summaries for her father's mercantile. However, none of her baths back home in Virginia could hold a candle to this moment, nor the time she'd bathed beneath the dusky sky during her time with the wagon train.

Kate soaked until the air grew sultry and then tipped her head back until her forehead met the waterline. Three soap scrubs and rinses later, her hair was clean and her skin was moist.

After abandoning the tub, she quickly toweled herself dry, twisted her hair into a dripping knot, slipped into the robe, and tied it at her waist. She pulled her room key from the pocket of her trousers, raced through the empty kitchen and stairway, then continued down the length of the upstairs hallway to her room. After fumbling briefly with the lock, she pushed the door open.

She gasped at what lay waiting on her bed.

CHAPTER NINETEEN
Laying Groundwork

KATE REACHED TOWARD THE BED, THEN stopped herself.

It has to be a mistake. It must be for someone else. A careless deliveryman probably brought it to the wrong room.

Laid diagonally across her bed was a dress that rivaled any she'd worn back home in Virginia, or left to rot along the trail. While endless yards of maroon velvet made the skirt full, the bodice was tight and the shoulders were low enough to showcase a décolletage. Ruffled lace trim across the bust line would conceal just enough to deem everything proper. Eyes wide, she bent to admire the intricate beadwork along the waist, the thin silk ribbon at the opening of each cap sleeve, and the perfectly spaced stitching—not a single gap or loop of thread to be found.

She slid her hands gently beneath each shoulder, then lifted and held the dress to her chest. Closing her eyes, she breathed deeply, reveling in the scent of a floral perfume. It reminded her of the balls and dinner parties she'd attended since turning sixteen. While she'd never cared for how guests engaged in rampant gossip and subtle speculation of another's personal worth, she'd enjoyed dressing the part.

She lowered the gown back to the bed, taking great care her work-roughened fingertips didn't cause a snag. She had no right to play dress-up with another woman's property.

Or was it? A deliveryman would have left it at the front desk. And she'd unlocked her door to get inside, so it must have come from someone with access to her room.

Someone with a key.

She backed away from the bed, intent on heading downstairs and finding Clara, but stopped when she noticed a small white paper lying on the floor. Scooping it up, she turned it over.

K,
Beauty as exquisite as yours deserves a dress to match.

Kate reread the paper several times, then frowned. The dress had obviously been given to her as a gift. But from whom?

****

Jake walked along the boardwalk toward the hotel, feeling more polished than a new pair of silver spurs.

After a visit to the mercantile and a chat with Albert, the owner, he'd left with a small white box, a stack of fresh clothes, boots, and a hat. While nothing was new, everything was in good condition. Albert's idea to allow hollow-eyed settlers to trade clothes for foodstuffs was both brilliant and generous. He'd helped many a starving traveler fresh off the trail get the items they needed to survive, while simultaneously offering clothes at reasonable prices to those who arrived with rags on their backs and money to spare.

Next, he'd visited the town's bathhouse for a much-needed dunk and wash, then the barber for a haircut and close shave. After that night's dinner with Kate, he planned to take her on a private walk, which would finish off his day rather nicely.

He intended to head into the hotel and wait in his room until a few minutes before dinner began at six o'clock, purposely leaving himself no time to engage in another solitary discussion with Theo. He patted the white box in his pocket, assuring himself again of its presence, then entered the hotel's lobby.

Sighting Theo, he muttered a curse to see his well-laid plan go awry.

"Good evening, Jake," Theo said, pushing himself back from his desk and rising to his feet. "I see you had a productive day."

Jake nodded, not fooled by the man's seemingly inane remarks. He had a reason for everything, and based on his bare desktop he hadn't been doing any paperwork. No, he'd been lingering at his desk, waiting for Jake to arrive. *But why?*

He pulled a wooden box from a shelf and set it on the desktop. "You a cigar man, Jake?"

"On occasion." Like Theo, cigars were something Jake tolerated but never enjoyed.

"It appears we've gotten off on the wrong foot. Again." Theo opened the box's lid, revealing a long line of cigars. "How about we step outside, have a cigar, and try to reach an understanding of each other?"

"On the contrary, I think we've already come to a perfect understanding of each other," Jake replied.

Theo silently raised the box until it was even with Jake's chest, then waited.

Out of sheer curiosity, Jake selected a cigar and then followed Theo back outside. He shut the door, then turned to see Theo had claimed the majority of the railing by standing with his lower back against it, his arms and hands resting wide on either side.

Jake chuckled at the man's not-so-subtle reminder that he owned the place.

"It's shaping up to be a nice evening," Theo said, using a gold cutter to neatly snip off the end of his cigar. After lighting it, he tossed the match into the street.

"Indeed," Jake replied, wishing he would just come to the point. He'd agreed to this strange meeting solely to figure out what the man was up to, not to discuss the weather. He accepted the cutter Theo offered and clipped off the end of his own cigar. After exchanging the cutter for a match, he dragged it across his boot heel to set it aflame, then calmly lit his cigar.

They smoked for several minutes before Theo broke the silence. "Let me ask you a question, friend." He blew a steady stream of smoke across the boardwalk, smirking as it hit Jake's chest. "Do you honestly think you can provide Kate with the lifestyle she deserves?"

Jake removed his cigar from his teeth. He took elaborate care in tapping away the flaky ashes, distracting himself from the sudden urge to push Theo over the railing, then hop over after him and finish the job. Dinner was only minutes away, and while his comment warranted a swift rebuttal—preferably a physical one—seeing Kate took priority. Finally, when he trusted himself to only speak, he replied, "I'm not your friend, and she's not your concern."

Theo scoffed. "A quality woman like her will never be truly happy with a worn-out saddle tramp like you."

"You may be right." Jake tipped his head back, blew a puff of smoke into the air, and watched the white cloud whirl away in the breeze. Then he faced Theo. "But you're sorely mistaken if you think she'll be satisfied with a ruthless schemer like you."

Theo grinned, seemingly undaunted by the warning. "Any woman's affections can easily be swayed—and won—by the man willing to toss the most baubles her way. You'll soon see I'm able to give Kate what you cannot."

As Jake watched Theo silently drop his cigar onto the boardwalk, twist it flat with his heel, then walk back into the hotel, he had the distinct feeling he'd underestimated the man.

CHAPTER TWENTY
Dinner and a Dress

KATE STOOD IN THE HALLWAY AT the base of the stairs, regretting how long she had taken to get ready for dinner.

Fastening herself into the dress had taken nearly half an hour, and only completed due to her overly limber arms and fingers and sheer determination. Once the wall mirror proved she'd gotten every button, she'd focused on her hair. The entire length was now captured into a shining, albeit messy updo atop her head. Styling her hair was still her weakness since she'd always had a personal maid, so several curls had already escaped their pins. Shoes had presented another problem. She'd had two options—dusty trail boots or barefoot. After considering how the long skirt would hide either choice, she'd opted for the boots.

Tucking a loose lock of hair behind her ear, Kate smoothed a wrinkle from her cap sleeve and stepped into the dining room. To her chagrin, Theodore, William, Margaret, and Jake were already seated and waiting.

"I apologize for my late arrival," she announced, then made her way across the room, holding back a grimace at how the skirt dragging along at her feet slowed her steps. She'd forgotten how cumbersome basic movements could be when done beneath a dress.

Theodore and Jake both scrambled from their chairs and reached for the back of the empty one between them.

Jake was quicker.

He winked as she approached, and she couldn't help but smile at his antics. Once she stood beside him, waiting for him to pull out the chair, he lowered his head and allowed his lips to linger mere inches from her ear.

"You're beautiful," he whispered.

She looked up at him in surprise, he winked again, and she dropped onto her chair with an ungraceful thud. Jake returned to his seat beside her as if nothing were amiss. As if he hadn't completely transformed himself. His hair—normally tucked under a hat or hanging over his ears in disheveled waves—was freshly trimmed and his beard was gone altogether. Pungent clothes had been replaced by new. And he smelled wonderful.

Kate longed to wander an exploring fingertip along his smooth jaw line and down his neck, then close her eyes, slide her arms around his waist, and nestle against his chest. Forever. Instead, she settled for taking a drink of water and fumbling her napkin into place across her lap.

"Kate," Margaret said, "I must admit I've only seen you in manly clothes, so I never knew you cut such a fetching figure, or had such flawless skin."

"I agree." Theodore nodded, his wide-eyed stare bordering on sheer rudeness. "You're positively stunning."

"Thank you," she murmured, fighting the urge to remind both of them she was still the same woman, just with a fancier covering.

Jake tapped his index finger twice against the back of her hand. Once their eyes locked, his intense gaze commanded, and received, her full attention. "You look exquisite tonight,

Kate. But then again, you always do."

Kate recalled the note with the dress, and how it contained the same unusual word, but Clara arrived before she could question him.

"Here is the first course of the evening," she said, placing a bowl of tomato soup on the table before each guest. "For those of you with delicate palates, there's crackers on the plate below each of your bowls. Or, if you prefer a stronger flavor, I'd be happy to bring out a fresh garlic roll."

Her enthusiastic tone rang false, and Kate noted the dark circles beneath her eyes. The poor woman must have worked all afternoon to put dinner together, all while coddling an interloper in her kitchen.

Kate tasted the soup and immediately nodded her approval. "This is delicious."

Theodore clapped his hands twice, then waited until all eyes were on him before speaking. "Yes, Clara has outdone herself with tonight's four-course meal. I had her prepare it especially in honor of you, Kate. I thought you could use a reminder that even in the territory, comfort and opulence are still available. You just have to realize who can provide them."

He launched into a long-winded description of the place settings, making special note of the gold rims on the glass stemware and plates, then moved on to declare the silverware as one of the few sets to survive the trip west, and the six crystal candlestick holders placed in a line down the center of the table as once belonging to English royalty.

Kate smiled appreciatively when Theodore's pauses indicated he expected a reply, all the while wondering if he thought her too simple to notice such things. On the contrary, she'd noticed everything he'd mentioned the moment she'd taken up her spoon. And then some.

She'd noticed everything he was so proud of wasn't half as fine as what she'd cast aside after Jake had convinced her of the need to lighten their wagon. She'd noticed Theodore's decision to load the table with finery and multiple courses had put a heavy burden upon Clara.

Most of all, she'd noticed Theodore was an attention-seeking braggart.

Clara arrived to clear their soup bowls and Theodore gustily announced the remainder of the menu course by course—the hearty venison and vegetable stew Kate had glimpsed earlier in the kitchen, a selection of cheese and bread, and finally peach cobbler topped with heavy cream for dessert.

William grinned and made a show of rubbing his middle. "I'm looking forward to everything you've just described. My stomach hasn't quit growling since we left Independence."

Margaret chimed in. "I love this food for the simple reason it's seasoned with spices instead of grit and insects."

"Trail rations can be tough to adjust to," Jake said. "But not much beats fresh meat, fish, or cackleberries cooked over an open flame and ate under an open sky."

Kate smothered a snicker when she saw the horror-stricken look on Theodore's face. He must have been a nightmare to travel west with.

"I think a change of subject is in order," he said, waving his hand in the air as if to flick aside their previous conversation. "I've always found it entertaining for guests to share the events of their day, especially since I typically spend mine at my desk going over paperwork."

"What an interesting idea," Margaret said, her head bobbing in enthusiastic agreement.

"We can skip Jake, since it's obvious he spent his day finally becoming acquainted with a scrub brush," Theodore said, shifting to face Kate. "What did you do today?"

She met his inquisitive gaze and smiled sweetly. "Since I too spent my day reacquainting myself with a scrub brush, I guess I deserve to be skipped as well." Ignoring Jake's burst of laughter and subsequent failure to cover it with a well-timed cough, Kate motioned across the table to William and Margaret. "How about you two? Did you have a productive day?"

"Yes, we did," William answered, completely oblivious to the recent volley of insults. "We rode all over the countryside, scouting land to file a claim on. Lots of potential out there."

Margaret leaned over and placed a quick kiss upon her husband's cheek. "The best part of my day was enjoying the beautiful surroundings without having to rush."

"Did you find a place?" Jake asked.

"Yes," William said. "It's about seven miles outside of town. Pristine, with no sign of a house or crops anywhere nearby. I'll be first in line when the claims office opens its door. Jake, you should be right behind me since there's competition scouting every available hillside. We came across several men today, all intent on discovering untouched land and declaring it for their own."

Kate's mood soured upon hearing William's news. If her father were here, he'd be plotting an agenda, broken down by weekly goals, for the next year or longer.

In four days and a wake-up she'd be in the land office, conniving to learn her future. Until then, planning anything was useless.

****

Jake gritted his teeth, regretting for the first time his decision to spend the day tending to superficial needs instead of focusing on his true highest priority—scouting for land. Tomorrow he'd hit the saddle at first light, and by nightfall he'd hopefully have several options to choose from if his first choice was signed on before he got to the claims desk.

His stomach roiled at the thought of riding out tomorrow without Kate by his side. Of standing on a hillside, alone, instead of with Kate tucked tight against him, his arm curled around her shoulders while they looked down upon a plot of land and declared it the perfect place to grow old together.

"Kate, what are your plans tomorrow?" Theo asked.

Instantly, Jake perked up. What was he up to now?

"I don't have any," she replied, her words and actions hesitant.

"I make it a point to visit my livery daily, and I can't help but notice all your horses need exercise. They've been cooped up in their stalls since you got here."

Jake was amazed at how smoothly the man could spout outright lies. If there was one redeeming quality about Theo, it was his obvious dedication to maintaining a high level of care for horses, his or otherwise.

"While your concern is admirable," Jake said, "I don't know why you're hiding how well you run your livery. I've been out there too and seen firsthand how your attendant, Mark, lets every horse roam about the paddock for several hours each day." He grinned at how he'd managed to correct the misimpression Theo had attempted, and how he'd cornered him. Arguing Jake's flattery would only lead to Kate questioning the care of her horses.

"You caught me." Theo raised his hands in a surrendering gesture. When he lowered then, he shifted his focus to Kate. "I was afraid of coming on too strong, so I used the horses as an excuse. What I actually want is to invite you on a ride tomorrow. Clara can act as chaperone, which will allow for your reputation to remain intact and give three of your horses the opportunity to stretch their legs."

Kate focused her full attention on Clara, who had just entered the room holding a silver tray laden with steaming bowls of chunky stew. She watched carefully as the woman served their second course.

After she left, Kate turned to Theo. "Clara deserves to rest after all she's done today, both for me and for everything she's gone through to prepare this meal. I don't want to burden her any further, especially for something as frivolous as a scenic horse ride."

Theo's eyebrows rose at Kate's admonishment, but instead of showing irritation he simply replied, "Another time then."

Jake let out a breath he hadn't realized he'd been holding. After evaluating the reality of his week ahead, he decided to eliminate any possibility of Theo spending time with Kate tomorrow.

"Kate, I've been meaning to explore the town a bit more, and tomorrow's as good a day as any. Care to join me?" He paused, and then added the one detail she wouldn't be able to resist. "We can stop by the land office and see how it's progressing."

Theo frowned. "Jake, certainly you have more pressing issues to attend to, like finding a place to live since you've declared my hotel to be unsatisfactory for your needs. I'd be happy to escort you about the town instead, Kate."

William slid his arm around his wife's shoulders. "Judging by how adamant you both are in trying to win Kate's affections, it seems like the rumors were correct—single women are a rarity out here. Glad I was smart enough to marry Margaret before we even hit the trail."

Jake grimaced at the truth behind William's words.

"Thank you for the offer, Theodore," Kate said. "However, Jake and I have a few things to clarify between us. We might as well stretch our legs while doing so."

Jake bit back a smile. Not only had she chosen to spend her day with him, but she'd also managed to use Theo's own line against him as her reason to decline his invitation. Oh, how he loved this woman!

Theo didn't reply, but instead made a point of checking everyone's stew bowl. When he found the majority empty, he removed a silver bell from his vest pocket and shook it three times.

Clara appeared with the serving tray tucked under one arm. "I'm just putting the finishing touches on the next course. It shouldn't be long." She whisked away their latest round of bowls and hurried from the room.

Theo rested an elbow on the table, slowly rubbed his chin several times, then snapped his fingers as if an idea had just occurred. "I know what we can discuss next." Theo turned to Margaret. "Forgive me if I'm being too forward, but I'm wondering how you're situated when it comes to clothing?"

Margaret shrugged. "I don't have much, but I'm a good seamstress so I'm able to make what I need."

"What about you, Kate? The dress you're wearing is in good condition. Did it come across the trail with you?"

Jake frowned. What was Theo getting at with this conversation?

"No," she replied quietly. "It was left in my room this afternoon."

To Jake's surprise, she didn't elaborate. Apparently she had no intention of telling the others he'd bought it for her. Why? He thought back for a moment, and then stifled a groan as he realized he'd forgotten to sign the note.

Beneath the cover of the tablecloth, he reached for her hand. "Kate, the moment I saw that dress I knew it would fit you perfectly."

Theo's lips twitched in amusement. "I'm guessing that moment was when you saw it lying on the floor of Emily's room? She's always been generous to you with her body; stands to reason she'd sell you her dress too."

"You're out of line," Jake muttered, then winced as Kate yanked her hand from his.

Theo ignored the warning and dug deeper. "In fact, Emily has visited my hotel several times looking for you." He lowered his voice to a brash whisper. "I prefer keeping her kind away from my guests, so when you two have *business* to attend to, I'd prefer it take place at the saloon."

"Kate, don't listen to him." Jake hated the desperation he heard in his tone, and the man who had put it there with his twisted insinuations. "He's lying."

"I most certainly am not," Theo declared, puffing up his chest in feigned indignation. "Are you implying you haven't had the pleasure of Emily's company? Or that she hasn't been trying to reconnect with you since your arrival?"

Kate fled the room.

CHAPTER TWENTY-ONE
Wavering

KATE STORMED INTO HER HOTEL ROOM, kicked the door shut behind her, and reached back for the first in the long line of buttons trapping her in the dress of shame. She freed the easiest ones and then clawed at the center of her back until buttons clattered to the floor like hail on a tin roof.

After several minutes her arms were weary, but anger and humiliation fueled her on until the dress lay in a twisted heap at her feet. Naked and near tears, she remembered how nearly every piece of clothing she owned was downstairs in the kitchen, soaking in the washtub or drying before the stove.

Kate snatched up the quilt, wrapped it around her shoulders and chest, and then plopped down on the edge of the bed.

How dare he! How dare Jake shroud her in his harlot's dress, then smile as she'd proudly paraded herself through the dining room? *Deplorable!*

She'd overheard Theodore informing Jake of someone visiting the hotel to see him while they'd been away in Champoeg, but it hadn't made sense. Until now.

On the second day across the trail, Jake had warned her of the presence of saloon girls and ladies of easy virtue in Oregon City. Now she understood how he knew of such things. Firsthand knowledge.

Cheeks flaming, Kate sprang to her feet and paced the room, her boot heels thumping a steady rhythm against the floorboards. She'd already suffered through a similar disgrace by her childhood sweetheart. Though Crandall's indiscretion—courting Kate and hinting at marriage all while impregnating the town trollop—had merely made her realize she'd been played for a fool. Seconds after learning the truth, she'd bid good riddance to Crandall and never looked back.

This was different.

She loved Jake.

Kate crossed the room to stand at the corner of the window and peer out at the town below. It wasn't as if she expected Jake to have a pristine past. He was thirty-one years old. But what kind of man was he to have sought solace in the arms of a saloon girl the same week he'd asked for her hand in marriage?

Of course, ultimately his proposal had meant nothing. Jake was, quite simply, a man who'd asked based on obligation, not love.

With a heavy sigh, Kate slumped against the wall and rested her damp cheek on the window's glass pane. She was so confused. Jake's final words before departing her room the morning after they'd returned from Champoeg had led her to believe he wanted to pursue a romance. Why else would he say he'd never been a quitter and didn't intend on starting with her?

Why hadn't he just been truthful and explained his interests were elsewhere?

Why would he think it acceptable to dally with a whore, and then buy the dress off her back to give away as a gift?

Three soft knocks on her door interrupted her thoughts.

CHAPTER TWENTY-TWO
Righting a Wrong

"WHO IS IT?" KATE CALLED, CLUTCHING the quilt tighter around herself while evaluating the number of steps to the knife hidden inside her saddlebags.

"It's me, dear." Clara's voice carried through the door. "I've got fresh water, your clothes, and a treat."

With a sigh of relief, Kate unlocked and opened the door.

Clara walked into the room, handing Kate a stack of folded clothes as she passed. "Here's everything you left drying downstairs." She set a water pitcher on the washstand and a dishtowel-covered plate on the bedside table. Brushing her hands together, she turned to face Kate. "I also went ahead and washed those clothes you had soaking in the tub. They're hanging by the stove and should be ready to wear by morning."

"Thank you so much! If you don't mind, I'll just be a moment." Kate hurried behind the dressing screen. She slipped into the camisole and calico, hung her nightgown on a wall peg, and then emerged with the quilt in her hand.

"I appreciate you bringing everything up." She folded the

quilt and placed it on the end of the bed.

"Sorry you had to wait so long." Clara grimaced. "Theodore had me so busy all afternoon I didn't have a chance to get to them earlier."

"Yes," Kate said. "That was quite an extravagant meal you prepared."

"Too bad you missed half of it." Clara raised a brow, then motioned to the covered plate. "I saved you some cobbler. No cream left though; Margaret's finally found something she'll eat."

Kate shifted her weight and let out a nervous chuckle. "I apologize if my leaving early caused you any trouble."

"No trouble for me." Clara's gaze wandered to the dress still lying on the floor, then settled on Kate. "Appears as though you can't say the same?"

Kate opened her mouth, intent on declaring everything was fine, but after seeing the sympathy in Clara's eyes she simply shook her head. "You're right. I can't."

Clara pointed to the chair by the door. "May I?"

Kate nodded eagerly. "Please."

"I knew trouble was afoot the moment I brought in the third course," Clara said, settling herself. "Your chair was empty and Jake's face was mottled with rage. Then things got exciting. I hadn't even set down the serving tray when Jake sprang to his feet, took a few steps as if he were leaving, but instead stopped behind Theodore's chair. He then leaned down and muttered something into Theodore's ear. I didn't catch what was said, but it must have been interesting since Theodore looked as though he wished the floor would swallow him whole. Jake then left the room without a backward glance."

"Where is he now?" Kate asked, struggling to sound composed even as her mind screamed of Jake's betrayal.

"I saw him leave the hotel shortly afterward. I'm not certain where he went, but I do know that he hasn't returned."

Kate gritted her teeth. "He probably went back to the saloon to buy another dress from a soiled dove."

Clara tapped her index finger against her lips several times, then threw up her hands. "Jake swore me to secrecy, but I don't think he'll mind me breaking my word if it clears up your confusion."

Immediate questions sprang to mind, but Kate stayed silent and waited for Clara to continue.

"Aside from how that dress is lying on your dusty floor in a careless heap, there's nothing improper about it. Jake bought that dress from a friend of mine."

Kate gasped. "What?"

"Jake came to me the day after you two arrived in town. He asked if I knew of anyone who could make you a dress. I told him I had a better idea. A woman I know had brought several dresses over the trail, but two kids and twenty pounds later she decided none would fit properly again. She put out word she was eager to trade them for food, supplies, or cash. Jake agreed on the latter and selected the one he thought would suit you best. It was delivered to the hotel this afternoon while you were repairing your calico."

Clara chuckled. "That's why I became so interested in—and a little bit pushy about—your bathing habits. I couldn't bear thinking of you in that fancy dress without a proper bath first. Do you like it?"

"I love it," Kate said, eager to assure her she'd done the right thing in breaking her word. "Thank you so much for taking the time to lay it out on my bed."

"Wasn't me," Clara said. "However, I did let Jake in your room, and then I stood in the doorway while he fussed and fidgeted over how to arrange it perfectly. I finally had to remind him you were waiting downstairs for an iron and he needed to hurry."

"I don't understand why he went through such trouble when he's..." Kate trailed off, embarrassed to continue.

Embarrassed to tell Clara her confusion as to why would Jake purchase such an expensive gift for her, all while carousing with a saloon girl.

Or was he?

A chill settled over Kate as she realized Theodore had obviously lied about the dress, so it stood to reason he'd lied about everything else he'd said about Jake. She bowed her head in chagrin.

Though Jake had all but pleaded for her not to listen to Theodore's assertions, she'd left dinner in a huff without giving him a chance to explain. She'd believed the words of a man she barely knew, and had been warned about, instead of a man who'd repeatedly proven himself as honorable.

"When he's what, dear?" Clara asked. "What were you going to say?"

"Never mind," Kate said, shaking her head for emphasis. Though she knew the truth of Theodore's lies, she had no intention of gossiping about him with Clara. After all, he was still her employer, and the man who'd given her a job and shelter when she'd had no other options. "It's nothing."

"A man doesn't buy a woman a dress like that one for no reason." Clara gestured to the floor. "What does Jake mean to you?"

Seeking a distraction from the question since she didn't know how to answer, Kate plucked the dishtowel from the plate and hefted a heaping spoonful of cobbler into her mouth.

Clara's smile faded and her cheeks went pale. "Don't take such big bites, dear."

Kate swallowed hard and gave up. Not only was this woman a stickler for manners, apparently she could also see through ruses.

"Jake asked me to marry him. It wasn't for the right reasons, so I said no."

Clara placed a hand over her chest. "Sometimes any reason is better than nothing at all, if you're interested in return. You'll have a lifetime together to win his heart."

Kate set aside the plate, got to her feet, and picked up the dress. Holding it over one arm, she brushed it clean with her palm and then laid it gently across the end of the bed.

"I was married once," volunteered Clara. "Harper was the best thing that ever happened to me. Not a day went by without me telling him I loved him." She smiled a gentle, knowing smile. "He loved me, too, just as much."

"What happened?" Kate asked quietly.

"A few days after our wagon train left Fort Hall, someone shot two deer and we stopped to cook them over a fire. We were all half-starved by then, so everyone got a plate full of meat. Harper couldn't help himself—he ate too much too fast, and choked. Men slapped him on the back and even turned him upside down, but he died." Clara blinked back sudden tears, then continued. "I could have turned back, but figured I had more opportunities at a better life here."

Kate wiped tears from her own cheeks. No wonder she'd felt an instant kinship with this woman. "I'm so sorry to hear of your loss. You have my deepest sympathy."

"I figured you'd understand, especially given what happened to your family and possessions on the trail." Clara leaned over and patted her hand. "Margaret told me."

They shared teary smiles, and then the remainder of the cobbler. Once the plate had been scraped clean and the dishtowel folded beneath, Kate decided to ask a question that had been bothering her ever since hearing Jim's news.

"Don't you find it unfair that men younger than me can own land, yet a woman cannot, no matter her age?"

"Things will change, dear," Clara replied. "Not in my lifetime, but probably in yours."

CHAPTER TWENTY-THREE
Reasoned Deception

Tuesday, November 14, 1843

JAKE SPENT MOST OF THE NIGHT lying in his bed with his hands tucked behind his head, staring at the ceiling and reviewing the events of the previous night's dinner.

He'd been so stunned when he'd first heard Theo's outright lie about where Kate's dress had come from that by the time he was ready to defend himself, Kate had already been up and running. He'd worked so hard to earn her trust it had physically pained him to watch her listen to the lies spewing from Theo's lips.

Except, to Jake's regret, not everything said had been a lie.

Though his transgressions were years in the past and weren't something he ever planned on repeating, Jake had spent time with harlots.

He knew for a fact Theo had done the same. During a visit, he'd imbibed too much and stumbled drunkenly into Jake while they'd passed each other in the saloon's upper hallway. Neither acknowledged the other at the time, but as was typical for Theo, he'd likely realized dinner was the perfect time to bring up Jake's sordid past. If Jake had told the other guests Theo had also been a regular participant in the debauchery on the upper floor, it would have just confirmed his own presence.

Though stars still hung bright in the early morning sky, Jake knew when he was licked. He'd get no sleep until nightfall. Leaving town and spending the day in his saddle was just the medicine he needed to cure his misery.

Tossing the bed's quilt aside, he got to his feet, buried the white box deep in the bottom of one of his saddlebags, and then made quick work of packing another saddlebag with what he'd need to scout out land. When he finished, he dropped the bag and his hat by the door and then rested his rifle nearby against the wall.

He dressed in the outfit he'd bought the day before, grimacing at the outright stank wafting over the ragged pile of clothes he'd worn on the trail. Upon his return, he'd need to reacquaint them with soap and a washtub.

As he slipped on his boots, he heard footsteps echoing softly down the hallway. At first he paid them no mind. He'd heard many other guests on his floor walk by his room on their way downstairs.

This time the footsteps stopped at his door. And waited.

Jake eased his pistol from its holster and checked to see that his rifle was within easy reach.

"Who is it?" he bellowed, opting for intimidation over manners.

After a long pause, the answer finally came. "Kate."

He quickly replaced the pistol in the holster and set it aside. After taking several deep breaths, he opened the door to see Kate standing before him, wearing the dress he'd bought for her.

"Hello," she said quietly.

"Hello," he replied, trying to hide his surprise at seeing

her.

Kate gave him an uneasy smile and then ran fidgeting fingers across the sleeves and bodice of her dress, pulling at seams and ruffles that were already straight. "I'm here for our walk around town," she said, her eyes and tone oddly hopeful. "If you're still interested."

He considered her words carefully. If she was seeking him out, perhaps she was willing to overlook his past?

Kate apparently took his silence for hesitation. "I'm so sorry about last night! You were so sweet to buy me this wonderful dress, and you've been nothing but kind to me, and given me no reason to doubt you about anything ever. You're such a good man. I'm so sorry! I wish I'd stayed for the whole dinner. I should have stayed by your side when Theodore was saying such horrific lies about you."

"Kate, what he said isn't all—"

"Please, Jake." Kate's voice cracked. "Please, just hear me out. I know about the dress. Clara told me everything. How you asked her where you could buy me a new one. How you picked out this one and laid it out on my bed with such care."

She paused to rub her palms over the sides of her hips several times, leaving two damp streaks on the dress's fabric. When she realized what she'd done, she clasped her hands together at her waist and continued. "Jake, asking about the walk was just an excuse. I'm really here to tell you I know Theodore is a liar and I don't believe a word he said last night."

A chill settled over him. How could he admit that Theo hadn't lied about everything? How could he taint his lovely Katie—still pure and so naive as to the ways of the west—with the knowledge of his past indiscretions with loose women?

He'd much rather take her on a walk.

Using the side of his foot, Jake pushed his loaded saddlebag behind the open door, hiding it from Kate's view. He had three full days until the land office opened; he could spend today with her.

"Kate, let's try this again." He grinned and held his hand out before her, palm up. "I've been meaning to take a walk around town and see how it's grown and changed since my last trip out. Care to join me?"

She slid her hand over his. "I'd love to."

CHAPTER TWENTY-FOUR
Reunions

AFTER A QUICK BREAKFAST OF EGGS and toast at the town's restaurant, which Kate happily noted wasn't nearly as dingy or rough as Theodore had claimed, she stepped back out onto the boardwalk and began walking with Jake at her side.

"We were on the trail for so long; I think it will take me some time to get used to living in a town again," she said, eyeing the buildings sprawled along the riverbank and up the hillside, and the range of mountains along the horizon.

Jake nodded his agreement. "It's a much different view than horses, forest, or grass and a campfire. Lots of changes here since my last time through. In addition to the hotel, there's a mercantile, a mill, an apothecary, a restaurant, a tannery, and countless new houses. It looks like there are plenty of buildings going up across the river as well. Only a matter of time before more businesses open with the amount of wagon trains due to arrive next spring."

"Spring?" Kate asked, wondering how travelers would dare cross the mountains during the winter months.

"Many people start out late like we did and then spend

winter near a fort, hunkered down in their wagons."

Kate sympathized with those in the unfortunate situation of enduring months of frigid weather and deep snow while cooped up in the back of a wagon. "I'm always amazed at what people are willing to tolerate for the opportunities and land out here."

"Speaking of land," Jake said, taking her hand to help her off the boardwalk steps and onto the street between the blacksmith and apothecary, "I'll be out of the hotel from sunup to sundown for the next few days. I need to start scouting for a claim."

"I'll miss you," Kate murmured.

"I'll miss you too." Jake put his hand on her arm, pulling her to a stop. "The other day when I left your hotel room, I should have been much clearer about my intentions toward you, and your future. Our future." He paused to gather both her hands in his and tuck them against his chest. "I'm a good listener, so when you said you wanted to be romanced and swept off your feet I vowed to give it my best attempt."

"When did I ever say such a thing?" Kate asked, her tone teasing, yet happy.

Jake's smile faded. "When you turned down my proposal."

"Is that why you got me this dress?"

"It's impolite to ask questions about a gift," he chided, then lowered his voice to a whisper. "Did it work?"

Kate grinned impishly. "I'd say it's a good start."

"Hey!" An unfamiliar shout broke the moment. "That you, Jake?"

Kate turned and saw a tall, broad-shouldered man dressed head to toe in fur approaching them. "Who's he?" she asked.

"A trapper who comes down out of the woods about three times a year," Jake replied. "He's a good, honest man. Little rough."

CHRISTI CORBETT

"Well, if it isn't Jake Fitzpatrick." The man smiled and clapped Jake heartily on the shoulder. "I thought that was you. When did you get back?"

"About a week ago," Jake replied.

While Kate awaited an introduction, she couldn't help but stare at the stranger's hat—a gigantic circle of fur with the face of a dead fox protruding from the front, a bushy tail hanging from the back, and four paws dangling down the man's chest.

"Trail give you any trouble this time over?"

"Some," Jake said, then motioned toward where Kate stood, still waiting. "Rob, I'd like to introduce you to Katherine."

Uncertain whether customs in the west dictated she should step forward and curtsy, present her hand for a quick touch, or something else entirely, Kate opted for a simple nod and to stay silent by Jake's side.

"Glad to see you finally got yourself hitched, Jake." Rob's grin widened, revealing a twisted line of chipped, tobacco-stained teeth. "I always said it would take a special kind of woman to get a wanderer like you to settle down."

"We're not married," Jake muttered.

Rob yanked the fox face hat from his head and shifted his full attention to her. "Ma'am, if Jake don't mind, I'd like to take you to dinner. Tonight."

Kate's cheeks warmed as she struggled for the words to gently refuse the sudden invitation. He apparently mistook her hesitation for a scheduling conflict and tried again.

"Tomorrow night?" he asked, his expression a mix of desperation and hope.

"You're kind to ask, but no." She reached to pat the man on the shoulder, then thought better of the gesture and settled for a sympathetic shake of her head.

Rob shrugged his shoulders and tugged his hat into place. "Worth a shot."

"We're going now," Jake said, settling his hand on the back of her waist. "I expect we'll be seeing you around again soon."

Taking her cue from Jake's slight push against her back, Kate took a step forward and allowed him to maneuver her past Rob and up the three steps leading to the boardwalk. Jake took his place at her side and their walk began anew.

Within seconds, their progress was again halted by an unfamiliar gruff voice. "Fitzpatrick!"

To Kate's surprise, Jake laughed and waved at a short, barrel-chested man standing in the middle of the street, watching them. Judging by his beefy hands and the thick leather apron covering him chest to toe, Kate guessed him to be the town's blacksmith.

Jake cupped his hands around his mouth and shouted, "You still slinging shoes out here?"

The man grinned, then ambled over. After shaking the hand Jake offered, he turned to her. "Hello there, ma'am!" His booming voice echoed down the boardwalk, leaving Kate to wonder if his hearing was intact. "I'm Travers. You got a name?"

"Go easy on her," Jake said, his grin indicating to Kate he was friendly with this boisterous man. "It's her first week here."

"I'm Katherine. It's a pleasure to meet you."

"Nice to meet you." Travers dipped his hat in her direction. "Good for you on finally getting this wild one —" he motioned to Jake, "—to settle down. Never thought I'd see the day."

"You still haven't," Kate said. "We're not married."

Travers looked to Jake in surprise. "She's not belonging to you?"

Jake hesitated, then shook his head.

"Well, that's good news for me!" Travers clasped his hands together. "Katherine, would you consider an afternoon stroll with me tomorrow? Or, if you enjoy fishing, I know of a perfect spot down by the river."

To her frustration, Jake again kept quiet. Why wasn't he telling these men of their burgeoning relationship? Granted they weren't married, but he could at least declare his interest or intentions.

"I appreciate the invitation, but I decline," she answered softly, all while hoping Travers wouldn't pursue the idea further.

"I'll be around if you change your mind," he replied, then turned to Jake. "You staying put this time, or you heading back east again come spring?"

"Staking a claim and putting down roots," Jake said.

"Good." Travers glanced across the street and frowned. "My forge awaits, so I better get back to the shop. Stop in anytime."

After exchanging farewells, their walk continued. Jake was a knowledgeable guide and Kate an eager student; she made detailed mental notes of the town's layout and the businesses she intended to visit.

They also met several more men from Jake's past. All were happy to see him back in town, and many approached to either shake his hand or slap him on the back. Most then eyed Kate and congratulated him on catching such a fine lady. She deftly corrected each man, ultimately earning three additional dinner invitations and one hasty marriage proposal.

She declined every offer.

An hour later her legs were tired, her hair was frizzing, and her mood had soured from having the same conversation with nearly every man she'd met. Yes, she was unmarried. Yes, she could cook. Yes, she planned on staying in or near town. It was as if she was the only available female within five hundred miles!

As for Jake, he'd kept quiet while she'd handled every inquiry, intervening only when one of the men had neglected his manners and gotten too nosy while prying for details. His standoffish behavior puzzled Kate. Why, when they were alone, was he so willing to say the romantic words she longed to hear, yet when in the company of his acquaintances he wasn't so eager to proclaim himself her suitor?

After Jake exchanged a round of goodbyes with yet another man who'd intruded on their time, Kate rubbed her hands over her arms. She needed a proper coat, or at least a shawl, to shield her skin against the damp air.

Jake noticed her gesture and frowned. "You're cold. I'd offer you my coat, but I didn't bring it along. How about we visit the mercantile next? Albert keeps it warm."

She pointed to a brown building about twenty feet down the street. "Is it that one over there?"

"Yes. Since I figured you might want to buy some necessities, I arranged our journey so it's the last business we'll visit. We can fill our arms with whatever you need, and since the hotel is only one street over, it won't be too hard to carry everything back."

They began walking again.

"Kate, you handled yourself well today, meeting all those men. They might be a bit rough and their manners could use improvement, but if you decide to open a mercantile they're your future customers. I don't know much about being a businessman, but I do know one thing—building relationships is important. They'll remember you as being kind, yet willing to speak your mind. And a little headstrong."

To her surprise, Jake let out a groan of frustration. "I admit, while I'm thrilled to see you're fully capable of standing up for yourself when men are seeking your affection, it's hard to watch. But I knew if I interfered, it would portray you as just another weak woman who needs a man to fight her battles."

Guilt flooded through Kate. He had been silently hanging back not from indifference, but to let her shine.

Oblivious to her inner turmoil, Jake smiled and held out his right arm. "I'd better help you. The boardwalk steps near the river tend to be slippery this time of year."

She twined her left arm around the crook of his elbow and gathered a few folds of her skirt in her right hand. Lifting the mass of fabric, she followed Jake down the steps and onto the street.

Two men slithered out from the alley and blocked their path.

Kate sensed these men were different from the others she'd met so far. There would be no friendly conversations with either, especially given how they were already glaring at Jake.

"Looky looky who's back in town, Cyrus," said the man with a bald head and a dark beard that ended in a point just below his chest. He was big—well over six feet tall—with enough belly to show he liked his food and drink, but enough muscle to make any reasonable man think twice about taking him on.

Kate felt Jake's arm muscles tighten beneath her hand.

"When did you get in?" Cyrus asked. He was tall too, but wiry. His crooked nose and sunken cheekbones gave him the look of a man who had started, and finished, many fights.

"Last week," Jake replied coldly.

"That's a pretty woman you got there." The bald man's words were obviously for Jake, but his beady eyes focused solely on Kate, looking her over from head to toe.

"You're in our way," Jake said.

Both men hesitated briefly, then shuffled a few steps toward the alley they'd come from. Without taking his eyes off the men, Jake propelled her across the street and urged her up the boardwalk steps. When he hurried her away from the mercantile, she finally spoke up.

"We're going the wrong way," she said, struggling to keep up with him.

"They're watching. Keep walking." Without breaking stride he lowered his lips to her ear. "We'll cut through the upcoming alley and head back to the mercantile using the next alley over."

She nodded. "Who are those men?"

"The big one is Murray James. If his size doesn't give him away, you can still tell it's him because of his gait. A man as big as him goes through boot heels quick, but because he'd rather spend his money on a bottle than a cobbler, Murray's usually limping."

Jake glanced over his shoulder then slowed their pace.

"His buddy, the one with the hump on his back, is Cyrus Montgomery. He's so thin most men dismiss his ability to hold his own, but I've watched him take down a man double his size with three punches."

"Do they live in town?" she asked.

Jake shrugged. "I'm not certain, though I would assume they've holed up somewhere close since they're known to frequent the saloon in the afternoon and linger through the evening. At least that's what they spent their time doing the last time I was here. I do know that when you see one of them, watch out, because the other is probably somewhere close by. They're mean. Avoid them."

They emerged from the alley and Jake smiled while motioning to the mercantile with an exaggerated sweep of his hand. "Are you ready to meet your competition?"

"Competition?" Kate asked.

"Yes, for your store." He shifted to stand before her, and then gave her a long, curious look. "Kate, you've only ever spoken of what your father wanted. What do you want?"

She let out a sigh of disappointment. By now, after all they'd been through together, how could he not know? She wanted his assurance she wasn't facing an uncertain future alone.

"Jake, I want..."

Kate trailed off when she saw his face go pale and his focus shift to something just beyond her shoulder.

CHAPTER TWENTY-FIVE
Emily

KATE TURNED TO SEE A GROUP of women standing on the boardwalk in front of the saloon, shrieking and carrying on like gold coins were falling from the sky. Some held cigars; some clutched heavy glass tumblers filled with amber liquid. Every dress boasted a pinched waist and plunging neckline, and many were hemmed above the knee. Men she now recognized were milling among them, laughing loudly while taking liberties with wandering hands.

Ignoring the scandalous sight in favor of finishing the conversation with Jake, Kate started to turn back to him until a movement caught her eye. One of the women had broken free from the crowd and was hurrying toward where they stood. She was shouting something, but a brisk wind and the steady clang of the blacksmith's hammer against his anvil made her words impossible to understand.

Eyes wide, Jake took hold of Kate's arm and began backing away, muttering about how he'd forgotten to show her one final business.

The raven-haired woman grew nearer, and her repetitive

words clearer. "Jake, I need to talk to you! Please, Jake!"

Kate twisted her arm from Jake's fingers, dug her heels into the dirt, and stayed put.

Once the woman saw he wasn't going anywhere, she slowed her pace to a suggestive saunter. By the time she stood before Jake, she'd placed a gloved hand on each hip—a gesture Kate knew full well was designed to accentuate the curves of her hips.

"Hello again, Jake." The woman's voice was husky, her tone seductive.

"H—hello," Jake stammered in return.

Undaunted by his subdued greeting, the woman cunningly raised her chin and brought her elbows back, which showcased her ample chest in an outrageous display and tested the seams of her purple satin dress.

Kate's stomach roiled as she rose to her toes before Jake, her lips puckered as if she expected a greeting kiss.

He quickly sidestepped her advance.

Undeterred by the obvious slight, the woman looked down at Kate as if she were a lump of manure needing to be scraped off her shoe. "Who's your friend, Jake?"

Kate squared her shoulders and returned the stare with an unwavering one of her own.

Jake's cheeks flushed crimson and he shifted his weight from foot to foot. "Emily, I'd like you to meet Katherine."

"Emily?" Kate asked, certain she'd heard wrong. "Your name is Emily?"

The woman's lips stretched into a grin and she slowly nodded. "Yes. Perhaps you've heard Theodore Martin mention my name to Jake? I've stopped in the hotel several times trying to find him, but had no luck. Until today."

Kate bit the inside of her cheek as anger flickered to life within.

Emily was real, Jake was a liar, and he'd played her for a fool.

"I'll leave you two alone to get reacquainted," she said, struggling to take even breaths so she wouldn't faint in the middle of the street. She wanted nothing more than to get back to her hotel room, bury her face in a pillow, and sob until Saturday.

"No!" Jake blurted. "Don't go."

"My plans for the rest of the day have changed," Kate sputtered, barely containing her fury. She looked around for the closest building to escape into and saw the mercantile across the street. "In fact, I'm heading off now to see my competition."

"Honey, don't you know yet?" Emily laughed and tapped her gloved hand against the ample curves of her chest. "I'm your competition."

Ignoring Kate, Emily brought her fingertips to her mouth and kissed them. She then lowered her palm to her chin and blew into the air toward Jake. "I'm sure we'll see each other again real soon. You know where to find me."

Emily strolled toward the saloon, leaving Kate aghast and Jake with his head hanging low.

"I always wondered how you knew so much about soiled doves. Now I know why you made certain to mention them in that horrible speech you gave me the second day on the trail."

"Kate, they were just a few momentary lapses of judgment that meant nothing."

Kate drew in several ragged breaths, then continued. "I'm almost embarrassed to say this now, but if you would have told me the truth, I would have understood."

Jake frowned in confusion, but stayed silent.

"You're nine years older than me, so I'd already accepted that you've likely had relationships before you met me. I didn't expect you to have a flawless past, but what I do expect is for you to never lie to me."

"Kate, I—"

"Stop talking." Kate glared until he closed his mouth

again. "This morning I stood in your doorway and begged for your forgiveness, pleaded for your understanding. You had the perfect opportunity to tell the truth about Emily, and instead you stood there and said nothing as I put all the blame upon Theodore."

"Kate, I didn't tell you because I was ashamed."

"You should be even more ashamed that you're a liar."

Ignoring his pleas for her not to go, that it wasn't safe for her to be alone, Kate lifted the front of her skirt and ran across the street toward the mercantile.

CHAPTER TWENTY-SIX
Sing a Simple Song Well

KATE STEPPED INTO THE MERCANTILE AND closed the door behind her, taking comfort in the familiar clang of a heavy gold bell hitting the door's edge. The interior of the building was spacious, sparsely stocked, and laid out with an obvious eye toward growth. She breathed deeply, enjoying the mingled scents of fresh-ground coffee, leather, and tobacco.

Jake was right; the storekeeper did keep it warm. Stacks of wood beside a roaring fire in a stone fireplace showed the owner had no qualms about catering to the needs of his customers. Her father had done the same with his own store, insisting a comfortable customer would linger and buy more.

Her mouth watered at the sight of a small glass jar filled with peppermint sticks sitting on the counter. As a child, she'd loved the days when her father would point toward the same kind of jar on his store counter, then smile as she filched a stick for herself and her younger brother, Ben.

Though he'd often spoiled her, her father always had her best interest at heart and had done his best to raise her after her mother's death. Unlike most men of the time, he'd considered Kate an equal and he'd always been honest with her, no matter the consequences doing so would bring.

Too bad she couldn't say the same thing about Jake.

Kate quietly walked among the customers perusing the shelves and display tables. She would focus on purchasing the material she needed so she could then return to the hotel and get out of the dress Jake had bought for her.

This time she'd leave it on the floor.

"Can I help you find something, ma'am?" asked a man standing behind the counter. His eyes and smile were kind, his beard neatly trimmed, and beneath his buttoned black vest his shirtsleeves bore the crisp lines of recent ironing.

"I'm looking for fabric," she replied. "Also buttons and thread."

"Follow me," he answered pleasantly. He stepped from behind the counter and walked her to a small table that held three bolts of material—one navy, one red-and-white checked, and one with a floral pattern on a pink background. Beside them sat a bolt of white muslin and several wicker baskets of notions.

Kate ran her palm along the nearest bolt. The cotton felt rough against her skin and made her appreciate again the times long ago when she'd worn silk, satin, and velvet.

"We've only got a few basics right now," he said, giving her an apologetic shrug. "I'm expecting one final shipment of goods before winter sets in, but I'm sorry to say it's food staples such as flour and sugar, seed packets, and a few tools. By late next spring I should have many more choices."

Kate shook her head. "I can't wait that long. These will work perfectly for what I have in mind."

His stare grew curious. "I haven't seen you around town before. Are you new here?"

"I arrived last week," she said, then braced for a repeat of the conversations on the street.

"Well then," he said, smiling broadly. "I'd like to

congratulate you on surviving the journey. Did you travel across the oceans or by trail?"

"Trail," she replied, returning his smile with one of her own. She appreciated his acknowledgment of the kinship they, and so many others settling the west, shared. Each had risked everything to travel to an unknown land, an act that took a special type of courage.

"I came by ship myself, just last year. I'm Albert Wilson, and I co-own this establishment with my partner, George LeBreton."

"I'm Katherine Davis," she said.

"Welcome to Oregon City, Katherine Davis." He bowed low before her, then rose again and eyed a customer waiting at his counter. "I'll leave you to your shopping, but if you need anything you let me know."

"Thank you."

After he walked away, Kate began a careful evaluation of each bolt of fabric. She immediately dismissed the red-and-white checked option as one better suited for curtains and tablecloths. Besides, she didn't have the sewing expertise needed to match a strong pattern across seams. The navy was the softest of the three, yet it had no pattern to disguise the mistakes she knew she would make. Every slipped knot and puckered seam would show.

She tucked the last option—pink, with a pattern of hundreds of miniature blue daisies with green stems amidst a scattering of tiny maroon dots—under her arm. She dug through the nearest basket until she found a set of twenty white buttons. Thread selection was easy since the choice was either black or white; she opted for three spools of the latter.

She gave the other baskets of notions a cursory glance, recognized nothing, and recalled a phrase her mother had been fond of—sing a simple song well. Kate knew how to cut fabric and sew straight seams; better to do those well and make a passable dress than to also attempt fancy overlays or attaching ribbons and other adornments, and ultimately make a mess of the entire thing.

Adding the bolt of muslin to the one already under her arm, she headed to the counter. Two customers were ahead of her, leaving her eyes and mind plenty of time to wander.

Could she realistically open a competing mercantile? Albert and his partner were already established in town and poised to expand once stocking the shelves wasn't a problem. Judging by the steady stream of customers through the door since she'd arrived, they also had a loyal clientele base.

She didn't even have a building.

Again, she considered her mother's favorite phrase. Starting a mercantile meant long hours, uncertain profits, and competing against two men who already had a strong foothold in the community. On the other hand, she knew plenty about the business of horses, and if she could get the land she needed, she was more than capable of starting a ranch from the ground up.

The desire to fight for a dream that wasn't hers was fading fast.

"Find what you needed?" Albert asked as she placed her selection on the counter.

"Yes, thank you."

She told him the yardage amounts she wanted and watched as he placed the pink bolt on the counter and flipped it several times to create a mound of loose fabric. Holding the cut end in his right hand, he extended his right arm out straight, and brought the uncut fabric to the end of his nose with his left hand.

"One," he said softly, then repeated the action six additional times, and then twice with the muslin.

"Fastest way I've found to measure a yard of fabric," he said, grinning at the curious look she gave him. "I've perfected it to within a quarter of an inch. I could get out the yardstick and give you the exact amount, but I figure if you get a few extra inches and I save a few minutes doing it this way, we're both happy."

"I agree," she replied.

"How would you like to pay for these today?" Albert asked, reaching for his ledger and pen.

Embarrassment colored her cheeks as she realized since she'd started out her morning with the intention of sharing a walk with Jake, not making purchases, she'd hadn't brought along her father's pocketbook.

"I'm so sorry. It seems I've left my money back at the hotel. My father owned a mercantile back home in Virginia, and he allowed purchases on credit. Perhaps you would consider doing the same in this instance?"

Albert frowned. "Your father owned a mercantile back east?"

"Yes. I was in charge of bookkeeping, but he handled everything else. If you prefer, I could run back to the hotel and return right away with the money I owe?"

"Is your father here with you, intending on opening a mercantile in this town?" He studied her closely as he waited for her answer.

"No," Kate said. "He died along the way, about a hundred miles past Independence."

His expression changed from suspicion to sympathy. "I'm sorry to hear that."

Albert flipped open the ledger to a page with the words Credit Given at the top, and then methodically entered a description of her items, their prices, and the total amount owed. He then wrapped everything she'd bought in brown paper and tied the package with coarse string.

As a child, she'd loved to help her father wrap customer's purchases in similar paper, and then place her chubby finger against the string to hold it in place while he'd tied the knot. Her special job had been to carefully snip off the excess string and hand the package to the customer, making certain to smile and say thank you.

Albert folded his hands together, rested them on the counter, and gave her a long look. "Are you married?"

Kate shook her head.

"What do you intend to do out here?"

"Why do you ask?" she replied warily.

"I've had to travel to Champoeg quite a lot these last few months, and as a result we've fallen behind on our accounting. Given how your father's passing likely left you without a solid plan for your future, and we're hoping to have more customers than we can handle, maybe next spring you'd be interested in occasionally filling in as a sales clerk?"

Kate felt as though a huge burden had been lifted from her shoulders. Even if she didn't accept Albert's job offer, she felt confident that he would jump at the chance to buy every wagonload of supplies already in route to her and her nonexistent store.

"It's an interesting proposition, and one I'll definitely consider. Do you need an answer right away?"

Albert chuckled. "Take your time. We're not going anywhere."

"Thank you for your kindness," she said, smiling as he handed over her package.

She headed back to the door, a newfound confidence to her stride. She'd overcome everything traveling the trail had brought upon her and now, by Jake's own admission, she was adept at handling herself with men who got too persistent. And if Saturday's visit to the land office confirmed she couldn't get her land, Albert's job offer meant she at least had a way of earning a living.

Oregon City might not be such a rough place after all.

After closing the mercantile door behind her, she made her way down the boardwalk steps and halfway down the alley, where she nearly collided with one of the men Jake had warned her about earlier—Cyrus Montgomery.

CHAPTER TWENTY-SEVEN
Wilting Flower on a Strong Stem

"OH, I'M SORRY," KATE SAID, DEFTLY avoiding Cyrus's hand hovering near her shoulder as if to steady her. "I didn't see you there."

"Hello again, pretty lady." Cyrus's smile revealed three rotted teeth amidst a wide expanse of pink gums. His thinning black hair was neatly combed, a sharp contrast to his scraggly beard.

She took a step back to put space between them.

"Hello," he repeated, then fumbled the bottom of his shirt into his waistband, smoothed the lapels of his faded coat, and puffed out his chest.

Kate was well familiar with the ways of men who wanted to impress. During her twenty-first year of age, her aunt had sent fifteen men to her father's store to meet her. One week alone she'd sent three. Aunt Victoria had been determined to find Kate a suitor she deemed acceptable, though often the size of a man's bank account swayed her into overlooking that he was twenty years or more Kate's senior.

They'd been easy for Kate to spot; they either wandered

aimlessly until finally asking her for help, or lingered at the counter making idle conversation. They typically requested she accompany them on a stroll about town, smiled politely when she refused, and then left.

She'd simply exchange a few false pleasantries with Cyrus, then be on her way.

"It's such a nice day." She gazed at the sky for a moment before returning her attention to the simpleton standing before her. "Though, given the way those clouds are darkening, it looks like more rain again soon. I need to be going now; enjoy the rest of your day."

She took another step back, spun around, and came face-to-chest with Murray. Jake had warned her the two traveled as a pair, but she'd been so occupied with Cyrus she hadn't even heard Murray's approach.

"You should watch where you're walking," he said, running his thumbs up and down the length of his suspenders while giving her an appraising stare.

"As should you," she replied.

Taking full advantage of his stunned disbelief at her response, Kate slipped between the two men and hurried toward the street. She made it two steps before they caught up.

"Why you rushing off so fast?" Cyrus asked, lengthening his stride to match her progress.

"Yeah," Murray added. "You almost hurt our feelings." He was so close Kate could see the oily sheen covering his beet-red cheeks. "We was just trying to have a conversation with you."

Kate's boot caught the edge of her skirt and she stumbled, dropping her package. She bent to retrieve it, but Cyrus was faster.

"What do we have here?" he asked, ripping a hole in the paper and peering inside.

Kate reached to snatch her package from his hand, but he lifted it into the air above his head. She couldn't have reached it even if she'd jumped.

"What's in it?" Murray asked.

"Don't know. You tell me," Cyrus said, tossing it into the air above Kate's head.

Murray caught it and glanced inside. "Nothing good. Just some frilly things."

"I'm done playing games with you two," Kate said, hoping the hard edge in her tone would show the men she was serious. "I'll take my property and be on my way."

She held out an expectant hand, grimacing to see it tremble.

"You can have it back." Murray grinned and swung her package around until it was hidden behind his back. "For a kiss."

"Me too." Cyrus stroked his cheek with his filthy fingertips. "You can put mine right here."

Several furtive glances around the secluded alley convinced Kate to abandon her quest for the fabric's return and flee to the safety of the street. While both men were belly-laughing over their perceived cleverness, Kate slowly slid her hands down the front of her skirt. Once she'd gathered and lifted several folds, she bent at the waist, shuffled backward several steps, then straightened and ran from the alley.

Angry shouts and thumping footsteps followed.

She made it just past the empty hitching posts in front of the mercantile before they caught up with her again. This time Murray positioned himself directly before her while Cyrus sidled in behind, effectively pinning her in place.

To her dismay, a glance through the glass pane of the mercantile door revealed no customers inside and a handwritten note with the words Out to Lunch hung from the doorknob.

"Move aside," she said coldly.

"Now don't be like that, sweetheart," Murray said, inching closer. Kate's stomach roiled as the rancid stench of whiskey and onions assaulted her nostrils. "Me and Cy was just thinking since Jake ain't around we should all get to know each other better."

She wasn't fooled. These men had the same plans for her now as Henrick had once had for her back in the deep woods of the trail. And this time Jake wasn't there to save her.

"I'm not your sweetheart, and I want you both to leave me alone!" Kate almost didn't recognize her own voice, so high and shrill.

The street was deserted, but she thought she saw movement at the doorway of the blacksmith's workshop.

"A sweet young thing like you reminds me of an unbroken horse that needs to be taught a few lessons." Murray ran his fingers along her cheekbone and then leaned in close. "And I'm just the man to tame you."

Infuriated by the intimate gesture and words, Kate shoved his hand away. "Don't touch me!"

"You're feisty," Cyrus muttered in her ear, then slid his arm around her waist and pulled her roughly against him. "I like that in a woman."

"Hey!"

Kate turned to see Travers standing just outside of his shop, holding an iron rod with a red-hot tip in his gloved hand. "What's going on over there?"

He waited for an answer, which she valiantly tried to give, but she managed only a garbled scream of panic.

Travers shouted over his shoulder into his shop and then hurried toward her, his leather apron slapping against his legs with each step. Seconds later, a herd of angry men burst from his doors. They followed at his heels, then fanned out in a circle around Kate and the men.

"What's going on here?" Travers repeated, slapping the rod against his palm.

Kate took advantage of the momentary distraction Travers's question provided by planting the toe of her boot squarely between Murray's legs. Hard.

His face went pale and he dropped to the dirt, writhing in pain.

Kate fought her way free from Cyrus's grip and whirled to face him. "Animal!"

Cyrus's eyes widened as he finally noticed the steady stream of men spilling from nearby doorways and rushing toward them, presumably to come to Kate's aid. He raised his palms and started sputtering excuses and apologies for his behavior.

Ignoring his feeble backtracking, Kate leaped into the air and slapped her cupped palms against his ears.

With a howl of pain, Cyrus bent at the waist, clutching his ears and vowing revenge.

CHAPTER TWENTY-EIGHT
Blustering

YOU SHOULD BE EVEN MORE ASHAMED that you're a liar.

Kate's last words echoed in Jake's head long after he watched her enter the mercantile and close the door behind her. He'd been having such a wonderful time on their walk until Emily had stumbled over and ruined everything.

How could he face Kate again? He'd lied, and she'd caught him. Even worse, given her perceptive words to him about his potential past, she would have forgiven him if he'd simply come clean.

Knowing she needed time to calm down before she'd listen to reason—or pleading—Jake headed toward the livery to fetch his horse instead of following her into the mercantile. His bag was packed. He might as well leave town and scout land for the rest of the day. Or longer.

At the livery he greeted the caretaker, a young man named Mark. They held another conversation about the care his two horses and Kate's four were getting, and if there'd been problems with any. Again satisfied with the boy's answers, he walked down the hay-scattered aisle, stopping at the last two stalls on the left. He greeted Plug, slipped a bridle and blanket onto Nickel, and then brought him out of the livery.

Instead of stopping at the hotel to grab his saddle and packed saddlebags, he led his horse to the end of the street and onto the next. By now Kate would likely be done shopping. Hopefully her arms would be loaded with purchases, which would provide him the perfect excuse to offer to relieve her burden. Escorting her back to the hotel would give him ample time to apologize for his deceit.

He kept walking, and while he passed the saloon he made certain his hat brim was pulled low and his eyes were focused on the ground. He had no intention of coming face to face with Emily again, today or ever. Once he'd made it safely past the building, he raised his head and saw a surprising sight—men bursting from doors and leaping off the boardwalk to gather in a shouting circle in front of the mercantile.

His step quickened.

As he grew closer, the men gave a collective gasp, followed by a low groan. He tied Nickel to the closest hitching post and hurried to the edge of the crowd. When he was still several yards away he caught a glimpse of Murray's bald head hitting the ground.

"Animal!"

Jake's eyes widened. He knew that voice!

He pushed his way into the center of the circle, arriving just in time to see a tiny blur of fury wearing a maroon dress leap into the air and box Cyrus on the ears. Cyrus doubled over, shouting curses and threats between howls of pain. Judging by the way Murray lay sweating and squirming in the dirt, he hadn't fared much better.

Jake took quick note of Kate's disheveled hair, clenched fists, and flushed cheeks and had a fairly good idea of what happened. Or rather, judging by the appearance of Kate's dress—wrinkled and streaked with dirt, but still intact—what had almost happened.

He rushed to her, his arms open and eager to cradle her against his chest. The sight of fresh scratches marring the soft skin along her upper arms convinced him otherwise. Worried his hands would hurt her further, he opted instead to bend before her until they were face to face.

"What happened?" he asked quietly, ignoring the rising anger of the crowd around them.

She hesitated, then shook her head.

"Are you hurt?" Jake asked.

She bit her lip and shook her head again.

Jake moved to stand at her side, wanting to keep an eye on her even as he focused on the two men.

"You're asking the wrong person about being hurt." Cyrus spun wildly, pointing to the side of his head to show the closest men how a thin line of blood ran from his ear down his neck. "Look what she did to me! And to Murray!" He pointed to his partner, now on his knees and heaving his breakfast into the dust.

"You two are filthy, disgusting pigs who deserve everything you got!" Kate shouted, earning a round of cheers and applause from the crowd.

"Shut up!" Blind rage distorted Cyrus's lips into a twisted snarl. He lunged toward Kate.

Jake was faster.

He side-stepped in front of Kate to block Cyrus's advance, slammed his fist into the side of the man's nose, then swung his right leg sideways and kicked Cyrus's feet out from under him.

Cyrus landed face first in the dirt.

"We're just getting started. Get up!" Jake yelled. This man deserved the beating of a lifetime, and Murray was next.

Cyrus groaned and rolled onto his back, clutching his nose and gasping for breath.

"What about you, Murray?" Jake crossed the circle and gave him a swift kick to the ribs. Not a fair move by any means, but neither was attacking a woman. "Get up!"

Jake felt a strong hand settle on his shoulder, warning more than restraining. "They've had enough," Travers said.

A few men in the crowd nodded their agreement, while others muttered how they should be beaten longer and then dumped in the river. Mr. Parker, owner of the town's apothecary, mentioned a public hanging and someone ran off to find two ropes.

"They'll be no hanging of these men," Travers said, once everyone had quieted. "At least not today."

The uproar began anew, and Travers again urged everyone to silence. "As much as we want to hang these men for their crime, we have to keep within the guides set up by the Provisional Government." Travers eyed all the men. "We're trying to prove to the east that we can become a state, which won't happen if they get word of us running wild and acting lawless."

Jake glanced at Kate, standing alone with her arms clasped around her waist and looking as though she could either cry or scream. "They need to be punished for what they've done," he said, wishing he'd had ropes handy a few minutes ago.

"I agree," Rob the trapper said, stepping forward to stand beside Jake.

Albert Wilson entered the circle. "Travers is right. We'll arrest these men. They can sit in jail until we figure out the logistics of a trial."

Cyrus and Murray began protesting that everything had been a misunderstanding. When their tactic failed to sway the crowd, they declared it unfair to arrest them because they hadn't actually completed the act with Kate, only bothered her a little.

At that, four men had to physically restrain Jake from

going after them again.

Two ropes were finally found, and after Cyrus and Murray's hands were tied behind their backs, several men volunteered to escort them to, and secure them in, the jail at the end of town.

They were led away amidst jeers and taunts from the crowd.

CHAPTER TWENTY-NINE
Regret

AFTER CYRUS AND MURRAY WERE GONE and the crowd had dispersed, Jake finally trusted himself to speak to Kate again. "What can I do?" he asked, hating that she wouldn't look him in the eyes.

"Help me find what I bought from the mercantile," she murmured. "Everything's wrapped together in brown paper."

Jake immediately began walking a zigzag pattern, going from the center of the street to the edge of the boardwalk, his gaze darting a matching pattern. Kate found it first, several yards from where she stood. She bent to retrieve it and then let out a sharp gasp as she straightened again.

"What is it? What's wrong?" Jake hovered over her, wanting desperately to help but not knowing how, and afraid whatever he did would make everything worse.

She winced and pressed her palm to her left side. "Cyrus dug his fingers into my ribcage. Hurts."

Easing the rumpled package from her hands, he tucked it under his right arm and offered her the support of his left.

"Take me back to the hotel," she whispered, gripping his

forearm tight and leaning against him hard.

Thankful he'd agreed to Travers's offer to watch over Nickel, he guided Kate through the streets of town.

When the hotel was in sight, Kate lightened her hold on his arm. "I'm fine."

He wasn't fooled. The deep breaths she'd taken as they'd walked were meant to calm, but the unmistakable shudder as she let each out confirmed to Jake her confidence was all an act. She'd just been accosted by two miserable excuses for human beings, and now she was being escorted to safety by the man who'd lied to her.

Kate wasn't fine. Not by any stretch of the imagination.

They walked into the hotel, up the stairs, and to Kate's door without another word spoken between them. She pulled her key from a skirt pocket. After she failed several tries at placing it in the keyhole, Jake eased it from her shaking fingers, unlocked the door, and swung it open.

She walked inside and sat gingerly on the bed. The package dropped to the floor, abandoned.

"Kate, I just want to—"

"Don't." She shook her head wildly. "Don't lecture me. I don't want to hear it."

"I just want to make sure you're all right." He started to take a step into the room, but she held up her hand to stop him.

"Please, go."

He paused, his foot still hanging in mid-air. "Let me stay."

"No. I just want to rest in my room until dinner."

"If that's what you want," he replied uncertainly.

She answered him by rising from the bed, walking to the door, and placing her hand on the knob. Her expression left him no doubt of her desire for him to leave.

"I'll be back later to escort you to the dining room."

"There's no need. I'll be eating in my room tonight," she

said, then softly closed the door and clicked the lock into place.

He hated to leave her. He hated seeing her frightened by those ruthless men. But most of all he hated that she felt she couldn't confide in him, or show him her fear.

He walked down the narrow hallway, stopped at his own room to pick up his saddle and saddlebag, then headed downstairs and into the hotel's kitchen. Clara was at the stove, stirring something in a large pot.

"Hello," he said quietly, hoping not to startle her.

"Hello yourself," she replied, eyeing the pile of riding gear hoisted over his shoulder. "Going somewhere?"

"I'll be gone riding for the rest of the day. Maybe even overnight."

Jake's father had always insisted women had a sixth sense about trouble, and this one was no different.

"What's wrong?" she asked, though her tone made her words more a demand than a question.

"Kate had a rough day."

Clara frowned. "What happened?"

"I'll let her tell you. In the meantime, I'd consider it a personal favor if you could keep an eye on her for the next few days. She's going to need a friend."

"Of course." Clara dropped the spoon in the pot and wiped her hands on the apron tied around her waist. "I saw you two leave together this morning. Where is she now?"

"Upstairs in her room," he replied, grimacing at the quiver in his voice.

She studied him closely, then narrowed her eyes and planted her fists to her hips. "You two have a fight?"

"And then some."

CHAPTER THIRTY
A Visit to the Land Office

Saturday, November 18, 1843

KATE LEANED AGAINST THE WALL OF her hotel room, staring through the window at the long line of men standing outside of the land office waiting their turn to go inside.

She'd risen before first light and watched William and Jake—both had slept on the building's doorstep to guarantee they'd be first and second inside—step through the door as it opened. Fifteen minutes later they'd both come back out smiling.

It was the first time she'd seen Jake since Tuesday. After the debacle in front of the mercantile, she hadn't left her room. She'd told Clara it was so she could focus on sewing new underclothes and a dress, but in reality she needed time to bolster her courage.

Kate shuddered yet again at the thought of those disgusting men, their vile suggestions and their rough, callused hands. Thankfully the physical reminders were fading fast. The scratches on her arms were now only faint lines, and the pain in her ribcage had subsided enough to convince her that Cyrus's strong fingers had only bruised, not broken.

Hiding in her room also allowed her to avoid the two other men who had earned her fury—Theodore and Jake.

Kate rested her forehead against the glass and yawned. Again.

The last few days had been brutal.

Though she'd worked day and night, sewing until her hands cramped and her fingertips were raw from needle pricks, she still hadn't completed the pink dress. It lay on the end of her bed awaiting sleeves, a bottom hem, and yet another adjustment to the bodice. While any reputable seamstress would have shaken her head in disgust, pulled apart every seam, and started from scratch, Kate was proud of what she'd accomplished. Creating a set of new underclothes and a half-finished dress in less than a week was quite a feat considering she'd only learned how to sew a few months ago.

Downstairs the hotel's front door slammed closed, startling Kate from her recollections. William's booming voice and Margaret's resulting squeals of delight told Kate that he'd returned to his wife and shared the news he'd secured their land and their future.

She eyed the men lingering in the street just outside the land office. Jake wasn't there. After craning her neck and standing on tiptoe to better see the town, she finally caught sight of him heading toward the livery, his stride fast and sure. Minutes later, he emerged atop of Plug and rode out of sight.

Kate wondered when she'd see him again. Now that he apparently had a land claim of his own, he had no reason to stay in the hotel. And she had no idea where to find him.

By lunchtime, the line outside the land office building had dwindled to only ten men. After a quick prayer for strength and guidance, Kate slipped both deeds into the pocket of her trousers, slid her knife into the sheath strapped to her belt, and headed downstairs.

If the next hour went well, she could be settled in her new house by dusk.

With her hair in a single braid hidden down the back of her shirt and her father's hat pulled low on her head, Kate made her way to the land office. Even though she knew Cyrus and Murray were in jail for what they'd done, she kept a wary eye on every man who got too close and clutched the handle of her knife as she passed the alleyways.

To her relief, her trail clothes proved to be an effective disguise and she arrived at the land office without anyone giving her so much as a second look. Since the line no longer ran out the door, Kate walked inside and took her place behind the last man in the queue.

Only five men were ahead of her, but nearly twenty more lingered in the building, standing around and talking. All ignored her, giving her ample time to look around the large, open space. There wasn't much to see. A desk and a chair near the back wall were the only creature comforts in the room, and were currently occupied by a stern-looking man she didn't recognize. A fireplace along the left wall struggled to keep the damp chill from the room.

The man at the front of the line thanked the man behind the desk and then walked over to join the others warming their hands over the flames. Kate couldn't hear what they were discussing, just their murmurs and the scuffling of boots against the wooden floor.

Another man left the desk. Kate shuffled a few steps forward and then forced her legs to keep still. Flighty feet would only attract unwanted attention.

When only two men stood between her and the claims recorder, she caught her first glimpse of the maps spread across his desktop. Her heart pounded and she dried her palms down the sides of her trousers.

The next man finished his business. As he passed Kate, he slowed to give her a curious stare—out of only one eye due to the other being covered by a black eye patch—but said nothing.

With only one man in front of her, Kate could easily hear every word of their conversation. She listened.

"Mark, you're young," said the man behind the desk. "Seeing how me and your Pa go way back I'm willing to give you a chance, but are you sure you're capable of proving up a claim? While I see you're not taking on your full six hundred and forty acres, what you are claiming is still going to be a lot of work."

"Yes. I can handle it, sir!" Mark's answer was quick and confident, but his voice revealed he was more boy than man.

The dark-haired man behind the desk chuckled. "You're a land owner now, which makes you a full grown man. It also means you don't need to call me sir, or even Mr. Johnson. Claude is fine."

"Yes, Claude. I can handle it," Mark repeated.

Claude chuckled again, then hunched over his desk, pen in hand and ink pot nearby. Kate leaned slightly to the left and watched as Claude wrote a mysterious series of numbers and notations on several papers, then rifled through a stack of maps until he found one with the words Oregon City Region written along the bottom edge. After loading his pen with fresh ink, he drew an uneven rectangle near the top.

"There you go." He leaned back in his chair and smiled. "Now Mark, you remember it's on the south side of the river, not the north. Don't want you getting your land mixed up with the British side now."

The men erupted in laughter.

Mark turned around, and in his excitement he nearly collided with her. Once he'd recovered his balance he tipped his hat in her direction. "Sorry, ma'am."

A hush fell over the room.

Kate swallowed hard and stepped up to the desk.

"Good afternoon," she said, opting to ignore the

comments coming from the men at the fireplace, some quiet and some not.

"Good afternoon." Claude frowned, then added loudly, "Ma'am."

Several men pulled their hats from their heads.

"I assume you're in charge here?" she asked, punctuating her question with a forced smile.

"That's what they tell me," he replied, tipping back in his chair and placing a toothpick between his teeth. "What can I help you with today?"

Kate had done a lot of thinking over the past week and figured there was a good chance she wasn't the only victim. Perhaps others were unknowingly holding a forged deed, and had already brought them to this office with the intent to lay claim to the land they represented. This man might already have a lead on who was behind the scheme and who to seek out to get back her father's money.

Kate held out the counterfeit deed to the store. "Can you tell me anything about this?"

Claude sat forward in his chair again and took the paper from her hand. After studying it briefly, he looked up at her, his expression one of bewilderment. "This is a fake."

She nodded. "So I've been told. I'm hoping you can tell me something about who might be responsible for creating or selling it."

He examined it again, this time making the extra effort to skim through the entire document and also evaluate the back. "I've never seen anything like this before. Where did you get it?"

"It was purchased in Virginia, and I was under the impression it represented ownership of a mercantile here in Oregon City."

Claude leaned forward in his chair, propped his elbows on the edge of his desk, and gave her a cold stare. "We've got enough merchants already."

Kate matched his attitude with one of her own. "The issue of whether this town can support another mercantile isn't what I'm here to discuss."

She retrieved the deed from his desk and turned to face the men in the room, now silent and hanging on her every word.

"I am a victim of fraud," she announced, holding the parchment aloft. "This deed was supposed to lay claim to a building here in town, but it's a worthless forgery. Let it be known, I intend to find out who is responsible for stealing from me. I want back the money spent on this; it's rightfully mine."

She gave a curt nod to the room as a whole, tucked the deed into her pocket, and then turned back to Claude.

"In the meantime," she said pleasantly, "I'd appreciate you directing me to where this property is located." She held out the second deed. "Please."

"You threaten a room full of men, and then have the audacity to ask for information you have no right knowing?" Claude stared at her in wide-eyed astonishment. "You're a woman. Why are you in here instead of in a kitchen?"

"Better watch yourself, Claude," a man called out. "Don't you recognize her?"

"No."

"This is the woman who went after Cyrus and Murray the other day. And won."

Low whistles and murmurs rippled through the crowd.

Claude's eyes focused on the paper Kate still held over his desk. "That deed bought at the same time as the other one? From the same person?"

Kate nodded.

"Stands to reason it's fake too."

"Jim from the Champoeg land office assured me it was real, and that you would be able to tell me where it was." She was stretching the truth, but decided in this case the end justified the means.

Claude took the paper from her hands and set it on his desk without a glance. "I don't view it as legal for a claim to be made out west, then brought east and sold."

"I don't know that it is either," Kate replied. "However, it's a tough thing to enforce, especially since we're only a territory and not officially part of America. Yet." She paused to take a calming breath and then asked the question her future hinged upon. "Is it real?"

With an exaggerated sigh, he hunched over the paper and studied it for nearly a minute. He then retrieved the same map he'd used with Mark, titled Oregon City Region. After comparing the two documents for what felt to Kate like an eternity, he finally looked up again. "The description seems off. It could be a simple mistake. Men draw the landmarks from memory and errors are common."

"What does that mean?"

Claude shrugged. "Nothing, if you have a good relationship with your neighbor. If not, you'll be back in here wanting me to redraw your boundaries."

"So it's real?"

He nodded.

Kate's knees wobbled and she put a steadying hand on the edge of his desk. "You're certain?"

"Without a doubt."

"Thank you!" She straightened and reached for the deed, eager to return it to the safety of her pocket.

"Hold on there, little lady." To her dismay, Claude smirked and held the paper just out of her reach. "To you, it's worth nothing."

CHAPTER THIRTY-ONE
Lies and Consequences

"I DON'T UNDERSTAND," KATE SAID, EYEING her deed clasped in Claude's hand. "You just confirmed it's real, so why would you then say it's worth nothing?"

"You need to listen better." Claude grinned. "I said it's worth nothing *to you.*"

"Because I'm a woman?"

He nodded. "Exactly."

Kate wasn't a proponent of lying and didn't do it often or well, but she did know one thing—consistency was the key to not getting caught.

"Mr. Johnson, it seems I should have explained my situation clearer. I am married, but my husband hasn't arrived yet. He sent me west with the deed so I could set up our household before he got here next spring. I've already explained this to Jim from your Champoeg office. He understood my problem and wanted to help, but couldn't since he didn't have the correct maps. He knew you would, which is why I'm standing before you today."

"Hey!" a familiar gruff voice echoed across the room.

"Why'd you tell me you weren't married?"

Kate closed her eyes as she realized she'd overlooked one important fact—only four days ago she'd adamantly affirmed her single status to many of the men in this room.

She clenched her teeth and spun on her heel. The fur trapper, Rob, stood near the doorway with his arms crossed and the fox face hat perched atop his head. Thankfully he seemed more amused than angry.

She heard the scrape of chair legs against the floor and turned to see Claude, now standing, though he was so short Kate couldn't see much difference.

"You'll soon see I don't take kindly to being lied to," he muttered, then hopped onto his chair to address the room, arms outstretched.

"This deceitful woman wants to take what you've earned. She's come in here trying to wheedle her way into owning what belongs to you, your brothers, and your sons."

"What's that?" asked Mark, his tone more curious than angry.

"Gentlemen, she's after your land."

Taking advantage of Claude's position, Kate snatched her deed from his desk before he could stop her and then whirled to face the room again. "I have no intention of taking anything from any of you. All I'm after is what's rightfully mine, and I have the paperwork here to prove my ownership."

Another man stepped forward and tapped his finger against the deed. "Where did you get this?"

"My father gave it to me, minutes before he died." She heard a hint of hysteria in her voice and forced herself to calm before continuing. "Claude has confirmed it's real, and as soon as he does his job and tells me where to find my claim, I'll happily be on my way."

Worried more men would attempt to touch the deed or even snatch it away, she quickly folded it and slid it into her pocket.

"I'm not telling her anything," Claude replied, hopping down from his perch back to the floor. "Now, if she finds herself a husband and brings him in here, I'll be happy to tell him everything I know."

A grizzled man rushed forward and dropped to one knee before her. "Ma'am, I'll marry you right now."

His earnest expression softened Kate's indignation. She leaned over and whispered a gentle refusal, then held out her hand to help him rise. He waved off her assistance and slowly got to his feet.

"What'd she say, Jonathan?" someone shouted from the back of the room.

Jonathan's kindly smile turned leering. "That I was too much of a man for her to handle."

"I said nothing of the sort!" Kate insisted. Her denial was quickly lost in the rising din of the crowd. Amidst guffaws of laughter, several men began calling out their own offers of marriage, and two of the worst-looking ones took the opportunity to inch closer.

Kate clutched the knife handle in her right hand and raised her left hand to her mouth. After placing two fingers against her tongue and teeth, she filled her lungs and blew a piercing whistle that silenced the room.

"I don't intend to waste any more of your time," she said. "Or mine." With a measured calm she didn't feel, she turned her back on the crowd to focus on Claude. Crossing her arms over her chest, she gave him the sternest glare she could muster. "Where is my claim?"

He shook his head, but stayed quiet.

Kate eyed the Oregon City Region map lying so temptingly close on the desktop. Desperation told her to grab it and flee the building, but reality kept her still.

She'd never make it through the door.

Claude let out a frustrated sigh. "I'm responsible for upholding the law, and the law says only men can make claims."

"Actually, you're making an assumption based on precedent already set in the states, but since we're only a territory there's no official law regarding women owning land."

A man who'd spent his time leaning against a nearby wall straightened to address the room. "She's a fancy talker, ain't she?"

Kate warily focused her attention on the burly stranger, who had a gap between his front teeth wide enough to run a pencil through and an angry scar that ran along his neck from one ear to the other. "Not fancy, just informed."

"There's one thing I can't figure out about you," he said, crossing the room to stand before her.

Kate blinked fast but held her ground. "What?"

"You've got what it takes to make more money in one night than any of us in this room could hope to make in a month. Maybe even a year." He tapped the brim of her hat none too gently. "Smart girl like you should know better than to hide your best assets under baggy clothes."

Kate's cheeks warmed, but uncertainty kept her still. "What are you implying?"

"Accompany me to the upper floor of the saloon and I'll gladly empty my pocketbook to get you writhing beneath me for the rest of the day."

She slapped him across the cheek. Hard.

Would the impropriety and crude behavior toward her never end? Was she destined to hear vulgarities for the rest of her life, simply because she was a woman? A woman who'd dared to go after what was rightfully hers?

Rob the trapper appeared at her side, his eyes snapping with fury. "Too far, Wade. This here is a respectable woman, and you've gone too far."

Instead of slinking away, Wade leaned in close. "Respectable women are the downfall of soiled doves. Take some friendly advice from me and all the other men in here who appreciate generous women of questionable moral standing—go back east."

She planted her fists to her hips. "No."

Wade snorted, but to her relief he returned to leaning against the wall. After murmuring her thanks to Rob for defending her, she faced the room.

"Though my appearance and actions might suggest otherwise, I am a lady and deserve to be treated as such. While I understand I don't have your support, I demand your respect."

With her back straight and her head high, Kate marched through the subdued crowd and out the front door.

CHAPTER THIRTY-TWO
Overeager Witness

As the sun was taking leave from the sky, Jake rode his horse back into Oregon City. He'd spent the previous night sleeping in the doorway of the land office, had made his claim just past first light, and then spent the rest of the day learning the particulars of his property.

He was thrilled with almost everything it offered—woods, fertile flatlands, and water. Located three miles from the edge of the city, the southeast corner was a hillside with enough trees to build a substantial cabin and stable, and still have plenty left standing for shade and cover. Or, if he chose to wait on the cabin and focus instead on plowing fields for the following spring's crops, he could take up residence in the dilapidated dugout someone had built long ago at the base of the hill, probably with the intention of it being a root cellar.

The northwest corner boasted another hill, though it was dotted with shrubs instead of trees. The majority of his property lay between the hillsides—a wide valley perfect for raising cattle, crops, or both. A vigorous creek entered his claim at the eastern edge and continued across the center of the valley until it exited at the southwest corner about a hundred yards away from a massive, solitary oak tree.

The only thing his claim was missing was the one thing he wanted most of all—Kate by his side.

He rode Plug to the doorway of the livery, hopped down from his saddle, gathered the reins, and led him down the aisle. As usual, Mark poked his head over the door of the stall he was cleaning. "Howdy, Jake!"

Jake waved and continued on to Plug's stall. "How are Nickel and the four other horses doing? Any problems?"

"Nope," Mark replied. "Did you get your claim today?"

"Sure did." Jake pulled a brush from the wooden shelf on the wall and got to work.

Mark appeared at Plug's stall door. "Got what you wanted?"

"Sure did," he repeated, grinning. Mark tended to ramble, but he was a responsible young man with a solid head on his shoulders. And he took excellent care of the horses, which Jake appreciated.

Mark let out a low whistle. "You sure did miss a good show at the land office today."

"What happened?" asked Jake, more out of courtesy than interest.

"You know the woman who owns those horses you're always asking about?" Mark pointed at Nina and Old Dan, and then the two packhorses.

The brush slipped from Jake's fingers, bounced off the toe of his boot, and landed in the straw. "What about her?"

Mark grinned and began bouncing from foot to foot as he realized he finally had a story that captured Jake's interest. "Mr. Martin—you always call him Theo—said I could take a long lunch break today and go make a claim for myself, so I left here just after noon and headed to the land office. Didn't have to wait long at all, and I got exactly what I wanted. It's perfect. For starters, it overlooks the Columbia River, and—"

"What about the woman?" Jake demanded.

"Oh, yeah." Mark's cheeks reddened and his grin turned sheepish. "Sorry about that. Anyway, she put up a ruckus when she got told she couldn't claim land without a husband."

Jake's throat and chest tightened. "Who was she there with?"

Mark shook his head. "No one, far as I could tell. Like I was saying, I got in line to make my claim, not paying much attention to who was standing behind me. After I was done, I turned around so fast I almost knocked her over since she was standing so close. I didn't recognize her at first seeing how she was dressed like a man, but once I caught sight of those pretty green eyes I knew right away who she was."

Fear for Kate's safety and anger at her actions raged a heated battle in Jake's mind.

Mark chuckled. "She's got a temper when she's riled, that's for sure. First, she tells everyone in the land office how she's a victim of fraud, then she says whoever stole from her better watch out, and then Claude jumps up on his chair and starts talking about how she's gonna take land from everyone."

Jake grimaced. "That does sound like a good show."

"Wait, it gets better!" Mark laughed and clapped his hands together. "So then she talks with Claude until Rob—the guy who always wears the dead fox on his head—yells out that she's not married. She starts ranting about how laws aren't legal out here in the territory, and that makes everyone all kinds of rowdy so she let out a whistle that shut everyone up good."

"Anything else?" Jake dreaded to hear the answer.

"So then some guy named Wade comes up and asks why she's not working in the saloon. She didn't care for that too much, so she slapped him right across the cheek and then lectured everyone about how she deserved respect."

As Mark paused to catch his breath, Jake yanked his hat

from his head and began raking his fingers through his hair. Not four days ago she'd seen firsthand the dangers of wandering the town without an escort, but instead of steering clear of danger, she was determined to seek it out. She might as well have kicked a hornet's nest for the all the trouble she'd just stirred up.

"You know," Mark continued, "come to think of it, seems not many of the other men cared for what Wade said either, because after she left they threatened him and said stuff about him never talking to a lady like that again."

"What happened next?" Jake asked.

"While Wade slumped against the wall, holding a handkerchief to his freshly bloodied nose, all the other men started talking about how headstrong and gorgeous she was, and how they actually liked a woman who was willing to stand up for herself."

"That so?"

Mark shrugged. "They said it takes a tough kind of woman to survive out here, and she's just the type the west needs."

Jake groaned.

Once he'd found out Kate was taking her meals in her room, he'd opted to dine at the restaurant instead of Theo's table. For days he'd eaten his food while listening to amazed men speculate at how someone so tiny could have taken on two beasts like Cyrus and Murray. After her stunt in the land office, Jake figured she'd have at least twenty men besides Theo strongly pursuing her affections.

"Can you finish brushing Plug and then give him some warm mash?" Jake asked, eager to get to her as soon as possible.

"Of course."

At Clara's suggestion he'd avoided Kate for days, figuring time and space was what she needed. But after hearing what she'd been through today, he had to see for himself that she was all right. After he assured himself she was safe and unscathed, then he'd try again to convince her how dangerous it was to walk around unescorted. All she needed to do was ask and he'd take her anywhere she needed to go.

Jake entered the front door of the hotel and headed directly toward the stairs, but didn't even make it up one step before Clara scurried from the kitchen and halted his progress.

"Kate has again requested her dinner be sent to her room," she said.

"I have to see her. It's important."

"Jake, give her the time she needs." Clara placed her hand on his arm. "She'll be fine. She's a strong woman."

Jake knew firsthand how strong of a woman she was. He thought back to the day they'd traveled along a winding and icy mountain road. Kate had slipped and fallen, then tumbled down a steep hill until smashing into a tree. She'd gotten a nasty, painful gash in her leg that would have made most grown men weep, yet she'd sat stoically while he'd cleaned rocks from the wound and then stitched it closed.

He'd been her rescuer and protector countless times as they'd crossed the trail, but now that they'd arrived in Oregon City things were drastically different. Though he was thrilled with her willingness and ability to take care for herself, it also made him miserable to realize she was choosing to move on alone, without him by her side.

CHAPTER THIRTY-THREE
Similar Tastes

Sunday, November 19, 1843

Minutes after the sunrise lit up her room, Kate was up and pacing. After the previous day's calamity in the land office, she didn't dare venture outside the hotel alone again.

She was at a complete loss as to what to do next.

Though her father had left her plenty of money, she hated seeing it go toward hotel and livery fees instead of building her future. Albert's job offer was only on an as-needed basis, and wouldn't start until spring. The only thing she knew for certain about her claim was water ran through it, but riding along the banks of every river and creek within twenty miles of Oregon City in the hopes of sighting an abandoned house wasn't practical or safe.

She missed Jake, and though she'd spent far too many hours staring out the window at the streets below, she hadn't spotted him since he'd left town after making his claim.

Perhaps he'd left word with Clara on when he expected to return. Eyeing the remains of last night's dinner still sitting on a serving tray near the door, Kate decided to be helpful and bring it down to the kitchen.

Within five minutes she'd washed, run a brush through her hair and secured the entire length into a twisted knot at the nape of her neck, and donned the pink dress she'd finished late the previous night.

Tray in hand, she headed downstairs. And into an empty kitchen.

Kate's spirits dimmed at the thought of spending yet another day trapped between the walls of her room, then brightened as she recalled the endless adventures sitting on a shelf only one room away.

Books!

Keeping her footsteps light so she didn't wake the other guests, Kate walked down the hallway, through the lobby, and slipped through the heavy curtains covering the doorway to the parlor.

Though her original intent had been to peruse the titles Theodore valued so much he'd sacrificed space in his wagon to bring them over the trail, the sight of sheet music displayed atop the traveling trunk in the far left corner waylaid her plan. While she hadn't especially enjoyed her years of forced piano lessons, she did appreciate music as a whole. Apparently so did Theodore. As she browsed through the pages, she recognized several of the finest concertos and minuets, and even her favorite symphony—Beethoven's eighth.

She replaced the sheets as she'd found them and then spent time at the bookshelf. Once again she discovered they had similar tastes. After pulling a book down to take back to her room, Kate crossed the parlor to stand before the oak clock hanging on the wall. The octagonal shape of the face, the black roman numerals, and the gold pendulum swinging behind the glass-covered door brought on a rush of memories of her childhood.

Her father had kept a similar clock in his study.

Every Sunday evening following her fifth birthday, when

he'd deemed her old enough, he'd held her in the crook of his arm and let her watch as he inserted a gold key into a small hole and turned it until the wheels and springs inside were tight enough to keep time for another week. Then he'd allow her to restart the pendulum with a gentle push. Afterward she'd circle her arms around his neck and rest her head against his shoulder as he carried her up the long staircase and into her bedroom.

On her tenth birthday, he'd pressed the heavy key into her palm and watched proudly as she'd wound the clock and pushed the pendulum. He'd then placed her hand around his elbow and escorted her up the stairs and to her room, where a maid waited to assist her in bathing and dressing for bed.

The tradition had continued until the week her mother had taken ill. Her father's focus shifted to doing everything in his power to get her well, and most everything else had slipped his mind. Kate had kept up the Sunday ritual on her own until her mother's death, three months after her thirteenth birthday.

"Hello."

She jumped at the unexpected interruption, surprised to see Theodore standing just inside the parlor doorway.

"I apologize for startling you." He took two steps into the room, then halted. "I'll go."

"There's no need to apologize, nor for you to leave," Kate insisted. "I was lost in memories and didn't hear you come in."

"I noticed," Theodore said, walking toward the window on the opposite wall. "You looked so peaceful I hated to bother you, but I'd watched you for so long I felt I needed to either say something or leave." He smiled. "I spoke up because I couldn't bear the thought of leaving."

After sliding the window curtains aside, his gaze went to the traveling trunk. He studied the top for several seconds, then frowned. "I see piano music is part of your memories?"

Kate was mortified. "I'm so sorry. I should have asked your permission before rifling through your personal property."

Though Theodore waved off her apology, he spent nearly a minute adjusting the corners of the sheet music until the stack was a solid block, with every paper perfectly aligned with the one below. Once he was satisfied, he straightened and eyed the book in her hand.

Kate cringed. "I had no right to—"

Theodore held up his hand. "It's my issue, not yours. Think nothing of it. In fact, it's good to finally meet a woman with an obvious love for music and books."

She hesitated, and then shifted her hand to reveal the cover.

His eyes widened. "You speak French?"

She nodded. "Fluently, thanks to eight years of lessons from a private tutor."

"*Avez-vous jouer du piano?*" he asked.

"*Oui, bien que mon instructeur pourrait en désaccord.*"

"I too play the piano." He chuckled and held out his hand. "And I have the scars on my knuckles to prove it."

"Why would playing the piano lead to scars?"

"My teacher believed a sturdy slap with a strong ruler to be an apt punishment for fumbling notes."

She gasped. "Didn't your mother ever intervene on your behalf?"

His expression hardened. "My teacher was my mother."

Silence blanketed the room until finally Theodore spoke again. "I've found you can tell a great deal about a person by their book collection. Tell me, which ones did you bring along?"

"We left the majority of our books behind in Virginia. The accident that killed my father also broke our wagon beyond repair, so I had to leave nearly everything I owned behind, save for my Bible and what I could fit in my saddlebags."

"Such a shame." Theodore grimaced. "When I learned you'd arrived with only horses, I assumed it was due to Jake's propensity of demanding travelers abandon all they hold dear."

Unwilling to further a discussion about Jake or one of the three worst days of her life, Kate changed the subject to the first object that caught her eye. "The floor rug in here is beautiful. I would guess by the color scheme and pattern it's imported? Perhaps from Europe?"

Instead of answering, Theodore cocked his head and stared at her, his expression both appreciative and intense. Kate got the distinct impression she was being evaluated, but for what?

"You have impeccable taste and a good eye for quality," he said quietly. "I must admit, I'm thrilled to meet someone who can fully appreciate my upbringing, my lifestyle, and the things I can offer. This territory is rife with either garish saloon hags or farm women who value soil quality and beasts of burden far more than education. I've waited years for a woman like you to arrive, a woman who understands what living with wealth entails, and requires."

His brows furrowed and he tapped his index finger against his lips several times before continuing. "I understand now why you were so in awe the last time you ate dinner at my table. Seeing civilization again after so many months of living outside like an animal must have been exhilarating."

Kate raised her chin a notch. "Actually, I was more in awe of the lies spouting from your mouth." *And your determination to destroy Jake's reputation.*

"In all honesty, I'm mortified at my behavior that night." Theodore's shoulders slumped and he let out a long sigh. "Frankly, I haven't been myself since my wife died."

His voice cracked at the last word and he fumbled through his pockets until he found a handkerchief.

"I'm sorry," he murmured, dabbing at a solitary tear

sliding down his cheek. "It's been years since she passed, but as I've discovered, grief returns at the most inopportune moments." He gave her a sympathetic look. "Something I suspect you know all too well."

Kate nodded, astonished at how fast his demeanor had changed.

"I have no family out here, so I was elated when I got word of William and Margaret's impending arrival." He wiped his eyes and then let out another heavy sigh. "I had grand visions of gathering together to celebrate the birth of their child, birthdays, holidays, and everything in between. Once I learned they'd already made a claim, I did my best to assure their safety and comfort by hiring a team of men to build them a house. Unfortunately, that also means they'll be leaving the moment it's completed." He folded his handkerchief, returned it to his pocket, then stared dejectedly at his empty hands.

Kate felt a twinge of guilt for initially suspecting his display of emotion was more calculated than sincere. The fact remained he was a lonely widower in a desolate land, pining for his wife and family.

"It's hard to let go of a dream." She touched his forearm, tentatively at first, then gave a firm squeeze before pulling away.

Theodore quickly raised his head. "Where are my manners? I'm rambling on about myself and I haven't even asked if you'd like to sit down and join me for my Sunday morning ritual, a cup of tea."

It didn't escape her notice that all traces of Theodore's misery had vanished and his confident smirk had returned. He was indeed an accomplished actor, but Kate had spent years under the tutelage of her driven and calculating aunt, who specialized in the art of emotional manipulation.

She smiled. "Yes, I'd love some tea."

With an elaborate bow, Theodore motioned her toward

the three mahogany chairs upholstered with cream-and-teal velvet she'd avoided her first night in town. She sat and then watched Theodore swing his silver bell side to side three times.

Kate wondered how many times Clara had been tempted to hide that bell.

Within a minute, Clara appeared carrying a tray with a silver teapot, a plate of sugar cubes stacked in a pyramid, a carafe of heavy cream, and one cup sitting on a saucer. Sighting Kate, she faltered.

"Oh, I didn't realize you had company, Mr. Martin." She set down the tray, then straightened. "I'll bring another set right away."

"Thank you, Clara," Kate called out to her departing figure.

Once she was out of the room, Kate turned to Theodore. "She's sweet and kind. You're lucky to have her assisting you in your hotel."

He was so focused on dripping cream into his tea drop by drop that he either hadn't heard her, or had ignored her altogether.

Clara returned with a cup and saucer on a smaller tray, as well as a duplicate plate of sugar cubes and another carafe of cream. "It's good to see you venturing out of your room."

"You didn't need to go to such trouble," Kate insisted. "I could have used the sugar you already—"

Clara's grimace and a slight shake of her head told Kate not to pursue it further.

After Clara had quit the room, Kate filled her cup with tea and added two sugar cubes and a splash of cream, then sat back in her chair and watched Theodore, now so engrossed in holding a sugar cube halfway into his tea and watching the crystals melt he was oblivious to anything around him.

"Well then," he said once he'd finally made the tea to his liking and gotten comfortable in his chair, "I feel I must again apologize for my blunt behavior during our last dinner together. I thought you already knew of Jake's proclivity toward saloon women. Given your response that evening, I quickly learned different."

He returned his cup to its saucer, steepled his fingers together, and brought them to his chin. "My intention was never to upset you or bring you more pain. Is that why you've been hiding in your room all week? Because of what I said?"

"No. I met some of the men in town. I don't want to go into further detail, so I'll just say they were far from gentlemen."

"Oh, you poor dear." He pursed his lips and gave her a sympathetic look. "I won't pry, but I'd like to give you some advice."

"Advice?"

His tone turned authoritative. "Any time you leave the safety of the hotel, you should have an escort, and even then it is imperative you stay far away from the saloon." He paused to give her a curious look. "Where was Jake while you were being accosted in front of the mercantile, or when you were in the land office?"

"I was alone," Kate replied warily. "How is it you are reluctant to pry, yet you know so much about my whereabouts?"

He chuckled. "Maybe you don't realize it yet, but you are the talk of the town."

"What?"

He raised his palms and brows. "Take no offense, but out here an unmarried woman—especially a beautiful one—is a rare commodity and therefore is in high demand." He frowned. "What I have yet to figure out is why you're in Oregon Territory to begin with."

"Like you, my father was a widower and decided to come west with the intention of starting over. He planned to run a mercantile in town, and eventually start a horse ranch.

My younger brother and I were going to help."

"Did you consider returning home after they died?"

Kate nodded. "I wanted to, but it was already too late in the year and we'd come too far to turn back. Jake said we had no choice but to continue west."

Theodore brought his cup to his lips and peered at her thoughtfully over the edge of the rim. "Will you be heading east come spring?

"No." She hesitated. "At least, I hadn't thought so. But now that my father's deed to the mercantile has been proven to be a forgery, I'm not certain. I'd love to find out who is responsible and expose their scheme to the world."

Theodore's cup slid from his fingers and tumbled down his chest, spilling the remains of his tea down his vest and onto his trousers.

"Oh no!" Kate exclaimed, quickly setting her own cup aside to grab the stack of linen napkins from the tea tray. She handed half to Theodore, who was now standing and grimacing at the wetness spreading across his clothes. As she blotted away the few spots on the velvet chair, he removed the pocket watch from his vest pocket, checked it over, and patted it dry.

"Were you burned?" she asked. "Should I get some butter from Clara?"

He waved away her offer. "No. I'm fine, really. The tea was lukewarm so there's no harm done."

She returned to her chair and placed the damp napkins on the serving tray. "I think your vest got the worst of it. Your chair should be fine."

He joined her again, this time sitting in the dry chair beside hers. "I'm more concerned about you, Kate. What do you intend to do now?"

"Thankfully my father was a sound businessman with good instincts. He left me with enough money to tide me over until I can figure out what to do next."

"What about the other deed?" he asked quietly.

She drew back in surprise. "How do you know about that?"

"I'm a well-connected, well-respected businessman. Little happens in this town that I don't know about." He sprang to his feet, shoved his hands into his pockets, and began pacing along the far wall. "Where are the deeds now?"

"Upstairs, in my room." Instinct told Kate to lie. In truth, they were hidden within a pocket Kate had sewn into the lining of her pink dress.

Theodore stopped pacing and stared at her. "If you get land, then you'll rarely come into Oregon City."

Kate shrugged. "I suppose so."

"You'll be so busy trying to survive you won't have time to track whoever it was that sold your father that deed."

Kate got the odd impression he was talking to himself rather than to her. She stayed silent, sensing the man was battling a conflict deep within. He started pacing again, but this time he made it only one length of the room before stopping.

"Kate," he said, his eyes gleaming with excitement. "I know a legal loophole that will allow you to claim your land."

CHAPTER THIRTY-FOUR
Any Person

"THERE'S A WAY OUT OF YOUR troubles," Theodore said. "A way for you to either claim the land your deed represents, or a different plot altogether."

"How?" Kate demanded. "How is it possible?"

"One specific word makes it possible. 'Person.'" Theodore clasped his hands behind his back and started pacing the room again. "Allow me the liberty of backtracking, so I can explain it clearer. About a year ago, many influential men in the area—myself included—realized the need for self-government. This need ultimately led to a series of meetings to discuss the issue. These 'Wolf Meetings', as many have deemed them because the first one dealt primarily with the trouble the wolves were creating for livestock, expanded from discussing animals to creating the Provisional Government of Oregon."

"How does this relate to my deed?"

Theodore staggered, then stopped pacing altogether. "I'm getting to that point. Bear with me, because it's complicated."

If an audience was what this self-important braggart

wanted, Kate would happily listen to him recite the full history of how America had been founded, topped off with a reading of the entire Constitution, if it meant he'd help her get her land.

His pacing and rambling began anew. "On July 5th of this year, the newly formed Provisional Government voted to adopt the Organic Laws of Oregon."

Kate pondered how serendipitous it was that this event occurred on the same day of her father's death. Her future revolved around that day in more ways than one.

Theodore noticed her distraction and paused to stare at her with one brow raised. "Are you paying attention? Because here's where it gets interesting."

Reminding herself yet again how the end justified the means, Kate made a show of sitting straighter and folding her hands on her lap.

"I'll skip the details of the various sections and articles of the document, and concentrate on the portion that pertains to your specific situation—the Law of Land Claims." His smile and tone turned smug. "While I warned everyone the phrasing was vitally important and we needed specific restrictions based on race, gender, and citizenship, they scoffed at my concerns. While I foresaw how their vague wording might eventually lead to problems should a willful woman come along, they deemed it inconceivable that an unmarried woman would want to own land." Theodore let out an arrogant laugh. "It seems you're about to benefit from their negligence."

Kate perched on the edge of her chair, waiting for him to clarify. She lasted only a few seconds before blurting out, "I still don't understand what the word 'person' has to do with getting land."

Theodore stood behind his original chair across from hers and smoothed his palms over the damp spots on his vest several times before continuing. "There's always been a deep-rooted tradition that only a man—or a man *and* his wife," he amended, "could get land. As a result, they anticipated no problem with using the word 'person' in Article One of the Land Claims Law."

"Which says what?" she asked.

"I remember it verbatim since I fought so hard against it. 'Any person now holding, or hereafter wishing to establish, a claim to land in this territory, shall designate the extent of his claim by natural boundaries, or by marks at the corners arid on the lines of such claim, and have the extent and boundaries of such claim recorded in the office of the territorial recorder…'"

He trailed off and stared intently at Kate, who by now was grinning and bouncing her heels against the floor.

"I see there's no need to continue, since you obviously understand how you will take advantage of their error?"

Kate's feet stilled as she recalled Claude's adamant denials. "I do, but I still don't know that Claude will be agreeable to—"

"I'll handle Claude," Theodore replied firmly. "You'll get your land, but I insist you abandon your threatened pursuit of whoever is responsible for the fake deed. Twisting the intent of the Claims Law is going to upset enough men as it is; you don't need to bring more danger upon yourself by poking around where you don't belong. You've already seen enough of the elephant coming out here, wouldn't you say?"

Kate grimaced. "Indeed I have."

"So you agree? You're going to let the issue of the fake deed go?"

"I agree," Kate said, taking care to keep her smile bright and eyes neutral. She had absolutely no intention of following his demand. One day she would learn who had stolen from her and have her revenge.

"Good," he said, his tone brisk and efficient. "I'm leaving for Champoeg in a few hours. Unfortunately, I've got a prior business engagement that will take me out of town for the upcoming week, but the following Monday morning we'll go to the claims office and find out what you need to know." He pursed his lips and tapped his finger against his temple. "Better yet, since your land deed has a map of the boundaries drawn at the top, why don't we just take our horses on a leisurely ride and find it ourselves?"

Kate hesitated. Intuition told her something was wrong, but she couldn't place why she was so uneasy about his proposition.

"Clara can act as escort if you're concerned about your reputation," he added, apparently mistaking her misgivings for a concern for propriety.

"Since I'm already well-known for gallivanting alone through the town, I don't think it's an issue," she replied.

"Perfect," he said triumphantly. "We'll leave Monday the 27th at nine o'clock sharp. In the meantime, I'll arrange for a special lunch just for the two of us today. We'll have privacy and be able to get to know each other better."

"Thank you, but I have to decline."

"Very well," he said pleasantly. "We'll do it another time. I'll keep asking until you say yes, and one of these days you will."

He said it with such conviction that she had to laugh. "How do you know that?"

"I'm a confident and patient man, but above all, I'm persistent."

His smile was friendly, but his words filled her with trepidation and the sudden urge to return to her room.

"Thank you for the book, and for the helpful conversation." She gripped the arms of the chair and leaned forward in preparation to rise, but Theodore quickly sidestepped around his chair and sat on the edge of the tea table, effectively blocking her exit.

"Kate, in the interest of time, I'm going to be blunt. My

hotel and my investments in the shipping industry have served my pocketbook well. One example is the role I played in financing the Star of Oregon venture; by the time all the details were worked out, I'd tripled my worth. However, I've come to realize I want what the west won't be able to offer in my lifetime—culture. I want to go to the opera, listen to a symphony, enjoy seven-course meals prepared by French chefs, attend ballroom dances, and all the other things that a wealthy lifestyle entails."

"Why are you telling me this?" she asked.

"Because I want to return to Boston next spring, and I'd like you to come with me. As my wife."

"I'm not interested in moving to Boston," she said quietly. "Or being your wife."

Theodore knelt before her and cupped her chin in his palm. His touch was gentle, yet a shiver of fear ran down her spine at the possessive look in his eyes. "I intend to convince you otherwise."

To Kate's immense relief, Jake stepped into the room.

CHAPTER THIRTY-FIVE
Confidence Lost

JAKE WALKED INTO THE HOTEL'S LOBBY with his saddle slung over one shoulder and his rifle resting on the other. He grimaced to see Theo's empty desk. His room was already paid through next Sunday, but he'd wanted to settle up for two additional weeks. Afterward he'd planned to head to the mercantile and buy a saw, an ax, and an augur, then spend the rest of the day at his land, marking which trees were the straightest and most easily accessible. Hard work was just what he needed to distract him from the disaster his relationship with Kate had become.

He had six months to prove up his claim. Ten seconds after walking into the dugout he'd decided what to do first—build a cabin. Staying in Theo's hotel for the next few weeks wouldn't be ideal, but would far outweigh sleeping on the floor of a dark, dank dugout. After one night the pain in his leg would be excruciating.

While waiting to drop more of his precious wages into Theo's soft palm, he lowered his saddle to the floor, propped his rifle against the wall, and then glanced out the window. To his dismay, grey clouds darkened the sky and promised rain. As he contemplated the whereabouts of his oilskin rain slicker, Jake heard an unexpected sound coming from the other side of the parlor doorway curtain.

Kate's laugh.

Stepping closer, he frowned to hear Theo's voice as well, though the heavy fabric made it impossible to hear specifically what was being said.

Jake rationalized his next move. Given she wanted nothing to do with him anymore, he could simply walk out of the hotel and leave her to her own devices. On the other hand, he hadn't seen her for five days, which made him downright negligent in keeping the promise he'd made to her father. Telling himself it was what Elijah would have wanted him to do, Jake shoved the curtain aside and walked into the parlor.

What he saw next made his jaw clench until his teeth ached.

The woman he loved, the woman he'd proposed to only eight days ago, was allowing that deceitful, corrupt, vindictive, pitiful excuse of a man to kneel at her feet and caress her cheek. Though she looked more surprised than sorry to see him, at least she had the decency to pull away from Theo's touch.

"Hello, Jake," Theo said, rising to his feet. "As always, your presence is both uninvited and inopportune. What do you want?"

He glared at Kate. "Faithfulness and trust, which I apparently won't find in here."

Kate's chin quivered, but instead of replying, she turned to Theo. "Thank you for the tea and the advice. If you'll excuse me, I need to check something in my room."

"Of course," he said, extending his arm in a grandiose flourish to allow her passage. "I'll think of you often this coming week while I'm in Champoeg, and I look forward to our ride together a week from tomorrow."

She nodded curtly, then brushed by Jake without a word.

Ignoring Theo's unmistakable look of triumph, Jake returned to the lobby, grabbed his saddle and rifle, then stalked out the door.

It is better to dwell in a corner of the housetop,
than with a brawling woman in a wide house.
Proverbs 21:9

It had been his father's favorite verse from the Bible. Growing up, Jake hadn't understood the reasoning behind it. Until now. While he would regret losing creature comforts like a warm, dry room and regular meals, he knew he couldn't handle watching Kate entertain offers from a man like Theo. His claim had shelter—however primitive—and water. This week in the hotel would be his last.

While building a cabin wasn't an easy task to begin with, and being cold and wet while doing it would only increase the difficulty, at least he'd be working toward his future instead of sitting around and pining over what he'd lost.

Fueled by anger and despair, Jake strode through the main door of the livery and down the aisle. He stopped just short of Plug's stall when Kate emerged from the shadows and blocked his path.

"Those were strong words back there, Jake. Care to explain further?"

"No." He attempted to step around her, but she was faster. This time she positioned herself in front of the door latch. Unless he physically picked her up and moved her aside, he wasn't going to ride out anytime soon.

Fine, then. If she wanted a confrontation, he was ready.

"I'm not surprised to see you here." He dropped his saddle, leaned his rifle against the wall, and crossed his arms. "I've heard you're good at harassing people to get your way."

"What's that supposed to mean?"

Jake scoffed. "I know all about your recent exploits in the land office. Threatening a room full of men, Kate? What were you thinking?"

She curled her hand around the top of the door and stuck her foot onto the bottom board, then pulled herself up to meet him eye to eye. "I'm thinking I refuse to allow my father's land to sit untended because of the idiocy of a few uneducated men."

"What do you intend to do now?" he asked.

"Get the land and work it," she quickly replied. "Losing the mercantile is a setback and will slow me down, but I won't let it stop me."

"I figured. You're used to getting what you want, so I'm certain you'll come up with a way around the law."

"I already did." Her lips tightened as if trying to hold back a grin. "The law has been incorrectly interpreted to imply women can't own land. An assumption I plan to correct as soon as—"

"As soon as what?" he asked. "Theo comes back to town?"

She jumped at his harsh tone. "Yes. Technically, he was the one who pointed out the specific detail, so he's going to—"

"Self-serving of him, don't you think?"

A long, low roll of thunder interrupted her and she glanced down at his saddle with a worried frown. "Where are you going? There's a storm coming."

"I'm leaving, Kate. Your actions in the parlor made it clear you're with Theo."

Her brows furrowed in confusion. "I'm not *with* him. We're just going riding. With Clara as our escort. He offered to help me and I accepted. There's nothing more to it."

"Trust me. That's not what he thinks." Jake recalled the rumors he'd heard from the other travelers with his and Theo's wagon train. Many had alluded—and some declared outright—that Theo had thought little of his wife when she'd been alive, had exploited her death for sympathy, and had snuck out of Boston under the cover of darkness to escape her family's outrage that he'd lost their entire fortune at the card tables. "Kate, he's a convincing smooth talker. And you're so busy putting status over character you're falling for his lies."

Her eyes widened. "Lies? You're one to talk of lies."

Jake yanked off his hat, tossed it onto his saddle, and ran frustrated fingers through his hair. "Yes, I should have been honest about Emily. But I was ashamed, so I kept it from you."

Lightning crackled close by, followed seconds later by another long rumble of thunder. With a wary eye on her horses she hopped down from the door, but made no attempt to leave.

"Kate, do you remember our conversation the night we met Henrick?" he asked quietly.

Her shoulders slumped, but she still didn't drop her gaze. "This is different."

"That night you told me you trusted me above all else," he continued, pressing his point. "And I responded by promising never to take your trust for granted. Why, then, won't you heed my repeated warnings about Theo?"

"You don't understand."

"You're right. I don't understand. Waking up with you in my arms after that night in the cave was the best morning I've ever experienced." He grabbed her by the hand, pulled her through the doorway of the livery, and jabbed his index finger toward the hillside overlooking the town. "Up there is the very spot I declared my love for you. Days later, I proposed marriage to you. I offered you everything I could give, and it wasn't enough."

Emotions tightened his throat, forcing him to choose his next words carefully. "You're not the woman I thought you were, Kate."

"I guess not," she whispered, slowly turning away from him. She started walking, but only managed a few steps before he grabbed her by the shoulders and spun her around to face him.

"This is how we end?" he demanded, ignoring the raindrops pelting his clothes. "After all we've been through?"

"Yes." He felt her muscles tighten beneath his palms. "Take your hands off me."

Without hesitation he lowered his arms and took two steps back. After a long moment he forced himself to look away from what he wanted so badly, but couldn't have. He'd blown it. Completely.

"He's waiting for you," he said, pointing down the boardwalk to where Theo had stepped outside the hotel and lit a cigar, unaware of the turmoil only twenty yards away.

As Jake watched Kate walk away, he realized the frigid rain was good for something—disguising his tears.

CHAPTER THIRTY-SIX
Stolen Knowledge

Monday, November 20, 1843

BRIGHT STARS LITTERED THE SKY AND provided the light Kate needed to slip undetected through the quiet, empty streets of Oregon City. Her trail clothes, boots, and her father's hat with her hair tucked underneath completed the desired look of a small man, while the leather sheath strapped to her belt protected and concealed her knife.

She was done.

Done hiding in her room and lying on her bed feeling sorry for herself and her father's broken dreams. Done visiting the livery and staring at her horses, as trapped in their stalls as she was in the hotel. Done watching her father's money being squandered on hotel and livery fees when she had a perfectly good piece of land out there somewhere, possibly with a house and barn.

She was done waiting for nothing to happen. It was time to act.

When she was less than ten yards from the mercantile, she heard the plodding hoof steps of a tired horse. Worried the rider might catch sight of her and get inquisitive or seek conversation, she fled down the alley.

With her back and palms pressed against the rough boards of the mercantile, she waited for the solitary rider to pass.

Kate craned her neck and listened until the horse's footsteps faded and silence returned, then leaned forward and first looked side to side, then back down the alley. After her fourth inspection of the moonlit surroundings revealed no one in sight, she knew she had to go at that moment or risk losing her courage.

The land office was one building away; she could be there in less than fifteen seconds. She tiptoed to the rear of the building, stopping below the nearest of the two windows. The sill was above her head, but after an anxious search she found a discarded wooden barrel to solve her height problem.

Dragging the barrel into position took longer than she liked and made significantly more noise than she'd hoped, but her work paid off when she crouched atop it and discovered it held her full weight. Thankfully the lid only emitted a small squeak as she rose to inspect the window.

She groaned to discover she'd have to remove it whole.

Without shifting her legs, she slid her knife from its sheath. Using the edge of the blade, she began prying at the bottom edge of the pane. Piece by piece, she carefully removed each section of decorative trim and stacked them neatly between her boot heels. When the last one was free, she hopped to the ground and moved them to the soft grass. Then she climbed back onto the barrel and got to work on the frame.

To her dismay, her knife left several gouges in the damp, weathered wood, but less than ten minutes later she managed to tug out the frame and rest it against the wall below. After one final glance around to make certain she was alone, she put her hands on the windowsill and kicked mightily while pulling herself up. Seconds later, she swung her legs over the sill and dropped hard to the floor inside.

She quickly lit one of the four taper candles on Claude's desk. Drafts through the gaping hole in the wall threatened the flickering flame, but ultimately it won the fight against the darkness.

Lowering herself to her knees, Kate laid out her father's land deed flat on the floor, then rifled through the stack of maps on the desktop until she found the Oregon City Region one she'd seen Claude marking boundaries on. She laid it on the floor next to her deed, spinning it so the edge marked north was farthest from her.

Her fingers skimmed lightly over her father's deed, stopping at the number written across the top—326-05. She said the number aloud, then continued quietly chanting it as she shifted her attention to the map. Recalling that her father had said the claim was approximately two miles from town, she orientated herself on the map by locating the river that marked the edge of Oregon City, then scanned the surrounding area for the same number within one of the countless lopsided rectangles.

"Found it!" she declared, jubilantly slapping her hand against her thigh.

A swift but thorough study of the boundaries ensued. To her delight, a wavering line identified by the words Squire Creek entered her claim at the northeast corner and continued through the center until exiting along the western edge. Other than a large circle labeled with the word "tree" in the northeast corner and the words "white rock" in the southwestern corner, there were no landmarks to memorize.

At least she knew the name of the creek, and that her property sat north of town and approximately two miles west of the river. That knowledge, combined with the landmarks she'd noticed on the claims between hers and the edge of Oregon City, would lead her to her land.

Seeing many of the claims had names written below their

corresponding numbers, she leaned in close to see if she recognized any, then froze when she saw the name written in the rectangle nearest her claim.

Jake Fitzpatrick.

Two distinct thumps sounded on the boardwalk just outside the front door.

Leaping to her feet, Kate grabbed the map and slid it between two others on the desktop, shoved her deed into her pocket, blew out the candle, and scurried to the window.

There she encountered her first problem.

She was too short. No matter how she tried, her arms weren't strong enough to pull herself up and over the windowsill.

Frantic, she scanned the room for something to stand on. Claude's desk chair was an option she quickly abandoned; leaving it under the window would be an obvious indication of mischief, and might lead to an angry investigation.

Another search revealed a wooden box in the corner.

With the fear of discovery looming, she lugged it across the room, jumped onto the highest edge, and hoisted herself into the open window. With her stomach against the sill, she teetered as her legs swung a wild search for the barrel.

Strong, unforgiving hands gripped her calves, then guided her feet to the barrel's lid.

Kate jumped to the ground and stared into the piercing blue eyes of her second problem.

CHAPTER THIRTY-SEVEN
Another Option

JAKE HELD BACK A GRIN AS he silently watched Kate replace the window and trim with shaking fingers.

She certainly was a resourceful woman.

When she'd finished, he didn't say a word, just walked alongside her as she made her way down the alley and through the streets. When they arrived at the boardwalk steps in front of the hotel, she went up first, then stopped at the top and turned to face him.

"How did you know?" she asked.

"You're a rotten criminal, Kate." He smirked. "I heard you walk past my hotel room at three o'clock in the morning. I looked out my door and figured you were heading for trouble. So I followed you."

"The only thing I took was knowledge," she declared.

Her words were spoken with confidence, yet Jake knew different by how she fidgeted with Elijah's hat. Whenever she was nervous, she held the brim between her thumbs and index fingers, then inch by inch she would make her way along the circumference of the brim.

"Find what you were looking for?"

Her expression turned guarded. "Yes."

"That was a foolish thing to do, Kate. Did you even consider what might happen if you'd been caught?" He paused to wipe sudden sweat from his forehead, then added sternly, "By someone other than me?"

"I had no other option," she said, her fingers beginning their third circuit around the hat brim.

His voice softened. "You had one option left."

"What?"

"Me." He tapped his finger against his chest to further his point that while their relationship might be over, she could still count on him. "Though you declared me free from the promise I gave your father that I'd watch over you, I have no intention of breaking my word to him. If you're ever in trouble or need advice, you can come to me. Always."

Her lips parted and she let out a long sigh, though he couldn't tell whether it was from relief or reluctant acceptance.

Jake followed her through the hotel's front door and up the stairs. When he reached his door he waited, telling himself it was to make certain she got into her room safely rather than wanting to appreciate the view of watching her walk away.

"Kate?" he called when she was halfway down the hallway.

She turned. "Yes?" she asked quietly, likely expecting another lecture.

"You're the most extraordinary woman I've ever met."

To his surprise, she winked at him before heading on to her room.

CHAPTER THIRTY-EIGHT
Her Claim

KATE TOSSED AND TURNED IN HER bed, unable to do more than doze fitfully now that she knew where to find her land. Checking her father's pocket watch revealed only seven minutes had passed since the last time she'd last held it in her shaking fingers.

"Six o'clock," she murmured.

Sunrise was still over an hour away, giving her ample chances of catching at least a few minutes of sleep. She closed her eyes and forced herself to take ten deep breaths in the hopes of calming her nerves.

No such luck.

Fed up with fighting the urge to finally see what she'd worked so hard to achieve, Kate tossed aside the quilt and sprang from the bed, giggling with glee. She dressed in the trail clothes she'd draped over the end of her bed frame less than two hours before, secured her sheathed knife at her side, pulled on her boots, and walked out the door. She stopped into the kitchen and grabbed two apples from the bowl on the center island, then jotted a note to Clara stating she'd be gone for breakfast and lunch.

At the livery, Nina eagerly accepted one of the apples, crunching happily while Kate saddled her and slipped on her bridle. Minutes later, she'd tucked the second apple into her coat pocket, rode through the livery doorway, and headed north out of town.

With frequent checks to make certain the river still was on her right side, she guided Nina through the dense woods covering several steep hills. The morning air was crisp, invigorating, and reignited her worry of what she would find.

What if she couldn't chop enough wood to keep a fire going day and night to provide warmth? What if the walls were rotted and threatening to crumble? What if the chimney had collapsed, caving in the entire roof?

What if there wasn't a house at all?

At the crest of the third hill Kate stopped to button her coat and slip on her leather gloves, then looked down upon the wide valley spread out below.

A trail!

She stayed still, allowing only her gaze to explore the land before her. Few things invited trouble like trespassing. So far she'd been fortunate not to encounter other riders or landowners. Jake's name written on the rectangle nearest her claim was also something to consider, but not today. Today was about her finding her land. Nothing more.

The trail began at the base of the hill, curved to the left, and continued on for about half a mile where it made an abrupt turn to the right and then disappeared.

"What do you think, Nina?" Kate leaned forward and scratched just below her mane. "You up for taking a look?"

Nina's ears pricked up and she swung her head to nudge Kate's leg.

Kate laughed. "I agree. Let's go."

Keeping a vigilant watch on her surroundings, she urged Nina down the hill and onto the well-worn path through the overgrown grass. She followed the trail to where it turned sharply to the right, then sighted something that left her wavering a fine line between cheering and sobbing—both from relief.

A white rock.

According to the map in the land office, it was the landmark that designated the southwestern corner of her land.

Though the urge to leap from the saddle and kiss a rock the size of three loaves of bread was strong, Kate instead set Nina to a rapid pace along the trail, which she surmised ran along the western edge of her claim. About half a mile farther, the trail intersected with a creek wide enough that Nina needed a running start to jump over it, then disappeared around the left side of a hill dotted with low brush.

Kate pulled her horse to a stop, worried at what she hadn't yet seen—a house. Perhaps the row of pine trees growing on the right side of the trail were the previous owner's attempt at creating a wind break? If so, her house might be close.

She squeezed her legs against Nina to get her moving again, then guided her to head east. Five minutes later she rode up to an obviously abandoned, but still standing house. Hopping from her saddle, she left Nina's reins dragging on the ground and walked a wide circle around the building, happily noting all four walls and the stone chimney were intact.

The second time around, she went slower and noticed more.

It was shaped like a rectangle, and Kate's counted-off footsteps gauged it to be about fifteen feet long and twelve feet wide. An overflowing rain barrel sat at the back right corner. The roof extended about four feet over what could be only loosely described as a front porch, since there were more floorboards missing than present and the thin logs serving as a railing were tilted at a precarious angle. To the left of the front door was a square hole. At one time the window had been covered by sheep hide, but time and the elements had left the covering in tatters.

Kate was surprised to see the house was built from boards rather than logs. They were too evenly matched to have been shaped by hand tools, so whoever built it had gone to a lot of work and expense hauling boards from the lumber mill back in Oregon City. Given how a few had shrunk from exposure to the weather and how all were withered to a dull gray, she would have preferred a cozy log cabin.

On the third time around, Kate paid extra attention to the surrounding area and found a fenced section that looked to have at one time been a kitchen garden, and two oak trees on each side of the house. They would serve as wind breaks in the winter and provide shade in the summer. After checking on Nina to make certain she was still munching away at the grass, Kate headed for the other building set about twenty yards away.

The barn was built like the house, but larger and with a loft. Fitting four full-grown horses inside would be easily manageable. The water trough out front was sturdy, but would need a thorough cleaning to remove the plethora of bright green moss clinging to the outside.

On the way back to explore the inside of her house, the side of her boot brushed against something hard. Looking down, she noticed a handle sitting atop a small wooden door. She tugged to no avail.

Curiosity and determination drove her to spend the next ten minutes on her knees, clearing away overgrown grass and clumps of stubborn weeds. Once the edges of the door were finally unobstructed, she lifted the handle, peered inside, and immediately let out a shriek of joy when she saw her own reflection.

A well!

Kate replaced the door, leaped to her feet, and skipped back to her house. She'd seen the outside; now it was time to go in.

Reaching the front door took longer than expected due to the need to gingerly test which of the porch boards would hold her weight, but finally she was able to grip the latchstring and give it a cautious pull.

Nothing.

She tried again, this time pulling the string harder, but the door still didn't budge. Upon closer inspection she found the problem stemmed from the dry, cracked leather hinges.

She'd have to push it open.

When tentative pushes and grunts of frustration yielded only a hair's width of movement, Kate pressed her shoulder against the door and shoved it aside inch by painstaking inch until she could finally slip inside.

The room was spacious, with a floor-to-ceiling stone fireplace centered at the back wall. A glance up the inside of the chimney found it solid and thankfully clear of any bird nests. A bedstead was built into the back left corner, and the kitchen was in the back right corner. Two l-shaped shelves hung parallel above a sturdy cupboard with a butcher-block top.

A pine table sat against the right wall, and Kate noted two matching pine chairs nestled beneath. On the wall above the table was a unique shelf; a two-foot long log had been split in half and both sections lay side by side upon a board that was set deep into the wall. It was rough, but sturdy. The house didn't have a stove, but she wasn't worried since she'd spent the previous six months cooking meals over an open flame.

The straw tick mattress smelled of mildew, cobwebs covered every corner, and everything was covered with a layer of heavy grime, but a few days of deep cleaning would make it habitable. Kate was grateful the floor was made of wood planks instead of dirt, though she noticed several of the boards below the window were discolored and spongy. Hopefully nailing up a new sheep hide or even an oilskin would keep the rain out and allow the floorboards to thoroughly dry.

She spent the rest of the morning and all afternoon exploring her claim. Whoever had sold the land to her father had cared a great deal for the property at one point. It seemed surprises awaited her at each turn—a birdhouse nailed to the back of the barn, rose bushes growing along the outer edge of the porch, flat stones protruding in random spots from the fireplace to use as shelves, and a stone box to the right of the hearth that would hold several days' worth of wood.

One of the best moments of her day took place at the base of the massive, solitary oak tree marking the northeastern edge of her claim.

There, she'd eaten her first meal on her new land—the other apple.

CHAPTER THIRTY-NINE
Preparations

Tuesday, November 21, 1843

"GOOD MORNING, KATE. YOU'RE UP BRIGHT and early," Albert said, unlocking the door to the mercantile and motioning her inside. "What can I help you with? More fabric?"

"I'm here to pay my debt owed from the other day, and purchase a few additional supplies."

Albert eyed the list Kate handed him, then read it aloud. "Hammer. Saw. Ax and splitting wedge. A hundred nails. Two wooden buckets. Scrub brush. Soap. Washboard. Mineral oil. Thirty candles. Salt pork, bacon, fifty pound bag of flour, ten pound bags of sugar and cornmeal, five pounds of coffee, a sack of soda, and fifty feet of rope."

"That should cover what I need. For today," she amended. "Do you have any window glass?"

Albert shook his head. "Hoping for a shipment with next spring's wagons, but I can't guarantee they won't break on the way."

"Put me down for one, and in the meantime I'll take a sheet of oilskin."

He raised his eyebrows. "Are you shopping for Clara at the hotel?"

"No. For myself."

He gave a curt nod. "Good for you. Will you need delivery, or do you have access to a wagon?"

"Delivery, please." She paused, reconsidering. "Except for a candle, the scrub brush, soap, rope, and both buckets. I'll take those now."

"I'll have everything loaded up by this afternoon and either George or I can run it out to you before sundown. Where's it all going?"

Kate gave directions to her claim and explained that Squire Creek ran across the property, so she'd meet the driver on the south side, then portage everything to her cabin.

Albert grinned. "You mean Tom Baker's old place." He looked at her strangely. "How did you get that?"

"I've got the deed right here," Kate said, patting her pocket and hoping he wouldn't notice she'd avoided answering his question. All she wanted was to spend the next few days cleaning her house. She planned to be moved in long before Theodore returned from Champoeg the following Sunday and inquired about their upcoming date for a horse ride.

"Baker came out here a few years before I did," Albert said. "By the time I arrived in 1842, he'd already built on the land and decided he wanted to go back east."

Kate gave a noncommittal shrug, then changed the subject. "How much do I owe?" she asked, digging into her pocket.

Albert explained he wasn't certain everything she'd requested was available and said he'd send word of the amended list and total cost with the wagon. Kate settled up for her previous purchase, then left with the cleaning supplies in hand.

She rode Old Dan out to her claim, rolled up her sleeves,

and got to work.

First she pulled every loose board from the porch, figuring it was better to straddle the few intact boards rather than risk busting through a weak one and breaking her ankle. Then she cut off a section of rope, tied it to the handle of one of the buckets, and headed to the well. After returning to the house with a bucket of clean, fresh water, she shoved the door aside and spent the remainder of the morning and the entire afternoon scrubbing every flat surface inside the house.

Early in the evening, while she was standing over the well pulling up her eighteenth bucket, she sighted a wagon traveling along the trail.

She swung onto Old Dan and rode out to greet Albert at the edge of the creek. To her delight, the wagon was filled with nearly everything she'd requested, though she discovered she'd have to wait until the final shipment of the year arrived to get the ax and splitting wedge, since they'd just sold their last ones earlier in the week.

Albert offered to help transport everything across the creek and to her house, and she gladly accepted. An hour later they exchanged a round of goodbyes and he headed back to town.

After carefully tacking the sheet of oilskin over the window, Kate pulled herself back into the saddle and returned to the hotel, happy with her productive yet tiring second day as a landowner.

CHAPTER FORTY
Adapt and Overcome

Wednesday, November 22, 1843

Kate woke early and had Nina saddled and ready to leave town before sunrise. On the ride out to her claim, hints of blue broke through the clouds, solidifying her decision on the first task of the day—to wash her mattress.

While she was grateful Tom Baker had left the straw tick behind, the fabric shell needed a thorough washing and the straw was musty and crushed flat.

"We're almost there, girl," Kate murmured to Nina as they rounded the now familiar white rock and headed toward her creek. "We'll stop to get you a drink and then you can spend the day grazing while I work on my claim."

"My claim," she repeated, looking across the surrounding land with a newfound sense of pride. It was perfect, and it was hers.

At the house, Kate broke her first sweat of the day battling the sagging door hinges until she had enough space to squeeze her mattress through. Then the real work began. Once she managed to slide the straw tick off the bedstead, she dragged it out the doorway. After positioning the open end over the edge of what remained of the porch, she scooped out the flattened straw. Tucking the tick under one arm, she grabbed the soap and scrub brush, mounted Nina, and headed for the creek.

Wrangling a giant fabric sack through three rounds of soaping and rinsing took nearly two hours, revealed four holes, and rendered Kate's hands and arms trembling with frigid exhaustion.

Figuring her clothes couldn't get any wetter than they already were, Kate rode back to her house with the soap and scrub brush resting between her legs and the clean straw tick slung over her shoulder.

Drying clothes on the trail had been simple; during their months on the prairie she'd spread them on the grass to dry in the hot sun, and in the later months when they'd traveled through dense forests she'd hung them over a rope stretched between two trees.

Since she didn't yet have a clothesline and didn't like the look of the darkening clouds, Kate opted to drape the fabric over her porch railing, taking care to spread the weight evenly.

A rumbling crash far off in the distance commanded her attention and sent her on a slow circle around the house, eyes and ears alert to anything amiss. Once she assured herself nothing was wrong, warming up took priority over identifying the source of the distraction. She went inside, shoved the door closed, and promptly discovered she had no wood to start a fire.

Two tugs into the long process of opening the door, the porch railing collapsed.

Minutes later, as Kate stalked back to the creek to wash fresh mud off her freshly washed straw tick, she heard the same rumbling crash. It wasn't thunder, though a glance at the pregnant clouds hovering overhead confirmed a storm was indeed brewing.

The air again went silent, and she focused on scrubbing and rinsing the fabric sack in the creek. Again. Once she'd finished she headed back to her house, fabric slung over her shoulder. Again. Except this time she wasn't riding Nina so the return trip took three times as long.

The first raindrop hit when she was half a mile away from her house. By the time she climbed over the boards of her porch, a steady rain poured. Thankfully she'd left the door open.

"Well, it looks like fixing the oilskin is the next project," she muttered when she discovered a puddle by the window. After spreading the straw tick over the bedstead to dry, she checked her tack job on the window covering.

Intact.

Looking up, she sighed to see a drop of water fall from the ceiling. Then another, and another. The leak was small, but if left untended, the puddle would eventually reach and rot the nearby bags of flour and sugar.

After positioning a scrub bucket on the floor to catch the rain, Kate grabbed her new hammer, filled her pocket with a handful of nails, and headed outside to the pile of boards she'd pulled off the porch yesterday. She selected three of the strongest ones, then upended the rain barrel and used it to climb onto the roof.

A year ago, if someone had told Kate that one day she'd be crawling across a rotten roof in the middle of a rainstorm to attempt a haphazard patch job, she would have laughed until she cried.

Now, she just wanted to cry.

She lined the three boards over where she thought the leak was, nailed them in place, then went back inside and watched the spot above the bucket for two minutes.

Success!

While she was thrilled with what she'd accomplished, she also knew much more work was ahead, starting with chopping enough wood to build a fire and drive the chill from her house and clothes. Food wouldn't hurt, either.

Filthy and soaking wet, Kate headed back outside. During her initial exploration of the barn, she'd seen abandoned tools sitting on a small wooden workbench. She hadn't given them much thought since they were rusted, but since she hadn't been able to procure an ax and splitting wedge from the mercantile, the tools were worth revisiting.

The idea proved worthwhile. Kate emerged from the barn minutes later with a hatchet in hand and hurried through the rain toward a fallen tree halfway up the hill behind her house. After taking several chops at the trunk, she inspected her work and found she'd barely gouged the bark. The blade needed sharpening.

Her wood-gathering skills had been long perfected from her months on the trail, so she settled for filling the crook of one arm with branches, all over two feet long but none bigger around than the circumference of her index finger. With her free hand, she took hold of the end of a larger, longer branch, and dragged it alongside her as she walked down the hill.

This time, the rumbling noise she heard was her own stomach.

Inside again, she expertly snapped the thinnest branches short and arranged them in the fireplace. Though the outer part of the wood was wet, the tree had apparently been down for years, leaving inside the bark reasonably dry. Soon she had a small, yet strong fire.

Eager to cook her first meal in her new house, she moved two steps to the right and entered the kitchen, where she promptly remembered the box from her time on the trail still sat in her hotel room. While she had all the supplies to put together a full meal, she had no utensils, pots, pans, or plates.

Kate warmed her hands until the fire dwindled down to coals, then rode back to the hotel, hunching her shoulders against the rain.

CHAPTER FORTY-ONE
A Splendid Discovery

Wednesday, November 22, 1843

JAKE TOSSED HIS SAW ASIDE, JOGGED backward several feet, then stopped and watched as another tree crashed to the ground with a satisfying thud that made the ground shudder.

His fifth felled tree of the day.

He'd woken early and headed directly to the town's restaurant, leaving an hour later with a belly full of steak, three eggs, four pieces of toast slathered with strawberry preserves, a cold glass of milk, and a slice of fresh apple pie to top it all off. The perfect meal to fuel his determination to work until dark.

The rain didn't bother him since he had an oilskin slicker and a fire blazing in the dugout stove. He'd developed a nice rhythm over the course of the day—down a tree, fetch his ax and chop a few branches into firewood, then head into his dugout to warm up and drink coffee. The following week, after he'd chopped off all the branches from each tree, he'd put his horses to work dragging the logs to his planned building spot near the solitary oak tree at the southwestern corner of his claim.

For now, Plug was grazing in the flat valley below and Nickel was locked up tight in the livery. As were all Kate's horses, except for Nina.

He'd checked with Mark, who was clueless on the subject—stunning, since he knew what was happening with almost every other person in town. All the boy knew was the past two days Kate had left town at sunrise on horseback, rotating between Nina and Old Dan, and typically she didn't come back until after sunset.

That night when he returned to the hotel, he planned to ask the woman he was certain would be well-informed as to Kate's whereabouts—Clara.

A gust of wind whipped through the trees and made the bottom edge of Jake's slicker flap wildly against his legs. A stinging burst of rain soon followed. Deciding it was the perfect time to take a break, Jake picked up his saw and headed to his dugout.

Inside he had all the makings of a ladder—his augur, two logs that were both eight feet long and the circumference of his forearm, and a sturdy branch about an inch thick. If he worked until dusk he'd have a good start on finishing the ladder long before it was needed.

After he'd built up the fire until the room was so warm he could work comfortably without his coat, Jake rolled up his sleeves, knelt beside the logs, and began boring out the first hole that would hold the cross steps. An hour and sixteen matching holes later, his arms burned from exhaustion, but he was proud of what he'd accomplished. A peek out the door confirmed darkness loomed, so he banked his coals and rode back to the livery.

He breathed a sigh of relief to see Nina safe in her stall. He breathed another sigh of relief when he remembered Theo would be gone until Sunday, so he didn't have to worry about running into him during his upcoming attempt to pry information from Clara. Jake hung his slicker on a hook in Plug's stall to drip dry, then walked directly to the hotel's kitchen. Sighting Clara standing at the stove, her back to the door, he pulled off his hat.

"Ma'am?" he asked.

She whirled, spoon in hand. "Oh, hello."

He hesitated, not wanting to disturb her, but desperate for information about Kate.

"Don't just stand there," she scolded. "Come in, sit down, and tell me what you want."

Knowing better than to argue with a determined woman in her own kitchen, he obeyed. "Have you seen Kate?" he asked.

"Have I seen Kate?" Her eyebrows shot up as she repeated his question. "Of course I've seen Kate. She came in here a few hours ago dripping wet, half-starved, and yammering on about how she'd fixed her leaky roof."

"Dripping wet?" Jake frowned. "Why wasn't she wearing her oilskin? She had it on the trail."

"That girl is so excited about finally finding her claim she's forgotten her common sense." Clara slammed a cutting board onto the center island, dumped a pile of carrots next to it, and started chopping. "Do you know what she ate on Monday?"

Jake shrugged. Judging by Clara's irritated tone and the demolished carrots it wasn't anything good.

"An apple! That's it, an apple." Clara waved her knife in the air. "Yesterday she bought herself a mess of supplies at the mercantile, but today when I asked her why she hadn't cooked herself anything, she said she'd forgotten to chop wood and bring out any pans." She let out an exasperated sigh. "Right then I fixed her up a hot bath and a hot meal. Then I told her starting tomorrow I'd be packing her a basket of food to take with her every day until she can get a handle on things."

Jake grinned. Kate had thankfully met her match in this

woman.

"What about you?" Clara put her hands to her hips and gave him a stern look. "Did you eat anything today?"

"Yes," he said, patting his stomach. "I had a good breakfast over at the restaurant."

Her lips twitched as if holding back a smile. "Theodore's gone until Sunday, so there's no need to keep missing my meals."

Jake sheepishly glanced around the kitchen. "Anything lying around I could have now?"

"Of course." Clara dished up a mound of stew, set two pieces of cornbread on the edge, and handed the plate to him with a sympathetic look. "A man the size of you won't get far on just one meal a day."

"Thank you," Jake said, then bowed his head in prayer.

Clara waited until he'd taken his first bite to continue. "Now, back to Kate. She's floundering, yet she's too stubborn to admit it. She's going to work herself to exhaustion." She cocked her head and studied him, leaving Jake to wonder at the mischievous glint in her eyes. "You should check on her. See how she's doing."

"I agree," he sputtered, talking through the food in his mouth. Clara's expression instantly changed to one of obvious distress and he winced in shame. His mother had taught him manners; he'd better use them. After swallowing what was left in his mouth, he wiped his lips and continued. "I'd be happy to check on her. Where's her claim?"

"I don't know exactly, but she did mention she enjoyed her first meal—the apple—beneath a lone oak tree that sits next to the creek running across her land. She said the tree marked the corner of her claim."

Jake's jaw went slack as the glorious realization hit—their claims shared the same landmark. He and Kate were neighbors!

CHAPTER FORTY-TWO
Overwhelming Advice

Thursday, November 23, 1843

KATE SPENT THE DAY WORKING HER claim. During the morning hours she'd cleaned the barn, readied the stalls for her horses, and made plans for the future. The list was both endless, and just the beginning of what it would take to survive and thrive.

Fence off a paddock so her horses could run free. Till up the garden soil so she would be ready to plant in the spring. Buy seeds. Repair the fence surrounding the garden to keep out rabbits, squirrels, and all the other critters plotting to abscond with her food. Build a chicken coop so she could have eggs and meat. Buy chickens. Fence off an area to keep a pig. Buy a pig. Learn how to butcher a pig. Buy a cow for milk, butter, and cheese. Learn how to milk a cow, make butter, and make cheese.

And of course, chop wood. She'd found what she believed to be a sharpening stone in the barn, but after hacking away at the fallen tree she wasn't sure if the stone had made the hatchet blade sharper or duller.

Either way, she'd worked from the afternoon into the

evening and managed to chop about four days' worth of wood, so she was happy. For now. Once she had an ax, she'd make real progress on creating a substantial woodpile. In the meantime the stone box to the right of the hearth was overflowing, and the rest she'd stacked on the strongest section of the porch, figuring it was a good idea to keep it within easy reach.

She'd forgotten her oilskin slicker the previous day, and had paid the price in the form of wet clothes and a chill that had settled deep in her bones and taken hours to leave, even after a steaming bath. This time she'd remembered to bring it along, but the day had been unseasonably warm.

She'd taken full advantage of the weather and spread out her straw tick on the grass near the house. By the time the sun sank below the hillside behind her house, it was bone dry. The next day she planned to sew the holes she'd discovered during washing and then stuff it with hay from the loft in the barn.

After laying the tick over the end of her bedstead, Kate grabbed Clara's wicker basket off the table, pulled her door shut, and whistled for Old Dan. He'd spent his day grazing the flatlands of her claim.

She rode into the livery and right by Mark, the caretaker. He was friendly enough and certainly good at caring for horses, but was also too inquisitive. She figured the less anyone knew about her the better, so she'd become adept at giving evasive answers to his nosy questions about where she'd been each day.

The ease of opening the door to the hotel made Kate again vow to figure out a way to repair her own door. Her arms and floor were bearing the burden of the worn-out hinges.

She trudged into the kitchen and found Clara standing at the center table, kneading bread dough.

"Welcome back!" she said, sighting Kate. "I'm a day late in saying this, but congratulations on your special day."

"What's so special about yesterday?" Kate asked, taking a seat on what had become her favorite stool.

"You arrived two weeks ago yesterday, so it's an anniversary of sorts."

Kate sighed. Had it only been two weeks since she'd stood on the hillside above Oregon City and blissfully listened as Jake whispered tender words in her ear? Felt his lips against hers in a thrilling kiss that hinted of a lifetime of slow caresses and passionate love?

The only thing she'd thought about more were the words he'd spoken to her only four days ago. The words she'd repeated to herself so many times they'd become burned into her mind, her heart, her soul.

You're not the woman I thought you were, Kate.

One day she'd venture along the borders of her claim and see if she could figure out where he'd settled. One day she'd do the neighborly thing and exchange friendly words and baked goods while discussing the weather, the water, and a litany of other mundane issues landowners battled in their daily quest for survival.

First she'd have to discover how to face him without dissolving into anger, or tears.

"You've been busy, so it probably seems like much longer." Clara gave the bread dough a final thump, dropped it into a metal bowl, covered it with a towel, and set it aside. "Especially given all that's happened since you got here."

"There's an understatement," Kate replied, placing Clara's open-topped basket on the edge of the table. "Thank you again for going to the trouble of putting together such a wonderful, filling selection of food. It was such a relief today to not have to stop working mid-project and cook. You're very thoughtful."

"I'm more worried than thoughtful. Are you certain you're up to living alone?"

As if she had another choice. "I'll be fine," Kate replied,

then changed the subject. "How are William and Margaret?"

"Theodore hired a team of fifteen men to build them a fancy house and a barn. Given how he offered a bonus if they finished before the deadline, I think they'll be moving out to their claim early next week."

She turned out another mound of dough onto a floured section of the table, punched the center, and began kneading with practiced ease. She then separated the dough into three equal sections, formed them into loaves, and set them into greased pans. After slashing the top of each loaf four times with a knife, she placed them in the oven.

"That ought to be enough for tonight's dinner, and a little extra for you to take along tomorrow." She rubbed her hands together, sending clumps of sticky flour flying. "Do you know how to bake bread?"

"I know how to make biscuits, pancakes, and cornbread," Kate replied. "Plus, I'm learning a lot by watching you."

"Good. Do you have your daily, weekly, and seasonal chore lists?"

Kate stared at her in weary confusion.

"I've found if I keep a strict schedule I don't get overwhelmed. Monday I do the washing, Tuesday the ironing, Wednesday is for gardening, Thursday is baking, Friday is catching up on everything I've fallen behind on, and Saturday is more baking. Sunday, I rest."

Kate grimaced. With such a busy week, no wonder she allotted time for rest!

Clara continued. "Of course, there are the daily chores—sweeping, mopping, dusting, washing dishes, getting water, caring for animals, chopping wood, and keeping a fire going. Don't forget the seasonal chores; they'll depend on your land and whether you plan on raising crops or cattle, but you'll want to at least plant a garden, ride your fence line and check for breaks, make soap and candles, do your butchering as needed, and if you get sheep, you'll need to shear them and card the wool into yarn."

Kate slumped forward, resting her elbows on the table and her forehead in her hands. She hadn't considered, nor knew how to accomplish, even a quarter of what Clara just mentioned.

"Of course, you can set up your routine however you like," Clara amended, probably upon seeing the despair Kate couldn't hide. "Don't worry, dear. Anything meant to be learned won't be learned in a single day. With time and practice you'll do fine. Of course, it's always easier to share the workload with someone else, especially someone you love."

In the days before her mother's death, Kate had listened attentively as her mother had spoken countless words of wisdom in a desperate attempt to instill precious lifelong knowledge within her thirteen-year-old only daughter. Clara's offhanded comment reminded Kate of something her own mother had said only hours before her death.

There is nothing better in this world than to share your life with the man you love, and who loves you in return.

Clara pursed her lips and waggled her finger at Kate. "Don't forget, it's important to take a day of rest."

Kate nodded.

"Speaking of forgetting," Clara said, untying her apron and tossing it onto the table, "I almost forgot to give you some things."

She walked out the room and returned minutes later, lugging a burlap sack at her side.

"Here are kitchen items you'll surely need—a jar of sourdough starter, a sack of potatoes and carrots, a mixing bowl, a spatula, and a loaf pan for bread. There's linens, too. A feather pillow, sheets, a braided rag rug to put by your bed so your first step of the morning isn't such a cold shock, and a heavy quilt, because winters are damp and cold out here. There are also two dishcloths, a tablecloth, and a few yards of fabric I thought might be perfect as curtains."

Kate frowned. This was beyond generous; something else had to be afoot. "You've been saving all this for a reason. What is it?"

Clara's expression turned pensive as she pulled out the stool across from Kate, then sat with her hands primly folded against the edge of the table. "You've seen the curtains hanging in the parlor doorway?"

"Yes," Kate replied.

"Those were the first of many things I traded to Theodore for room and board after I arrived in Oregon City. I brought several trunks of household goods across the trail, and ended up giving him nearly everything before he figured out my plight and offered me a permanent job." Clara reached across the table and gripped Kate's hand with astounding strength. "Every time I see something of mine in this hotel, it reminds me all over again of the future I lost the instant my husband died." Tears slipped unheeded down her cheeks. "When I arrived I had no way of getting land, and I'm too old to try now. Please, take everything in that bag and put it to good use."

Kate couldn't say anything over the lump in her throat, so she simply nodded while blinking back unshed tears.

Clara walked around the table and wrapped her arms around Kate. "You be careful," she whispered. "Make sure to come visit anytime you need a good meal, a hot bath, or advice."

CHAPTER FORTY-THREE
Reflections

Friday, November 24, 1843
THE SCYTHE WAS DULL, BUT EFFECTIVE.

Within an hour of the first swing, Kate cut almost enough grass to fill the straw tick, and had simultaneously cleared a walking path from her porch to the barn. One time around the house garnered the remainder needed to finish the job.

Then, she discovered a problem. While one blade of grass was lighter than a feather, her petite frame was no match for an unwieldy bag over two feet taller and two times wider than herself. Next time she'd fill it inside the house, but she had no intention of redoing work she'd already completed. Or cleaning up the mess.

With her fervent desire to sleep on a comfortable bed instead of her hated bedroll utmost in her mind, Kate spent the next hour shoving and yanking the mattress onto the porch, through the doorway, across the floor, and onto the bedstead. By the time she finished making up the bed with Clara's sheets, quilt, and pillow, she was slick with sweat, exhausted, and eagerly looking forward to what would come next.

Unpacking!

Every flat surface of her house was covered with supplies from the mercantile that needed to be organized and stored in a logical manner, and her saddlebags and packsaddles were filled with the few treasures from home that had survived the trail. The burlap sack from Clara awaited exploration as well.

After building up the fire and slipping out of her trail clothes, she spent time with a washcloth and soap until she was clean, then put on the pink dress.

She tackled the kitchen first. The parallel corner shelves on the wall were sturdy and wide, and easily held her single metal dinner plate, two mugs, and one serving spoon. She set the spider pan and iron kettle on the hearth. Everything else from the cooking supply box had been lost in the Columbia River.

She stowed the bags of flour, sugar, cornmeal, and coffee against the wall between the kitchen and table, leaned her father's rifle in the corner by the window, then emptied Clara's burlap sack onto her bed and found a place for each item.

Eight nails hammered into the wall by the end of the bed created an improvised closet for hanging up her worn calico, her two dresses that she hadn't yet figured out how to wash properly, the maroon dress from Jake, her silk camisole, and her trail clothes. She added another nail for her pink dress, then pounded two more into the wall to the left of the door for her father's hat and her coat.

Her nightgown found a home beneath her pillow, and she folded her mother's lace coverlet and laid it carefully across the foot of the bed. Her bible and china teapot fit perfectly on the small shelf above the kitchen table, while the supply box found a new purpose as both storage for the rolled oil painting of her mother and her father's pistol, and a low display table for her mother's silver brush, comb, and mirror set.

Kate dug deep into her remaining saddlebag and removed the final item—her mother's silver jewelry box. She lifted the lid and lovingly brushed her fingertips against the four treasures laying atop the red velvet lining: her mother's gold wedding ring, her father's pocket watch, the pearl ring her closest friend, Marie Ann, had given her as a going away present, and a small metal box containing two pinches of dirt—one from her father's grave, the other from her brother's.

Closing her eyes did nothing to staunch her sudden tears, nor her thoughts of how different these past two weeks would have been if they'd made it across the trail. Ben would have loved frolicking in the creek and climbing the tree at the edge of the claim. Her father would have made fast friends of nearly every influential man in town, and by now would have a line of sellers eagerly describing their horses available for purchase.

And perhaps she and Jake wouldn't be at odds.

Angry with herself for allowing emotions to overshadow her achievements, Kate scrubbed the tears from her cheeks, set the jewelry box beside the silver mirror, then rose to her feet.

Crying and wallowing over what could have been accomplished nothing. Success in life was how she'd honor her family's memory, and right then she had everything she needed, and plenty of extra comforts she hadn't had while on the trail—a roof over her head, easy access to water and wood, and a soft place to fall at the end of a hard day.

Her horses were provided for as well, due to Tom Baker's diligence and her decision to fill her mattress with grass instead of hay. Thankfully the barn's roof had fared better over the years than the house's, which meant every stalk of hay stuffed in the loft was dry and usable.

She had nothing to complain about, and a lot of work to accomplish before bedtime.

With her father's hat on her head and her threadbare coat buttoned to her neck, Kate headed back up the hill to the fallen tree and spent two hours chopping up another day's worth of wood and stacking it on her porch. After a hearty dinner of salt pork and biscuits, she washed and dried the dishes, then got the idea to step outside and enjoy the sunset.

What she saw when she opened her door both startled and amused her.

Jake's black-and-white paint horse, Plug, was grazing less than fifty feet from her barn, ripping and chewing mouthfuls of grass as if he didn't have a care in the world. Which he likely didn't. Plug was known to wander, and since he always returned when beckoned, Jake typically made no attempt to curb the horse's adventurous spirit.

But what if Jake's hurt?

It had happened before, when he'd suffered his broken leg. Plug had taken advantage and run off then, so maybe Jake was again lying on the ground, incapacitated. Or worse.

Kate edged toward Plug, taking care to make no sudden movements or sounds lest he spook and run off before she could catch him. When only ten feet separated them, his ears twitched and he raised his head.

Their eyes locked.

As she dared one more step forward, a piercing sound filled the air. A sound Kate was well familiar with—Jake's whistle. She watched Plug lope along the edge of the creek and past the oak tree, where he quickly disappeared from sight.

The map in the land claims office had been right. She and Jake were neighbors.

CHAPTER FORTY-FOUR
An Offer Declined

Monday, November 27, 1843

KATE ATE A HURRIED BREAKFAST OF leftover biscuits while wearing her trail clothes, coat, hat, and leather gloves. Her house was chilly since she hadn't built up the fire when she'd gotten up that morning. No need to waste precious wood when she planned to spend the coming hours riding the borders of her claim, trying to figure out where best to put her paddocks. And hopefully catch at least a peek of Jake working his claim.

A soft knock at the door changed everything.

With one hand on the knife sheath strapped to her waist, Kate pulled her door open an inch and peered at the man standing on her porch, a picnic basket slung over his forearm.

"Kate? It's me, Theodore." He frowned when the door didn't budge farther. "Are you all right in there?"

Holding back a sigh of disappointment that it wasn't Jake waiting outside, Kate dragged the door open another two inches. "I'm fine, just startled to see you here."

The last time she'd seen Theodore he'd proposed

marriage, yet she'd managed to slip away without answering. He wasn't the type to take rejection lightly. Or easily. Dissuading his affections and convincing him of the futility of future visits was guaranteed to disrupt her well-laid plans for the morning.

"I returned from my trip to Champoeg yesterday." His expression turned hard, resentful. "Imagine my surprise to find you'd left my hotel, especially after you'd agreed to go on a ride with me this morning."

Kate's grip tightened on the door handle. "While I appreciate your assistance and the information you shared, I saw an opportunity to take possession of my land, so I did."

He eyed her trousers, coat, and boots. "I see you're dressed for riding, so perhaps you anticipated I'd find you?"

"Yes. I mean no." She stammered through a flustered correction. "Yes, I'm planning on a ride, and no, I wasn't expecting you to find me."

"Nevertheless, I did, which means we'll be able to proceed with our plans." He flashed a bright smile while brandishing the basket closer to the door. "Clara packed us a picnic."

She managed a weak smile in return. "I'll be gone most the day, and I'm sure you have things to do back at the hotel."

He dismissed her concern with a wave of his hand. "I'll always have time for you, Kate."

When she made no attempt to open the door further, Theodore's smile faded to a scowl. "It seems Jake's lack of manners has influenced you during my absence." He let out a harsh laugh. "Pardon my blunt words, but you are failing to realize I'm a busy man making time to help you. There's no malfeasance behind my visit here today. I simply want to take you on the ride you'd already agreed to, and let you know I've spoken with Claude at the land office about your situation."

He eased the basket off his arm and began swinging it at his side. "However, if you're too busy to hear the outcome of my meeting with Claude, I can leave. Or, if you'd like to discuss what happened like the civilized people we were both bred to be, you can let me in."

"I suppose," she said, uncomfortable with his insistence on the matter, but not wanting to offend him in light of how he'd gone out of his way to be helpful with the land office. She pulled the door open to allow him inside, then shoved it closed again.

"Would you like some coffee?" she asked, all the while hoping he'd decline.

Theodore wrinkled his nose in disdain. "Never touch the stuff, but I'd love some tea."

"Sorry. Fresh out."

"I'll bring you some on my next visit," he replied. He strode over to the table and set down the basket. "You seem overwhelmed. Agitated too."

"A bit," she replied, fighting the urge to demand he get to the point. With men like Theodore, it was always better to gently steer the conversation back to the subject of interest. "You mentioned a chat with Claude?"

"Yes. He's heard you've taken possession of your claim, and is curious as to how you found it in the first place?"

Kate stared at him warily, wondering how to answer the question without revealing she'd broken into the claims office. While she'd stolen nothing and had replaced everything, she'd still broken the law. Or at least what served as the law in Oregon Territory.

"Forgive me," he said, apparently taking her hesitation for distress. "I didn't mean to upset you. I'm just worried for your safety, especially since there's a few men riled up about how you've taken over this claim. They're simple-minded, so they refuse to listen to reason when it comes to the complexities of the land claims law. As for myself, I can't understand why you left my hotel for this unsuitable hovel." He dragged his fingertips along the seat of the nearest chair, stared at them briefly, then shuddered. "It's little better than a pig trough."

"I don't expect you would understand," she replied, unwilling to idly accept his insults. The chairs were clean, as were her floors and every other part of her house. She was proud of what she'd accomplished in the past few days, and all he'd done was to tear her down. *Pig trough indeed!*

"Kate, you're working yourself to exhaustion by slaving from dawn to dusk, trusting in dirt and animals to make a living, and abandoning the cultured and refined existence I know deep in my heart you enjoy. This is not the life a woman like you should be living."

Her cheeks flamed as she recalled her childhood sweetheart's similar words to her moments before he shattered her trust.

You're not the marrying type, Kate. You're too busy doing the work of a man instead of behaving like you want to marry one.

Oblivious to her irritation, Theodore left the basket on the table and crossed the room to stand before her. "You do recall my proposal? Say yes, and I'll give you the life you're accustomed to. What you deserve."

"I deserve the life I create for myself," she retorted, taking two steps back to put space between them. "Not one given to me by another."

Theodore matched her retreating steps with advancing ones of his own until Kate felt the unyielding door against her back.

"All I ask is that you consider what I can offer." He brushed his knuckles against her cheek. "Consider me."

Kate thwarted further advances by dodging his outstretched hand and then ducking beneath his arm.

"I don't need you to offer me anything, I'm doing fine," she insisted, uneasily shifting her hand beneath her coat to rest on her hip, within reach of her knife. "And if I run into trouble, Jake's claim is close by."

"How convenient," Theodore said, his scorn apparent from his tone and sneer.

Keeping her right hand on her hip, Kate marched to the table, snatched up the basket, and pushed it against Theodore's chest as she passed him on her way to the door. Three sharp yanks on the handle opened it halfway, and two pushes on the outside edge finished the job.

"Please give Clara my best," she said, motioning toward his waiting horse.

With the basket slung again over his forearm, Theodore pulled himself into his saddle, spent far too long adjusting the reins in his hands, and then, to Kate's great relief, rode away.

CHAPTER FORTY-FIVE
Deception

JAKE LAY AWAKE IN HIS BEDROLL, his fingers linked behind his head while he stared at the dugout ceiling. Though the dirt floor was a poor substitute for an actual bed, his first night on his claim had been warm due to a plentiful woodpile, and relaxing due to the knowledge he was done living under Theo's roof. But while he was pleased to learn the dugout was sturdier than he'd first thought, he faced an even bigger problem.

While he had a roof over his head, his horses needed a stable. Immediately. Paying livery fees to house them while he first built his cabin was out of the question. The weeks he'd spent on a hotel room had already diminished the thickness of his pocketbook enough that he worried of his ability to buy a plow next spring. Instead of further padding Theo's palm with his coins, he'd simply changed his plans. By using the trees he'd already felled and stripped, working from dawn to long past dusk, he should be able to build them a suitable stable within the next two weeks.

Urgency should help avoid further distraction by the

woman who'd taken up residence less than a mile away. Three days before, he'd figured out where Kate's claim was located. He'd ridden his borders, stopping on the southwest corner by the oak tree when he sighted a wisp of smoke rising from the stone chimney of the long-abandoned house. Since none of the other nearby claims had houses, it had to be hers.

He'd confirmed the assumption with the aid of a scope, sighting her stuffing handfuls of grass into a straw tick. He'd allowed himself the privilege of watching her for only a minute, then ridden back to his own claim. Since then he'd deliberately stayed away—partially from pride, and partially from uncertainty on how she would receive him.

Jake threw off the blankets tangled around his legs, got to his feet, and stretched the kinks from his back. As he brought his arms over his head, taking care not to push a hole through his ceiling, he decided it was high time he paid Kate a neighborly visit.

****

Jake followed the creek across his land until he reached the oak tree, and continued onto Kate's land. He rode in slow, then pulled Nickel to a stop at the corner of her barn, wanting to conceal his presence while he studied the markings on the horse waiting in front of her house. When his usual remedies—squinting and rubbing his eyes—hadn't proven effective, he reluctantly brought out his scope. With one look, disbelief and dread settled in Jake's chest.

The horse was Theo's and the saddle was empty.

Before Jake could begin rationalizing his next move, Theo came into sight. Jake backed his horse a few steps to further conceal himself, then watched the man go to his horse and mount up. After fiddling with his reins and then a basket hanging from his arm, he rode off.

Jake slid the scope back into his saddlebag. Judging by

the way Theo had stomped over to his horse, he wasn't happy with whatever had transpired during his visit.

Telling himself he'd much rather face Theo than the wrath of Kate after she'd figured out he'd been spying on her, Jake rounded the barn and rode a wide arc behind her house. He at least owed it to Elijah to investigate Theo's appearance on Kate's claim.

When he reached the trail to town that ran along Kate's western border, Jake stood in his stirrups and urged Nickel into a full run. Minutes later, he rode up alongside Theo, who seemed genuinely startled to see him.

"Stop!" Jake demanded.

Theo gave him an incredulous look. "No!" he shouted, kicking his horse in the ribs and sending him thundering down the path.

This wouldn't be Nickel's first time keeping pace with another animal while Jake negotiated with the owner, and his tractable horse didn't disappoint this time either. Seconds later, Theo gave up and pulled his mount to a stop.

When dust and chests had settled, he glared at Jake. "What do you want?"

Jake didn't mince words. "Why were you at Kate's claim?"

Theo's lips slowly twisted into a smug smile. "Envy isn't a trait I'd ever expected to see from you, Jake. I need to savor this moment."

"You've got nothing I want," Jake said.

"You're wrong," Theo replied, raising his chin in a futile effort to look down his nose at Jake. "I'm in control of the one thing you want, because I provide her with the one thing you can't—information."

"She's not the only one you're feeding information," Jake said. "Earlier this week, I had an interesting talk with Claude at the land office."

Was it Jake's imagination, or had the man paled?

"I don't know what you're talk—"

Jake cut him off, not interested in lies. "You're deceptive as always, and playing a dangerous game. Telling Kate how to get her land, then raising questions to the claims office about whether she has a legitimate right to her claim. What I can't figure out—yet—is why you're talking out both sides of your mouth."

"That has nothing to do with you," Theo snarled. "Stay out of it."

"No. I made a promise to her father to watch out for her, and if someone is trying to get her off her land, it has *everything* to do with me."

"Oh yes, that's right." Theo sneered. "Her father hired you to bring Kate, the younger brother, and himself out here. Perhaps if you'd been a better trail guide they wouldn't have died along the way." He began to dismount.

"I'd stay seated if I were you," Jake muttered, clenching his fists but otherwise staying still. Once he started, he knew he wouldn't be able to stop, and he neither wanted to drag an unconscious man back to town nor leave him for Kate to discover.

Theo settled his rump against the saddle. "Jake, consider this a friendly warning, but also your last. Don't poke your nose into my affairs, especially when it comes to the woman I intend to make mine."

Jake snorted at the absurdity. "Kate doesn't want a man who views her as a possession, as an object to be won."

"She'll learn eventually what I can give her is in her best interest. She already understands I'm an important man with enough money and power to buy most men fifty times over. That beats a saddle tramp any day of the week."

Hearing the same insult, again, brought on a stunning realization. "You're afraid."

"Of what?" Theo scoffed. "You?"

"Of what's going to happen when she realizes you've got

only money to offer." Jake recalled Theo's angry movements outside of Kate's house and realized she'd probably already rebuffed his advances. "In fact, I'd wager it's already happened. You offered her everything, and she wasn't interested in a man who considers his possessions as symbols of status and wealth, and his peers as pawns."

"Move aside, before I start to take serious offense to your words." Theo shifted his reins into his left hand and gave them an almost imperceptible tug.

Jake had been watching for the coward to attempt a retreat, and simply walked Nickel forward, effectively blocking his path. Theo gave up on sleight of hand tricks and opted to instead yank on the reins, eliciting a sharp whinny from his horse. Once again, Jake outmaneuvered him.

"I'll move after you answer my original question," Jake replied. "What were you doing at Kate's house?"

"Figures a man satisfied with eking out his living in the woods wouldn't be concerned with wasting away my day." Theo's fingers tapped an impatient rhythm on his saddle horn. "If you must know, Kate and I were having a rousing discussion on whether the harpsichord could make a worthy substitute for the piano in Beethoven's Sonata Number Fourteen. I believe the piano is better suited to portray the intricate movements, but she's got the peculiar idea the harpsichord might be up for the task."

Theo let out an arrogant laugh. "I assume by your slack jaw and dumbfounded expression you have no input on the matter? It's just further proof that you're unsuitable for her in every way imaginable." He raised his elbow to bring attention to the basket on his arm. "We also shared a delightful breakfast, followed by a tender moment. I won't get too descriptive, but since you blundered your way into my parlor and interrupted us once, you already know to what I'm referring."

Jake couldn't risk a response for fear of spewing bile.

"I'm hosting a social gathering at my hotel in less than an hour." Theo smirked. "Kate is on the guest list, and since any self-respecting man knows never to keep a beautiful lady waiting, I'll be on my way."

This time Jake made no attempt to halt his departure.

CHAPTER FORTY-SIX
Problem Days

Thursday, December 7, 1843

KATE LAY ON A PILE OF hay on the barn floor, her stomach tight from hunger, her eyelids drooping from lack of sleep, and her feet and hands numb from cold. According to her father's pocket watch it was just after midnight, which meant she had fifteen minutes until it was time to walk Nina again. Fifteen minutes to worry over everything she'd done, and still needed to do for the next few hours and days, to keep her prized mare alive.

Back home in Virginia she'd had a team of helpers, including stable boys and her father, whenever one of their horses had impaction issues. Here, she had no one.

No one to notice when or why her prized mare had gone from alert to lethargic, from pawing and pacing to flopping to the ground and thrashing about wildly, or when her manure had gone from normal to nothing. No one to review Nina's past weeks and help pinpoint the various reasons for her trouble—change of feed from quality grain to musty hay, and change of routine from walking for twenty plus miles a day to near constant idle stall time.

No one to help ease the fatigue that stemmed from round-the-clock monitoring of Nina's heart and breathing rates, temperature, stomach sounds, and gums. No one to quiet her frantic horse as twice a day Kate eased a tube up Nina's nose, down her throat, and into her stomach to deliver the life-saving mineral oil treatment. No one to walk the horse ten times around the barn every hour, day and night, praying the regular movement helped instead of hindered.

Kate was on her own, and the life or death of her beloved horse rested solely on her shoulders.

Though exhaustion whispered for her to snuggle into the hay and sleep until dawn, Kate got to her feet, straightened her shoulders, and went to Nina's stall. After a glance at the bare floor again revealed nothing, she sighed.

"Hey, girl," she murmured. She took a moment to scratch her morose horse's muzzle and ears before she led her out of the enclosure and began the now-familiar trek around the outside of the barn. At least the rain had subsided from downpour to drizzle.

Twenty minutes and a thorough evaluation later, Nina was back in her stall with her head again tied high to prevent her from rolling. One violent turn could potentially twist her internal organs and prove fatal within the day.

"I'll be back soon, sweetie," Kate said, forcing a cheery tone to reassure Nina. She hated to leave her horse unattended for even a few minutes, but her unrelenting hunger and thirst could no longer be ignored.

Kate trudged across the yard to her house, shoved the door open, and hurried to the dark fireplace. Her numb fingers initially fumbled through the motions to light a candle and then a fire, but eventually flames flickered to life. She moved to the kitchen and mixed ingredients to make a batch of pancakes—a simple, portable meal that could be eaten cold.

Daily chores had gone by the wayside three days ago

when she'd entered the barn and seen Nina with her head turned, eyeing her flank. From that moment, nothing else had mattered but keeping the mare calm, medicated, and alive. This marked the fourth day of round-the-clock care, and if Nina didn't pass her obstruction soon, there would be no hope.

Kate ladled lumpy circles onto the spider pan and then waited with a spatula in one hand and a mug filled with water in the other. Four pancakes were more than enough to sate her current hunger and keep her going until nightfall.

Anticipation of owning a claim had proved far better than the reality.

Once again, like her first month on the trail, Kate found herself totally unprepared for a new way of life. Except now she was alone. At least on the trail she'd had others to commiserate with, and to share in the daily struggles. Now she was isolated, with her horses as her only companions. And though they listened attentively when she confessed her worries, they made poor conversationalists.

She'd had such high hopes her first few days on her claim. But now, two weeks later, she was trying so hard and failing at everything. She couldn't keep up with the daily chores, much less weekly ones, and the seasonal ones Clara had mentioned weren't even a consideration anymore. As for the horse ranch, she could barely handle feeding and caring for her own four horses, so adding more to her herd held no appeal. Everywhere she looked she found work to be done, and now she knew all the money in the world wouldn't buy what she so desperately needed—the time, skills, or lately the energy to do any of it.

At this point, she was struggling just to survive.

Kate eased the spatula under the edge of one of the pancakes, peered beneath, and then flipped all four. Rising, she noticed the bucket resting in the middle of her kitchen table needed to be emptied. As did the one on the floor near the window, along with her iron kettle on the end of the bedstead, and Clara's mixing bowl and bread pan sitting side by side in the center of the room.

She was out of ways to catch the rain.

The roof had too many leaks, and she had too few pots. The only thing she could do—aside from nail old porch boards over the worst of the rotten sections—was to strategically place items throughout the house to collect the raindrops, and suffer through until Nina recovered enough to allow for a trip to town to place an order for lumber. And, hopefully, new hinges for her door. If not, the groove in her floor would turn from a mere annoyance to a true concern. Already the bottom edge of the door was losing a chunk of wood every time it passed over a split floorboard.

With practiced efficiency, Kate slid the pancakes onto her plate to cool. She longed for butter, jam, or syrup to adorn the stack, but her wants far outweighed her abilities to make her favorite toppings, so she had to settle for sips of water to ease down the meal.

Kate carried the plate, fork, and mug to the table and collapsed into the nearest chair. As she took her first bite, she stared at the chair sitting across from her, empty. Tears filled her eyes and flowed unchecked down her cheeks as she forced herself to take bite after bite of pancake, unwilling to allow emotion to keep her from the animal waiting faithfully in the barn.

It wasn't supposed to be like this.

She had everything she'd wanted—a house, a barn, land, and the freedom to do as she pleased, but the victory felt hollow without someone to share it with. Without Jake.

Kate swiped at her cheeks with the back of her hand and then swallowed hard, wincing as the lump of dough made its slow descent down her throat. She covered the remaining pancakes with a dishcloth and headed back outside.

Inside the barn, a long-awaited stench brought Kate's

hand to her nose and a smile to her lips as she peered into Nina's stall and saw what covered the floor.

Success!

CHAPTER FORTY-SEVEN
A New Normal

Tuesday, December 12, 1843

JAKE CLOSED THE MERCANTILE DOOR AND limped toward his horse waiting at the hitching post. After dropping the tool he'd just purchased into his saddlebag, he grabbed the saddle horn. Though every muscle in his arms throbbed in protest and his left leg threatened to buckle beneath him, he grimaced through the pain and fatigue and pulled himself into the saddle.

The physical aches he felt after building a stable by himself in less than two weeks were agonizing, but having no one to share in his joy hurt far worse. Loneliness and regret had made setting the final roof board in place a subdued rather than celebratory moment.

Jake guided Nickel out of town and onto the now familiar path toward his property. The path that took him along the western edge of Kate's claim. He'd put off checking on her, rationalizing his need to build shelter for his horses took priority over social calls. But now that the task was done and the drawknife he needed to smooth the rough edges of the pile of shingles awaiting placement on the stable roof was tucked into his saddlebag, he was out of excuses.

It was long past time he paid Kate a visit, especially given what had taken place minutes ago in the mercantile.

Jake heard the ring of metal against wood long before he spotted Kate on the rise behind her house, chopping chunks off a fallen tree. He rode closer, thankful, yet at the same time alarmed, that her back was to him and she was so preoccupied that she hadn't noticed his arrival. After all, if he could watch her unobserved, so could others.

Judging by the coat hanging off a nearby branch and the darkness under her arms, she'd been working for a while, yet she only had a meager woodpile to show for her effort. Half a day's worth of warmth at best.

Still in the saddle, he moved closer.

She'd lost weight. The shirt she wore—one he'd always enjoyed due to its tendency to stretch taut across her hips and chest—hung loose, now unencumbered by curves. Her hair looked different too—a frizzy mess that hadn't seen the working end of a brush in days. Maybe longer.

Still oblivious to his presence, she lifted what he quickly realized was a hatchet rather than an ax over her head. Then, with a noise that was more whimper than grunt, she brought it down against the tree. Instead of sinking deep into the wood, the blade bounced off the trunk, nearly hitting her ankle.

"Hello, Kate," he said, quietly so as not to startle her.

She whirled so fast her feet tangled and she wobbled briefly before steadying herself. The moment she caught sight of him, she bowed her head and turned away.

"What are you doing here?"

Jake frowned and slowly dismounted. He'd gotten only a glimpse of her, but it was enough to see hard work wasn't the sole reason for her unkempt appearance.

"I figured I'd take the liberty of inviting myself over to see how you've been doing," he replied, forcing a cheerful tone. "So, how you been doing?"

Her bony shoulders rose in a half-hearted shrug.

Jake eyed the hatchet still in her gloved grasp. Even he could see the blade was dull. At the rate she was going, she'd work until nightfall and not have enough wood to cook dinner. Certainly not enough to heat her house through the night.

"I've spent plenty of time working a woodpile," he said, taking a tentative step closer. "Mind if I take over?"

With her back still to him, she raised her hand to stop him. "I don't need help."

She brought up the hatchet again. This time when she attempted to hit the trunk, she missed completely. Thankfully the swing ended harmlessly between her legs rather than into one.

"You need an ax and a wedge for this job," he said, stepping closer and wishing she'd turn to face him. "Or at least sharpen the blade of what you're using now."

"I know!" she shrieked, her tone uncharacteristically shrill. "I know I'm working twice as hard as I should be, yet accomplishing next to nothing!"

"I'm only trying to help you, Kate."

His gentle tone and patience were rewarded when she shifted slightly, allowing him a peek through her hair to see her quivering bottom lip.

"I'm sorry." Her voice cracked, and she paused to take several deep breaths. "What I should have said was that I've checked the mercantile. There's no ax or wedge to be found, and since Albert got word the final shipment of goods for the year is stuck in the mountains, there aren't more expected until next spring." She brandished the hatchet in the air, unwittingly close to Jake's nose. "Until then, I'm stuck with this useless thing."

He placed a steadying hand on her back, then leaned down and pulled the handle from her grasp. To his surprise, she didn't fight him. To his even bigger surprise, she leaned against his arm for several glorious seconds before pulling away.

"Why won't you let me help?" he whispered.

"I can't rely on you," she whispered back, her head still bowed, hiding her face. "I've got to be able to do this on my own."

Whatever had sparked her earlier tirade—be it exhaustion or irritation—Jake had no intention of tolerating her hiding from him any longer. Something was wrong, and he wouldn't leave until he knew what it was and had done his best to fix it.

"Look at me, Kate."

Her hair swung in greasy, tangled strands around her face as she shook her head in adamant refusal.

"Katie," he pleaded. "Please."

After a long moment, she squared her shoulders, took a deep breath, and raised her face to meet his gaze.

It took every bit of resolve Jake had to smile instead of gasp. Dark circles below her red-rimmed eyes were the only spots of color on her face, and he suspected their glittery shine wasn't from crying. Due to either clumsiness or carelessness, she'd missed several of the upper buttons when putting on her shirt. Usually her décolletage was smooth, rosy, and guaranteed to tempt Jake to distraction; now the skin was nearly translucent and showcased a myriad of blue veins and bone bumps.

Jake steeled himself against the overwhelming urge to scoop her up in his arms and carry her to his dugout, where he could lavish her with hearty meals, a warm bed, and days of rest. He settled instead for asking her a simple question, even though he knew the troublingly obvious answer.

"Are you well?"

Her laugh bordered on hysterical, and ended in a horrific coughing fit that had him once again reaching out to steady her. After she recovered, she gave him a bitter smile.

"I've had better days. Nina suffered an impaction last week, and I've been nursing her back to health."

Jake nodded. Around-the-clock care for a horse was tough to deal with. It was little wonder Kate looked so worn out. Though he'd never wish infirmity on a horse, he was grateful to hear Nina was the reason for Kate's decline; exhaustion and hunger could be remedied far easier than illness.

After a brief discussion about Nina's care, Jake was impressed with Kate's skill at handling such a dangerous health issue alone. He also wondered what Theo had done to help during the crisis. Judging by Kate's appearance it hadn't been much, if anything at all.

"How's your house?" he asked.

Instead of answering, Kate bit her lip and stared off into the distance. Her distractedness, coupled with her appearance, settled the issue for Jake. What she needed was some tender care, coupled with firm insistence that she spend the next few days resting more than working. Since Theo obviously wasn't man enough to handle it, Jake would gladly step up.

"How about a tour?" he asked. "I'd love to see what you've done with the place."

Truth was, Jake could care less about what trinkets she'd put where. He wanted to see for himself her walls and roof were solid, her supplies were plentiful, and she had easy access to Elijah's guns should she need the protection they provided. And given her uncharacteristically docile temperament, right now was the perfect time to check on her.

To his relief, Kate offered only a brief show of hesitation before nodding her agreement, dropping her gloves beside the hatchet, and heading toward her house. He quickly tied Nickel to the closest tree, then followed Kate.

"Watch your step," she warned as she nimbly made her way across the porch. It was a mess of rotten wood and collapsed railings, neither of which concerned Jake. Front sitting was a luxury, not a necessity.

The door was another thing entirely.

He watched silently as she slammed her left shoulder and arm against the door. To his dismay it took five straining shoves for her to push it open far enough to slip inside. Her slim fingers grasped the edge, and Jake couldn't resist helping her as she pulled it open further, allowing him entry.

While she closed the door and then fiddled with a candle sitting on a nearby table, Jake stood still and waited for his eyes to adjust to the low light and his exposed skin to adjust to the frigid temperature. How long had it been since she'd had a fire? The fireplace was suspiciously missing the telltale orange glow of banked coals, and a test exhale confirmed his breath's ability to hang in the air as a white cloud.

The candle's flame flickered to life, revealing an unmade bed, unwashed dishes, and an empty wood box.

Jake's hand tightened around the hatchet he'd forgotten he was holding. "I left something outside. I'll be back soon."

He opened the door with one firm yank, closed it behind him, and then hurried back to where she'd been chopping wood. Ignoring the pain in his aching shoulders, Jake sank the hatchet blade into the fallen tree trunk. Working at a speed that bordered on frantic, he chopped for the next fifteen minutes without stopping.

His reward for his effort was the undisguised smile of relief Kate gave him when she answered his knock and found him standing on her porch with his arms loaded with wood, and a hefty pile of kindling stacked by his feet.

"Thank you," she murmured as he stepped around her.

He moved to the wood box and dumped what he carried, happy to see he'd filled it so far that two logs didn't fit, and instead toppled over the edge and rolled toward the kitchen. When he retrieved them, he couldn't help but to give a closer evaluation of the dirty dishes scattered across the top of the prep cabinet. All had sat there for several days at least, and none held the telltale marks of hearty eating—bacon grease, gravy splotches, pork gristle, or bread crusts. Instead, they all featured the dried batter he recognized from his leaner days before he'd had Kate's father's money to spend on needs and wants.

Eyebrows raised in trepidation, he turned. Kate stood by her kitchen table, her expression one of uncertainty and shame. Jake took note of how one of her hands grasped the back of one of the chairs so hard her knuckles were white, and the other hand was braced against the tabletop as if she were afraid of collapsing.

"How about you sit while I start a fire?" he asked, hoping her hatred of being seen as weak would be far overshadowed by her obvious need to rest.

To his great relief, she sat.

Jake hurried to the rickety porch, brought in the remaining kindling, and returned to her fireplace. He crouched before the hearth, where his suspicions were quickly confirmed as to the last time she'd had a fire—he had much more to do than stir the ashes and add fresh kindling.

As he worked to bring a roaring fire to life, he gave surreptitious glances to his surroundings.

She'd displayed everything she'd brought from Virginia in a manner that pleased the eye, and had a few items he'd never seen before, like a new quilt and pillow. However, the light of the growing flames revealed previously darkened corners where, to his relief he saw Elijah's rifle, and to his dismay, he saw less than half the food supplies she'd need to survive the winter. Another glance around the room exposed another issue—a plethora of pots, pans, and water-soaked rags positioned to catch raindrops falling from the leaky roof.

"I see you're checking everything I've done," Kate said quietly. "What do you think so far?"

"The house looks nice," he said, struggling for a way to

tell her she'd spent precious time decorating, when instead she should have focused on her basic needs like chopping wood and tilling soil in preparation to plant a spring garden. However, no good would come from him giving word to his disappointment, so he said nothing else.

"I'd hoped to accomplish more by now, but given all that's happened with Nina I've had to put off a few things. I'll get to it all, though. Eventually."

Jake plucked the tin coffeepot from the hearth, got to his feet, and turned to face her. "Mind if I make us some coffee?"

"I can do it," she replied, her tone hinting at the fierce determination he knew so well. He heard the scrape of her chair as she made a half-hearted attempt to rise.

"I'm closer," he said easily, moving to her kitchen cabinet in search of coffee and two mugs.

She settled back into her seat. "How have you been?"

Jake smiled at the ease at which they were able to fall back into simple, easy conversation. Of course, they hadn't spoken of anything of substance, but for now it was enough.

"I'm doing well," he said, tossing a handful of coffee grounds in the pot. "I've been busy working my claim, and just finished building a stable." He covered the grounds with water and then set the coffeepot near the fire.

"Good thing you've got a place for them, especially since it seems Plug likes to wander here as much as he did on the trail." Kate gave him a hesitant smile. "He's paid me a few visits."

"Some things never change." Jake chuckled at first, then his lips tightened at the thought of who else had paid Kate a visit.

He couldn't do it. He couldn't handle Kate speaking of Theo favorably, so he decided to avoid the topic altogether. Better to instead focus on honoring his promise to her father instead of how he'd lost her to a man like Theo, who was apparently content with allowing Kate to wither down to skin and bones and work herself to exhaustion. Even during their worst days on the trail her eyes hadn't shown the distinct haunted, hungry look they did now.

He grabbed two logs from the wood box and knelt again before the fire. Already the room felt warmer, but he still wasn't satisfied. After poking one of the chunks of wood into a better position, he turned to find Kate still seated at the table, her eyes closed and her head leaning against her hand.

She was asleep.

Quietly, he rose and moved to the kitchen.

An hour later he carried a plate loaded with pan-fried salt pork, cornbread, and hefty chunks of seasoned potatoes and carrots across the room. Kate awoke with a start as he set the plate on the table.

"Sleep well?" he asked, settling himself in the opposite chair, a mug of coffee in hand.

She nodded, her eyes focused on the pile of food sitting before her.

"I figured you could use a good meal," he murmured, sliding a fork, knife, and cloth napkin closer to her right hand. The action reminded him of the time on the trail when she'd been so out of sorts she'd refused to eat for days.

Thankfully, today was different.

Still staring at her food, Kate picked up her fork. Jake saw only the top of her head as she bent low over the plate and shoveled in the first few bites with the hurriedness of a feral dog that had discovered a discarded cow carcass behind a butcher shop.

Just as Jake was about to warn her not to eat too fast, lest everything make a return appearance, she set her fork down and straightened in her chair. With her eyes closed and her mouth full, she gave a low moan of pleasure as she slowly chewed.

He'd been there many a time and knew exactly how wonderful it felt the moment hunger pangs finally subsided enough to allow a person to finally enjoy the savory scents and tastes of a substantial meal.

"There's plenty more," he said, rising to return to the kitchen.

Kate's eyes flew open and she shook her head. "No, please," she said, grabbing his hands with her own to hold him in place. "Stay."

Her cheeks reddened and she quickly pulled her hands away, but not before he'd noticed their appearance. The skin surrounding several of her nails and knuckles had cracked open, and three spots showed telltale smears of dried blood. Her palms had felt rough against the backs of his hands, and he surmised them to be in far worse condition than her foot had been when she'd hurt it on the trail.

Jake forced himself to just stay still and sip his coffee while he considered what to do, and say, next. While he'd spent the past three weeks utilizing his carpentry skills to build a stable, a ladder, and the beginnings of a workshop to make furniture while he was stuck inside during the upcoming rainy season, she'd been huddled in a cold house, shifting bowls of rainwater beneath a leaky roof and fighting to open and close a heavy door.

While he'd been filling his belly daily with small game he'd hunted either with his rifle or snares and fish he'd caught from his creek using a bent sewing needle, she'd been surviving on pancakes and water.

While he'd chopped enough wood to last well into the summer months, she'd been spending hours each day with a dull hatchet, with little to show for her efforts.

Though Jake was amazed at Kate's tenacity and unbreakable spirit in light of all she had faced and overcome since taking over her claim, the fact remained she was unsuited and unprepared for solitary life on a desolate land.

Kate pinched her last bite of cornbread between her fingers and ran it across her plate, soaking up all the glistening remains of her salt pork. After popping the sodden morsel into her mouth, she smothered a belch into her hand, then gave him a chagrined smile.

"Thank you for this wonderful meal." She wiped her lips with a napkin. "As you've probably gathered, it's been a while since I've had a chance to cook."

"Kate, I'm worried about you."

"There's no need to worry." She waved her hand in the air as if to dismiss his concern. "I went into town yesterday. At the lumberyard I placed an order of enough boards to replace the roof and porch, with plenty left over for paddock fences. I also hired a man willing to help me catch up on what I neglected when I was taking care of Nina. After that, he'll do a few basic repairs and dig fencepost holes. His name is Zeke, and he starts Friday."

Long ago, Jake had been scornful of wealthy landowners hiring out their work instead of learning how to accomplish a task and then doing it themselves. Now he was just grateful Kate had the means to hire help. However, as he'd heard that morning in the mercantile, there was a problem.

He was glad he'd waited to speak until she'd cleaned her plate, wanting to make certain she was sated before he brought up what was bound to be a sensitive topic.

"Yes, it's true Zeke Waggoner is willing to help you. Help you right out of your petticoats." *Not that you wear them anymore.*

She gasped. "What?"

"Kate, that old codger's been talking everyone's ear off about how the 'fool-headed female' living out at Tom Baker's place hired him, and how much of her money he was planning on 'stealing from right under her nose since a woman don't have no business sense neither'."

Kate's jaw went slack. "He was as polite as could be when I spoke with him yesterday."

Jake shook his head. "He's got you duped, because just

this morning he stood in the mercantile and bragged to anyone who'd listen how he was going to be doing himself a 'mighty big favor getting wages from you without having to do nothing.' And hopefully get a good glimpse down your shirt to boot."

She closed her eyes, bowed her head, and began rubbing her temples. After nearly a full minute, she let out a long sigh and sat back in her chair.

"Admittedly I hadn't done much—" she paused, then corrected herself, "—make that any research on him. I hired him mainly because he fit my sole criteria—willingness to work. I'll fire him the moment he steps foot on my land."

Jake hated to even speak his next words, but if she didn't want to be with him, at least he could convince her to do what was best for her own sake. If it meant encouraging her to return to the security Theo's hotel offered, he'd do it just to make sure she was safe.

"Kate," he said gently, "running a claim seems to be too much for you to handle on your own, and you're starting to put yourself in danger. It might be time to consider moving back into town. Back to the hotel." He paused, his brows furrowed with concern. "It won't be what you wanted, but you'll be safe and comfortable."

"Safe and comfortable!" She jumped from her chair so fast it tipped over behind her. "My father and brother did not give their lives for me to be safe and comfortable! I came here to help my family fulfill their dreams, and now that they're gone it's up to me."

"What about your own dreams, Kate?" he asked, wondering yet again her thoughts of having a family of her own, and someone to share in the work and joy of owning a claim.

She stared at him for so long he almost dared to try again at telling her how much he loved her, but she spoke before he could begin.

"This *is* my dream now," she replied, her chin angled at the stubborn tilt Jake had grown to love. "It's a part of me, Jake. In the beginning I wanted it for my father and brother, and now I want it for myself. Granted it's changed some since running a mercantile is out of the question, but I still want to eventually create a horse ranch here. It's going to take a lot longer than I planned, but I won't give up. Ever."

"All right," he replied, keeping his tone calm, even though he wanted to cheer for her independence. "Then I'll do what I can to help make it come true for you. For starters, I'll be back in two days to help fix your roof and get a substantial woodpile started."

"Are you sure? I don't want to keep you from your own work."

He laughed. "I've just spent the last two weeks building a stable at record speed, so I'm not especially eager to get back to spending my days felling and dragging trees." He figured he was due a break while his body recovered from the strain.

Kate bit her lip, obviously still uncertain at what he'd proposed.

"If it makes you feel better, you can pay me back with steady supply of pies next summer once the blackberries are juicy and ripe for the picking."

She nodded, and her grin sealed the deal.

CHAPTER FORTY-EIGHT
Trouble in Town

Wednesday, December 13, 1843

KATE TUCKED THE SHARPENING STONE SHE'D just bought at the mercantile inside her saddlebag. The stone she'd found in her barn had long since proved ineffective, so she figured buying a new one was a practical investment in her future.

With the first of several planned errands completed, Kate pulled herself into the saddle and set Nina to a brisk walk down the street and toward the hotel. Her horse had recovered completely from her recent illness, and Kate had every intention of providing the best of care from now on, which would be yet another investment in her future. A future that looked remarkably promising.

Kate was still amazed at how a tasty meal, a thorough washing, and ten hours of sleep in a warm bed had affected her outlook on her situation. A week ago she'd struggled just to endure each passing hour of the day, and now she was ready again to tackle the world—starting with a visit to Clara, and then checking on her order from the lumberyard.

The men lingering on the boardwalk in front of the hotel

almost convinced Kate to keep riding. Almost.

Sighting Zeke as one of the three men content with flapping their yaps instead of being productive, hardworking members of society, Kate figured she might as well dismiss the man here on the street rather than on her own porch.

When Jake had first told her of Zeke's true intentions, she'd only been able to stare at him as disbelief and disappointment washed over her in waves, sinking her high hopes for what she'd planned for Zeke to accomplish. Then she'd gotten angry.

As she rode closer, the men quieted. When she dismounted beside the hitching post closest to the hotel's front door, they shifted to stand shoulder to shoulder. She didn't know the second man with Zeke, but recognized the third man with the gap between his teeth as Wade, who'd propositioned and then insulted her in the land office.

Kate swallowed her fear and straightened her spine. No time like the present to prove she wasn't meek, nor would she allow herself to be intimidated.

They watched quietly as she tied Nina's reins to the post. After she'd finished, Zeke smoothed back his bone-white hair and then broke the silence.

"Sure is a fine filly you've got there, ma'am," he said, not even bothering to hide the smirk playing across his lips.

"I agree," she replied, pushing aside the front of her coat just enough to reveal the knife strapped to her belt. Once Wade's low whistle let her know he'd seen what she'd purposely shown, she slid her coat back into place.

"Sure am looking forward to working with her." Zeke tipped his hat in her direction. "And with you, for that matter."

Kate stared at him, her emotions a clash between determination and disgust. "You'll never get any closer to her—or me—than you are right now. You're fired."

"Fired?" Zeke's stance went rigid, his gaze incredulous.

"Why?"

She lowered her chin and raised her brows, giving him a first and last chance to change his mind about pursuing the reason.

"Why?" he repeated, his lips curled into a wolfish snarl.

"I need an honest worker." She crossed her arms and gave him a scornful look. "After I got word of your recent boasting, it was clear you aren't the man for the job."

While Wade and the wiry stranger, who had shockingly tiny ears, were busy snickering and Zeke stammered protests and denials, Kate slipped by them and into the hotel. Once the door was safely shut behind her, she closed her eyes, yanked her father's hat from her head, and leaned her forehead against the wall until her heart and breathing calmed.

Footsteps sounded from the hallway and grew louder, then stopped. "Kate?"

She whirled to see Theodore standing in the doorway, staring at her in confusion. "Oh," she stammered, feeling a flush of embarrassment rise to cheeks. "Hello."

He took a step toward her, then eyed his desk and halted. "Are you all right?"

She nodded, eager to avoid discussing what had just transpired outside. "I'm sorry for interrupting you. I happened to be in town running errands and thought I'd pop in for a quick visit with Clara."

"She's not here." He took two quick steps to his desk, swept a stack of parchment paper into a drawer he'd hastily pulled out, then straightened to face her again. "She's with the doctor."

Kate's hand flew to her chest in alarm. "Is there a problem?"

"No, she's fine." He gave her a reassuring smile. "Clara and the doctor have begun dining together every Wednesday morning."

Relief flooded through Kate upon learning nothing was

amiss with her dear friend. "I'm thrilled to hear she's found happiness. She definitely deserves it."

"Speaking of happiness," Theodore said, "I'd love to extend this unexpected visit of yours into a lunch date. Are you free?"

"No, I'm sorry. I need to get back to my claim. I apologize again for disturbing you."

"Another time, then," Theodore replied, disappointment in his tone.

Kate opened the door a crack and peered outside. The men had moved to the street, but to her dismay, they were less than three feet from Nina.

Another confrontation loomed.

"Kate?" She turned again to see Theodore studying her closely. "Are you certain nothing is troubling you?"

Kate hesitated, then decided Theodore was the lesser of two evils when compared to the men waiting outside. "It seems I've upset a few of the townsfolk, and they've decided they want to continue a conversation I cut short by stepping into your hotel."

Theodore frowned, then strolled across the room to the door and eased it open several more inches. "Stay here," he warned, then slipped through the doorway, pulling the door shut behind him.

Kate heard low voices, and once she thought she heard Theodore shout, but couldn't make out anything specific being discussed. While she waited, a debate waged within. Not five minutes ago she'd been rife with confidence, yet now she was hiding like a simpering fool while Theodore fought a battle she'd started.

Suddenly disgusted with herself, Kate opened the door and stepped onto the boardwalk. She spotted Theodore in the middle of the men, who were now clapping him on the shoulders and back, their smiles more jovial than cruel. Spotting Kate, Theodore nudged the others and they dispersed without giving her so much as a second glance.

"Thank you," Kate said, making her way down the steps and onto the street. When she reached to untie Nina's reins, Theodore placed his hand over the knot.

"Though our last visit didn't end on the best of terms, nothing has changed when it comes to how I feel about you."

As Kate searched for a way to gently confess how she'd hoped differently, Theodore bent at the waist and ducked below Nina's neck. Before Kate realized what was happening, he'd smoothly maneuvered himself to stand face to face with her.

"What?" he asked, feigning innocence when Kate flinched and took a small step back. "I've given up trying to hide my feelings about you, so why are you surprised at my refusal to stand idle while you're suffering?"

"I'm doing fine."

He lowered his gaze to her boots and gave a slow perusal of her trail outfit, ending with her father's hat once again perched upon her head. "Your appearance today suggests otherwise."

Kate pulled the lapels of her coat tighter around her chest. "Work clothes aren't meant to flatter; they're meant to be practical."

Theodore let out a long sigh and held up his hands in a surrendering gesture. "It seems whenever I'm around you my tongue lets things slip that are better left unsaid. Perhaps once you learn how I've helped you out by calling in a few favors owed to me, you'll forgive my abhorrent behavior."

Kate mulled over what he'd said and opted to ignore the hidden insult in favor of questioning the most relevant part. "Why would favors owed you benefit me?"

"You don't realize yet the amount of trouble you taking over that claim has caused, but I do. Fortunately, I've taken a special interest in you, and my actions of late are the sole reason you're allowed to keep your claim." He bounced on his heels while she absorbed his declaration, then added a final shot across the bow. "For now."

"I must admit," she said, staring at him in disbelief, "I'm torn."

"Between what?" His feet stilled and he reached for her hand, which she pulled away before he could touch.

"Between scolding you for acting upon my behalf without my knowledge or consent, and waiting to find out what it is you've done." She heard the defiant tone in her voice and forced herself to soften it before she continued. "In the interest of my land, I'll choose the latter."

His expression turned placating, and he backed away from her until he leaned against the hitching post. "Claude is fed up with the stories he's heard of a single woman living on a highly desirable claim. Furthermore, though I've explained to him in great detail how the wording technically allows it, he has been hesitant to accept how a simple mistake gives you the right to land ownership."

"Then I'll go explain it to him myself," Kate said, untying Nina's reins and reaching for her saddle horn. "After I persuade him to listen to reason, then I'll finally have my name written on the official land record."

"Wait. I'm not finished." Theodore pursed his lips and gave her a stern look. "Three weeks ago you might have been able to eventually convince him to abide by the wording, but not now."

Kate racked her brain to recall what had occurred three weeks ago. Once she did, she kept quiet, not trusting her voice.

"As you well know, there was a break-in at the land office three weeks ago. It didn't escape Claude's attention that you left town shortly afterward, and are now living alone on the same claim that coincided with the deed you presented to him just two days beforehand."

Kate bit the inside of her cheek so hard she tasted blood, but thanks to hours spent listening to her vindictive aunt's tutelage on how to control her emotions, her expression remained impassive.

Theodore continued, oblivious to her distress. "As a personal favor to me, Claude has overlooked the box you moved inside his office, the barrel you left outside of it, as well as the scrapes on the window frame. If you go marching in there demanding what he doesn't feel you deserve, he'll become even more infuriated with you. Rile him up enough, and he might start taking his sworn oath seriously and try to send you to jail for fraud."

"I can't lose my house and my land. It's all I have left." She looked up at him, unable to conceal her desperation. "What am I going to do?"

"Best thing you can do is head back to your claim and stay there until I've handled Claude."

A shiver of uncertainty ran down her spine.

Theodore shrugged. "Of course, you can do what you want, but I'll warn you I've heard talk from plenty of men interested in your claim, and many are willing to do unscrupulous things to get it." He leaned forward to level his gaze with hers, and then drove the point home. "The two that immediately come to mind were let out of jail just last night—Cyrus and Murray."

The shiver turned to outright fear, and Kate hesitated no more. Minutes later, after securing a promise from Theodore to send word when Claude wasn't so irate at being outmaneuvered, Nina's thundering hooves carried her out of town.

CHAPTER FORTY-NINE
Fools

Thursday, December 14, 1843

JAKE WATCHED AS KATE BENT STUDIOUSLY over the final roof shingle, tapping a nail into place with his hammer. She was a hard worker; she'd listened attentively to his every word and together they'd worked through the afternoon fixing her roof. Their morning had been spent chopping up the remainder of the fallen tree behind her house. He'd brought his ax and wedge, and after showing her how to use her new stone to sharpen the blade of her hatchet, they'd managed a considerable woodpile. More than enough to get her past Christmas, and possibly to the first week of the new year.

Though it had only been two days since he'd last seen her, the color had returned to her cheeks and her stubborn streak had returned as well. They'd argued briefly over whether she'd go up on the roof with him. She wanted to learn all he knew about repairing a roof so she could do the job properly herself next time; he wanted her to sit inside and rest while he did the work.

He'd lost.

"All finished," Kate said, leaning back on her heels and wiping her cheek with the back of her hand. "Can I have my present now?"

"No." Jake smiled at the streak of grime she'd left behind. "You're adorable when you're dirty."

He'd given her several compliments throughout their day together, both because she deserved them, and to test whether she'd insist he stop.

She hadn't, which was encouraging. He wasn't certain she was being courted by Theo—pride and a touch of fear kept him from asking—but the fact she'd hadn't declared his flattery as improper since she was in a relationship with another gave him hope.

Kate slammed her fists to her hips in feigned frustration. "Quit trying to change the subject."

"What?" he asked, raising his eyebrows and placing his hand against his chest, attempting, and failing, to portray innocence. "I'm simply saying dirt suits you."

"What's in the blanket?"

Jake made a show of cocking his head and knocking on several of the nearest boards and shingles. "It's rotten in spots, but it'll hold through the rest of the winter."

"Is the present something to eat?"

"Next spring you'll probably want to put a whole new roof on." He loved how antsy and curious she was about what he'd brought her. Anticipating the look of joy on her face when she caught her first glimpse of what he'd made had kept him working late into the previous night, and he'd risen again early this morning to give it a special finishing touch.

"Are you at least going to give me a hint?"

He grinned. "Nope."

Ignoring her groan of disappointment, he collected his tools, swung his legs over the edge of the roof, stepped onto the rain barrel, and jumped to the ground. Kate followed.

"Thank you," she said, brushing her hands against her

trousers and giving him a bright smile.

"You don't even know what I brought you yet," he teased.

Her smile faded. "I'm thanking you for all you're doing to help me succeed."

"You can count on me." His heartbeat pounded in his ears and he felt lightheaded. "Anytime."

"Want some coffee?" she asked.

He nodded, then walked beside her as she headed around the house, stopping briefly to fetch her present from where he'd tied it to Nickel's saddle. Once inside, he built up the fire while she poured two cups of coffee, still warm from that morning. After she set them on the table, he placed the blanket-covered present in her hands. Her eager fingertips fluttered along the edges of the gift, testing and evaluating what lay inside with taps and pinches.

He chuckled. "Quit stalling and open it."

"I can't help it," she replied, gleefully freeing the first knot of the rope securing the blanket. "Anticipation is half the fun."

Indeed. He ached to slide his hands into the glorious waves of her hair, tilt her head and allow his lips to leisurely explore the smooth skin just below her earlobe. He longed to glide his fingertips along the curves of her shoulders, her waist, her—

"Oh, Jake." She gasped, pulling the final corner from the fuzzy wrapping and holding the mahogany picture frame aloft. "You remembered."

Of course he'd remembered. The day after her father had died she'd been forced to abandon nearly all she'd held dear, including the picture frame that held the painting of her mother. He'd watched in silent despair as she'd knelt in the grass and fought tears while cracking it open. As she'd painstakingly rolled up the canvas and stored it in her saddlebag, he'd vowed that one day, God willing, he'd build her a new frame.

"I know it won't replace the one you left on the trail, but I wanted to make sure you had a way to display her portrait."

"It's perfect." She faced him, her eyes glimmering with unshed tears. "Thank you."

Jake dared a step closer.

"As soon as Theodore lets me know it's safe for me to return to town, I'll buy a velvet ribbon at the mercantile and then I'll hang this frame on the wall."

Jake shook his head, dazed at hearing Theo's name in the midst of his wandering thoughts. "When did you see him?"

"Yesterday we had a long talk when I stopped in for a visit at the hotel," she answered, her eyes still shining with excitement as she lovingly stroked her fingertips along the frame's edges. "He's proven himself to be brilliant at negotiating the law, and figuring out how certain words will eventually allow me to keep my claim. I don't know what I'd do without his help."

Jake gritted his teeth. "If he's so helpful, then why did I find you half-frozen and half-starved as rain poured through your roof?"

"Jake, I—"

"Theo's never done anything to benefit anyone but himself." His words were hard with anger. "He's playing you for a fool."

"That's not true! He's working diligently with Claude and the Provisional Government to convince them of my right to own land. I just have to stay out of town while he figures out the details, and he'll let me know when he's made everything official."

Realization hit Jake, and suddenly everything was crystal clear. The scoundrel wanted Kate for himself, and the easiest way would be to get her kicked off her land, leaving her helpless with nowhere to go. Then he could swoop in and save her.

"Kate, he's convinced you he's helping when what he's actually doing is playing puppet master with your land. Your dreams. And you're foolish enough to let him."

Her cheeks flushed crimson. "You're saying that Theodore, the one who's been helping me keep my land, is actually trying to roust me from it? That's absurd."

Jake stared at her as anger fled and acceptance took hold. He'd tried everything, yet failed. No matter what he did, no matter what he said, he'd apparently never convince her of Theo's true nature.

"It seems I've been the biggest fool of all." Blinking hard against emotions and second thoughts, Jake walked out her door.

CHAPTER FIFTY
The Cloak

Sunday, December 24, 1843

LATE IN THE AFTERNOON KATE FINALLY ran out of projects to complete in the barn and returned to her dark house. It was little wonder the fire had gone cold; she'd spent the morning giving each of her horses a ride around the perimeter of her claim and then completed a detailed health evaluation for all four. After lunch, she'd polished her saddle to a gleaming shine with a soft cloth, rearranged the tools Tom Baker had left behind, swept the entire barn floor, tidied the loft, currycombed each horse, and braided Nina's tail.

Boredom and loneliness were her sole companions, and made for productive days and nights.

Kate knelt before the fireplace and stirred the pile of ashes. When she sighted the familiar orange glow, she added several thin sticks. Leaning close, she blew on the coals until they were red hot and continued adding kindling, and eventually logs. Once she was confident the fire wouldn't go out without constant monitoring, she filled the iron kettle and bucket with water and set them on the hearth to warm.

Might as well wash her work clothes. It wasn't like she had anything better to do. She didn't dare to go into town that evening for the Christmas Eve service at the church. Theodore's warning had left her wary of discussing her living situation with anyone, and even the thought of running into Cyrus and Murray again sent her into a panic.

She undressed in front of the fire, allowing the heat of the flames to warm her skin while she soaped and rinsed herself from head to toe. When she'd finished, she added soap to the wash bucket and dropped her trousers and shirt inside to soak overnight.

After wrapping herself in a towel, she stood before the wall where her clothes hung and pondered what to wear. While she knew the sturdy calico dress was the practical choice, especially if she was going to spend the evening outside at the working end of her hatchet, her fingers longingly brushed against the maroon dress from Jake.

Memories won over chores, and she plucked it from the hook. Though she was alone on Christmas Eve for the first time in her life, she could at least engage in frivolity on her own, starting with dressing in the gift from the man she'd once loved.

Still loved.

While she hadn't yet built up the courage to drop in to his claim for an unexpected visit, all week she'd found excuses to be outside. First, she'd entertained the hope that Plug might wander onto her property again. Catching him would ensure Jake would visit to reclaim his wayward horse. When the horse failed her, she'd simply abandoned the ruse she'd convinced herself of and settled for constant checks of their shared oak tree and the path to and from town that ran along the western edge of her claim.

All to no avail.

Jake hadn't shown his face, and once she was finally truthful with herself, she didn't blame him. She'd been so focused on convincing him of all Theodore was doing to earn her legal right to her claim, she'd all but scoffed at everything Jake had done. All the time he'd spent away from his own land, helping her so she could thrive on hers.

If only she'd focused instead on Jake. On telling him how she considered his company much more than a comforting break in the dull routine of her workdays. How much she missed his witty banter, handsome grin, and gentle touch. How much she longed for him to appear at her door for a short visit, or better yet, to stay forever. And most of all, how much she loved him.

Kate lowered the beautiful dress to the floor, stepped inside, and pulled it up. To her consternation, fastening it was no longer a breath-holding, spine-twisting struggle.

She needed to take better care of herself. Sew a sturdy coat to replace her patched, threadbare one, cook regular meals, sleep longer, and at least attempt to squelch some of the misery that came from missing Jake so badly her heart ached.

A hard knock at her door interrupted her fanciful thoughts.

Kate tensed, envisioning Claude on the other side, eviction paperwork in hand. Several deep breaths later she headed for the door, reasoning that even a man like Claude wouldn't force her from her land on Christmas Eve.

She pulled the door open. To her relief, she saw only Theodore.

"Hello! Come in!" she exclaimed, her enthusiasm due more to the fact neither Claude nor a crowd of angry men waving fiery torches were standing on her porch, rather than actual happiness at seeing Theodore.

"Thank you." He slipped past her, then stood in the middle of her room, holding a lumpy package the size of a stack of dinner plates.

"To what do I owe the pleasure of your unexpected visit?" she asked, already hoping he wouldn't stay long.

"I come bearing a gift."

She reached out a tentative hand and took the package from him. "You didn't have to get me anything."

"Kate, I share my fortunes with those I care about." His serious expression changed into a childlike grin of pleasure. "Besides, it's Christmas."

She sat on a chair and placed the package on her lap. After she untied the twine and pushed back the paper, she gasped to see a luxurious cloak made of wool that had been dyed a deep green. The inside was lined with brown velvet, and braided brown cording had been meticulously stitched along the entire bottom edge. It must have cost him a small fortune.

"Theodore, I don't know what to say. I can't accept such finery from—"

"Clara said the color would compliment the red in your hair perfectly." Theodore slid the cloak from her fingers and held it aloft until it unfurled before her. "Let's see if it's true."

Slowly, she rose.

Theodore settled the material over her shoulders, fastened the silver clasp at her throat, then stepped back to give her an appraising gaze. "It seems Clara was right."

"It's lovely," Kate said, "but I—"

"Clara and I couldn't bear thinking of you out here alone during the cold winter nights." He nodded toward the dwindling fire. "The wool will keep you warm."

"It does get cool at night," she agreed weakly. Was the gift from Clara, or Theodore?

He smoothed a wrinkle from one of the folds of fabric, then patted her on the shoulder. "I thought you might need it on our ride into town for the Christmas Eve service."

She sank into her chair, shaking her head. "I couldn't possibly go."

"Why?"

Kate bowed her head. "I don't expect I'm welcome there

these days."

"Nonsense." Theodore snorted. "If you're on my arm, you'll have nothing to fear. Besides, Clara is the one who sent me to get you. She would have come herself, but her knee has been bothering her enough to make riding problematic."

Theodore raised his eyebrows and a mischievous grin flitted across his lips. "Now, are you going to make an old woman's day and attend church, or am I to come back empty-handed and watch her cry?"

Kate relented. She did want to go to the service, and seeing Clara again was the deciding factor.

"I suppose we can't have Clara upset, now can we?"

CHAPTER FIFTY-ONE
A Stunning Confirmation

JAKE STEPPED INTO THE CHURCH AND squeezed himself into the last open seat at the end of the back row. He was grateful for everyone's effort at putting together a Christmas Eve service. The church building was lit up with nearly a hundred candles and lamps, and their glowing flames reflected a crowd of almost as many shining faces.

According to Travers, organizers had worried over whether the preacher would arrive in time, and whether anyone would venture from their far-flung claims to attend, but based upon the sheer amount of people now gathered to celebrate the birth of their savior, it seemed all the worry had been for nothing.

Was Kate there?

Jake's gaze skimmed over the crowds of bystanders who'd arrived too late to gain seating and were standing shoulder to shoulder along the outer walls. When he didn't see her, he focused on the seated guests, evaluating the backs of their heads row by endless row. Thankfully, he was tall.

Minutes later, Jake sighed with relief when he finally

recognized Kate's familiar brown hair with hints of red. She had come!

He'd spent the past week weighing his last moments with her and come to the conclusion he'd been unfair. She'd had to break the law just to learn the location of her claim, so it was little wonder she'd be willing to do almost anything to keep it, even garner advice from Theo. He knew firsthand what a liar and manipulator Theo was, yet he'd taken his word as gospel when he'd said he was courting her. Jake had berated himself countless times for never actually asking her about her feelings toward Theo and instead jumping to conclusions. For all he knew, she couldn't stand the man.

At the preacher's instruction, everyone rose to sing several hymns. Jake especially enjoyed "Amazing Grace", a favorite for both the message it gave believers and because the low notes were easier for him to sing.

When the songs were over and guests began again taking their seats, Jake finally caught an unimpeded view of Kate—and the familiar man sitting next to her; the man whispering into her ear, earning himself an endearing smile from her in return; the man sliding his arm around her shoulders and pulling her close.

The man was Theo.

Jake's world came to a sudden, unmistakable, crashing halt. His vision blurred and he had trouble catching his breath. He felt dizzy and wanted more than anything to get away, but he was trapped in place by the crush of people crowded around the end of his pew and clustered in the doorway. The exit was completely blocked, so even if he managed to squeeze his way out of his seat, aside from shoving people aside or walking on their shoulders, he was stuck.

He sat numbly through the rest of the service. When the preacher signaled it was over, he was the first to rise. It did no good; he had to wait while the masses around him swept out of the pews in laughing, hugging, joyful waves. Frozen with disbelief, he allowed himself to be propelled along in the surge toward the door.

Then, as he reached the entryway, he saw Theo.

The man was reaching to grab a green cloak from one of the many coats crowded on the metal hooks near the door. As he pulled it down and draped it over his arm, he turned and caught Jake's eye. After putting two fingers against his forehead in a mock salute, Theo smirked and disappeared back into the church.

Instead of fleeing, Jake stumbled backward into the corner, driven by an involuntary need to see Kate up close with Theo by her side. He had to know for certain; he had to see for himself that she would choose such a man.

Minutes later, he watched in silence as she appeared in the entryway, wearing the same green cloak he had seen Theo pull from the hooks. He slumped against the wall as Theo put his hand at the small of her back to usher her through the waves of people trying to leave through the single doorway.

Kate had made her choice. It was over.

CHAPTER FIFTY-TWO
A Gift Reconsidered

KATE FUMED THE ENTIRE RIDE BACK to her house.

Not only had Theodore misled her about Clara attending the service, he'd spent the entire time whispering in her ear, distracting both her and the other guests. He'd been intolerably rude, and she'd refused to answer any of his questions or respond to any of his comments. Since admonishing him would have attracted undue attention, she'd opted to give only tight smiles in the hopes of dissuading him from further interruptions. No such luck. By the end of the service she'd been so furious she'd just wanted him to escort her to her house and then leave. She wanted to be done with him. Forever.

As they rounded the corner and her house came into sight, she breathed a sigh of relief. "The preacher's service was enlightening," she said, mainly to break up the silence as they rode the last quarter mile to her house.

"I guess so," Theodore replied. "He could have shortened it up by cutting out those songs, though."

"Too bad Jake couldn't make it," Kate said.

"Probably for the best," Theodore replied. "A ruffian like him isn't suited for social situations."

The cloak clasp pressed against her neck and she wished yet again she hadn't accepted such an elaborate gift. The only thing keeping her from wadding it up and tossing it onto his saddle was the slim chance it was indeed from Clara.

When they reached her house, Theodore dismounted. "I'll wait here while you put Nina up for the night."

"You've been more than generous with your time already; there's no need to wait for me. I manage fine on my own."

"I insist," he said in a tone that wouldn't accept otherwise. "Your safety is my primary concern, so I won't hear of my leaving until after I've made a thorough check of your house."

Kate let out a heavy sigh, declining to point out the obvious issue of him neglecting to check the barn she was heading to, alone.

This man was so different from Jake and how he'd treated her, protected her with his every action. On the trail there'd been several instances when he'd adamantly put her first over his needs, and oftentimes his safety—when he'd gone out in a thunderstorm in search of Old Dan, when she'd fallen off a cliff and he'd climbed down after her, and most memorably when he'd warmed her by the fire when they'd spent the night in the cave.

Kate secured Nina in the barn and then returned to her house. She silently passed Theodore where he waited on the porch, shoved open her door, and then blocked the doorway.

"Thank you for a nice evening," she said, the words more a result of the manners drilled into her over the years by her aunt than a reflection of her true feelings.

"Aren't you going to invite me in?" He frowned and cupped his hands around his mouth, blowing to warm them. "I'd like to heat up by the fire for a few minutes before I go."

Kate acquiesced, reasoning that he'd be back on his way in less than ten minutes.

He followed her inside, removed his coat, folded it so the sleeves were perfectly aligned, and then draped it over the back of the closest chair. He then settled himself in the other chair and watched while she stirred the coals and began to build up the fire. Within minutes flames danced and crackled and their warmth began chasing the chill from the house.

"You shouldn't have to do such filthy work, Kate."

"I don't mind. I'm used to it now."

He rose and walked to stand beside her at the hearth. "It hasn't escaped my attention that you've never answered my marriage proposal. I've been patient. I gave you time out here, thinking you would come to your senses and realize what I have to offer. The life I can provide for you. For us."

"No," she said, then shook her head for emphasis.

"Perhaps I haven't been clear." He curled his fingers around her wrist. "I'm a successful businessman, and my wealth can provide you with anything your heart desires, starting with getting you out of this hovel." He looked around in distaste, then uttered a laugh that was more cruel than kind. "What more could you ask for in a husband?"

"I want the love of a good man, not money and things." She yanked her wrist free, gritted her teeth, and headed for the door. "I don't want you intervening with the land office or the Provisional Government anymore on my behalf. I don't trust you."

Theodore's quick strides brought him across the room to tower over her in less than two seconds. "Your trust doesn't concern me."

Kate opened the cloak's clasp, slid the material off her shoulders, and held it out before her. "I can't accept this. Please, take it and leave my house."

"Your house?" A smirk played across his lips and she shuddered at the menacing tone that had crept into his voice.

"We both know that isn't exactly the truth."

She held the cloak higher. "Take it and leave."

"Don't ever disrespect me by being ungrateful for a gift." He grabbed her forearm with one hand, seized her hair with the other, and then pulled her so close his face was inches from her own. Tears sprang to her eyes and she tried to cry out, but was crippled by fear.

"One way or another you're leaving this claim. Claude can send you to jail for fraud, or you can marry me." He let her free so fast she collapsed in a heap on the floor. "I'll see you again soon," he said, straightening his clothes with a few brisk movements. "In the meantime, I'm certain you'll see the wisdom in reconsidering my offer."

He picked up his coat and walked out the door.

CHAPTER FIFTY-THREE
A Cornered Wildcat

Tuesday, December 26, 1843

KATE HEARD THEM BEFORE SHE SAW THEM.

She'd just finished tidying up from breakfast and was sitting on the hearth, getting ready to sew another patch on her coat when she heard the first bang against her door. She'd had only enough time to grab her father's rifle, crawl under the bed, and pull her saddlebags in front of her before the door gave way with a splintering crack.

"Finally," muttered a deep voice she couldn't place. "I didn't think I'd have to give that door so many kicks. It's sturdier than it looked."

"Let's get to it then," said another voice.

Kate hid like a cornered animal and listened as two men began ransacking her house. At first, anger flickered to life and her finger tensed on the rifle's trigger. However, after a moment of consideration, she decided she wasn't confident in her ability to kill both men before they could turn on her. And since no one could hear her if she screamed, she stayed motionless and powerless to do anything to stop the systematic destruction of all she'd created. Though her cheek was pressed hard against the chamber pot, she didn't dare to move even a fraction of an inch for fear the noise would giveaway her location.

They started in the kitchen, running knives across the bags of sugar and flour and laughing as the contents poured onto the floor. They tossed her plates, cups, and all her cookware into the fireplace. They shredded her tablecloth, upended her table and one kitchen chair, then stomped apart the other. After her mother's teapot was dropkicked across the room, their boot heels twisted each of the shattered pieces into powder. The pages of her family Bible were ripped from the spine and flung into the air.

Fear kept back her tears as Kate watched two pairs of heavy boots cross the room and stop beneath where she'd lovingly hung her mother's portrait only two days ago.

"Purty," drawled one of the men.

Kate winced as she heard the telltale sounds of a knife piercing the canvas.

"Where did she go? I was hoping to have a taste of something sweet."

Kate's eyes widened as she finally placed the voice as belonging to Cyrus, her harasser from town.

"Hey!" She now recognized Murray's voice booming across the cabin. "He ain't paying us to hurt her. Just to bust things up and scare her."

Kate's eyes widened in disbelief. Who wanted her scared?

Murray walked to the bed. She winced as she heard the sounds of knives ripping through her bedding, and seconds later the quilt from Clara was tossed to the floor, shredded to ribbons.

"Reckon we ought'a mess with these clothes too?" Cyrus asked after kicking over the box that showcased her mother's silver mirror and her matching comb and brush set. Kate breathed a shallow sigh of relief to see the jewelry box merely fall to the floor, unopened.

"He said destroy everything except that green thing," Murray replied.

They cut into the maroon dress from Jake first, followed by the two she'd never bothered washing since they were far too sophisticated for daily wear. They ripped holes into her pink calico she'd taken such pride in creating, and Clara's purple-and-gold rag rug. The straw tick was opened with one quick slice, and they spent several minutes scattering grass and the feathers from her pillow across the floor.

Murray stood in the center of the room and snickered. "That ought'a earn our pay."

"We headin' to the barn to tear it up some?" Cyrus asked.

"Nah, we're only supposed to do the house."

Kate was grateful she'd left her knife in the barn, along with her father's pistol and his hat.

"Let's get out of here before anyone gets nosy," Murray said. "Especially the one he warned us about."

"Who, Fitzpatrick? He don't scare me none."

"Me neither, but let's get out of here anyway."

The men stomped through the splintered door, but Kate didn't dare move until long after she heard their horses' hooves pounding along the hillside. Only then did she slowly uncurl herself and crawl out from under the bed to evaluate the damage.

The house was still standing, but everything inside was destroyed.

Everything except the cloak.

CHAPTER FIFTY-FOUR
Distractions

JAKE SPENT HIS MORNING THE SAME way he'd spent Christmas Day—lying on his bedroll, staring at the white box with the slim gold ring nestled inside.

He'd lost her.

By the time the afternoon sun was high in the sky, he was determined to forget, at least for the moment, how bleak and alone he felt. He grabbed his coat and hat, then headed to his stable, saddled Nickel, and rode for town.

After tying Nickel to a hitching post in front of the saloon, Jake passed through the building's swinging doors and into a crowded room rife with debauchery and sin. A polished oak bar spanned the entire length of the left wall, and the rest of the room was filled with drinkers and gamblers sitting in battered chairs, clustered around battered tables. A staircase at the back wall led to the upper floor, where coins could buy companionship.

Jake headed straight to the bar.

Once he'd settled himself on a stool and propped his boot heels against the long brass rail bolted inches above the floor, the bartender ambled over.

"What'll it be, friend?"

"Something strong enough to make me forget my own name." Jake slapped a pile of coins on the bar so hard the sound echoed against the walls. "Don't give me that rot-gut whiskey, either. I want the bottle you keep back for yourself."

The bartender's eyebrows rose, but he said nothing. Less than a minute later, he set a heavy glass tumbler in front of Jake and poured two fingers' worth of whiskey from a bottle.

Jake brought the glass to his lips and tipped it back. The amber liquid slid down his throat with a satisfying burn.

"Another!" he growled, slamming the glass back onto the bar.

The bartender obliged.

This time, the burn felt sweeter.

"Leave the bottle," Jake commanded before the bartender could replace the cork.

****

An hour later, Jake was drunk and drinking more.

A soft rustle and familiar low, honey-smooth voice interrupted his brooding. "I knew you'd come for me."

He turned to see Emily standing next to him, clad in a black corset and red thigh-high stockings held up by lace garters. She eyed the pile of coins sitting on the bar in front of him, then slithered closer.

"I've waited for weeks." She lowered her eyes and stuck her painted lower lip out in an exaggerated pout. "Good thing I'm a patient woman."

"Among other things," he replied, twisting too fast on his stool in his rush to face her directly.

"Whoa there," she said, catching him by the arm.

"You smell good," he murmured, grinning as she pushed him back onto the stool, then spun it until his back was pressed against the bar. "Like a flower."

"Do you remember the time we spent hours in a field of daisies?" she asked, arching her back in a not-so-subtle ploy to accentuate the curves spilling out the top of her corset.

"I do," he replied, spreading his arms wide and resting his elbows on the counter in an attempt to keep his balance.

She stepped between his knees, slid off his hat, and twirled her fingers through his hair.

He gazed at her through a fog of hazy confusion. "What do you want?"

After she leaned over and whispered into his ear, Jake felt his face grow warm.

CHAPTER FIFTY-FIVE
Intuition Confirmed

KATE SPENT THE AFTERNOON PEERING THROUGH her broken door in search of more vicious visitors and picking through her possessions, all while trying to avoid the sight, and significance, of the untouched cloak hanging on her wall.

Jake had been right all along. The revelation startled, then shamed.

She'd been so intent on convincing herself of the need to tolerate a man like Theodore to be a success that she'd willingly pushed aside the one man she knew deep down she could always count on, believe in, and trust.

She'd been so determined to get her land she'd ignored Jake's warnings, as well as her own small voice deep within telling her Theodore was dangerous.

She'd been so focused on telling herself that she desperately needed the knowledge and connections Theodore had to offer, and that he was just being friendly and helpful with no ulterior motive.

She'd made a terrible mistake. In ignoring her intuition she'd lost sight of who she was, what she stood for, and the man she loved.

Kate stared at the cloak, recalling again Murray's declaration. *He said destroy everything except that green thing.*

Murray's words were all the proof she needed that Theodore was the man behind the directive, and she had no intention of letting him get away with such savagery.

Kate headed out to the barn. It was time to go into town.

CHAPTER FIFTY-SIX
Bottles and Blathering

As Old Dan carried Kate closer to Theodore's hotel, her need for an immediate confrontation faded, replaced by a more compelling urge—to see Jake. Despite all that had been said between them lately, deep down she knew she could count on him. Always.

Though she'd never set foot on his claim and didn't know what section he'd be working, she was willing to spend the rest of her day searching. She tightened her hands around the reins in preparation of turning Old Dan around and heading back out of town, but caught sight of something that stopped her cold.

Nickel was tied to the hitching post in front of the saloon.

She frowned. A glance around confirmed no nearby buildings he'd have reason to enter; he had to be inside the saloon.

Kate dismounted and secured Old Dan beside Nickel on the hitching post, dread settling low in her stomach at what she'd see upon her first time ever going into a saloon.

"Let's get this over with," she muttered, then pushed the

swinging doors apart and walked into a dim room that smelled of liquor and failure.

Immediately it began.

"Hey boys! There's that saucy little lady from the land office!"

Kate wasn't certain if the shouted words were a taunt or a compliment, but opted to ignore them, and all the subsequent catcalls and appreciative comments, in favor of scanning the room in search of Jake.

Nothing.

Like most of the patrons, the saloon's windows had been neglected of a proper washing for weeks or longer, making it difficult to see faces clearly. Once her eyes adjusted, she sighted a man standing behind the bar that spanned the length of the left wall. Thinking he might be able to help, she headed toward him.

She'd taken only a few steps when the wiry man with oddly small ears that had lingered at Zeke's side the day she'd fired him sidestepped before her, blocking her path.

"What'cha doin'?" he asked, eyeing her father's hat.

"It's not your concern." She heard the defiant tone in her voice and forced herself to soften it before she continued. "Let me pass."

"An' if I don't?"

"Ma'am?" questioned a deep voice she'd heard before, but couldn't quite place.

She glanced around, searching out who'd spoken. To her surprise she saw Rob, wearing his familiar fox face hat, heading her way.

"Don't pay Percy no mind," Rob said, clapping his meaty palm on the tiny-eared man's back. "He's nothing but a pig-stealin', dystentary-havin', high-smellin' kind of guy. By the way, anything of yours ever comes up missin', you check with Percy. He's got an aversion to leavin' things be, but he's so stupid it's easy to catch him."

Rob watched closely as Percy gave her a good-natured smile and an exaggerated low bow, then wandered off toward the collection of tables overflowing with playing cards and surrounded by chairs filled with men.

"Ma'am," Rob said, eyeing her with obvious concern, "I don't mean to pry or tell you how to conduct yourself, but I'm wondering if you're in the right place?"

Kate squared her shoulders and raised her chin. "I'm looking for Jake Fitzpatrick."

"You should just go." Rob pursed his lips. "No need for you to see him like this."

Kate hesitated, then shook her head.

Rob sighed, then nodded toward the back wall of the room.

No wonder she'd missed sighting Jake when she'd initially glanced around the room. He was sitting at the end of the bar with his head bowed low and his hands over his face.

"Thank you for your assistance," she murmured to Rob, who shrugged his shoulders in acknowledgment, then stepped out of her way. As she strode across the room, she couldn't help but notice how every man who wasn't already staring had turned to silently watch her progress.

"Jake?" she asked, taking note of the nearly empty bottle before him and how his right shoulder was pressed against the wall, seemingly holding him upright. "Are you all right?"

"Kate?" He raised his head and stared at her in bleary-eyed confusion. "What are you doing here?"

She clasped her hands together tightly. "I need to talk to you."

"I'm busy." He let out a heavy sigh and his head and shoulders drooped low. "Besides, you'd rather talk to Theo."

"No." She shook her head for emphasis, then watched in dismay as Jake's hand knocked over the bottle, sending it crashing to the floor. The sound reverberated around the room like bullets shot through a tin bucket.

"All right, Fitzpatrick," said the bartender as he came around from behind the bar, with broom and dustpan in hand. "I think you're done here."

"Katie," Jake murmured just before his eyes fluttered closed and he slumped against the wall.

Kate put her hand out—wanting to help but not knowing what to do—but a woman rushed by her in a blur of heady perfume, stained satin, and tired lace.

Emily.

"I'll take care of him," the harlot insisted, draping herself around Jake's neck and pressing her voluptuous, exposed curves against his arm as if she belonged there. As if she had the right to touch him.

Trouble was, Jake didn't protest.

"Sorry, honey, he's made his choice." Emily ran her gloved fingertips along his upper arm as she gave Kate a slow, appraising gaze from head to toe. "I always knew he wouldn't be satisfied with a woman like you."

Kate cleared her throat, but ultimately said nothing. There was nothing left to say.

Turning on her heel, she stumbled blindly toward the swinging doors and pushed her way through them into the cool, evening air.

CHAPTER FIFTY-SEVEN
Confessions and Apologies

Wednesday, December 27, 1843

JAKE AWOKE TO A TICKLING SENSATION on his nose and opened his eyes to find the head of a dead fox less than a foot away from his face.

"What the—?"

"Good morning," Rob replied cheerfully, giving Jake's cheek a final nudge with the snout of his fox hat and then tossing it on the foot of the bed. "Though, technically it's already the afternoon. I was wondering if you'd ever wake up. How you feelin'?"

"Like I got kicked in the gut by a team of horses, then fell in the manure pile and slept there for a week." Jake eyed his favorite cup now resting in Rob's hand. "Any coffee left?"

"Nope," Rob answered, taking a purposely sloppy sip and then smacking his lips so loudly Jake's head throbbed.

Jake looked around at his dugout and realized he'd slept on the floor. "How did I get here?"

"Me." Rob grinned. "I dragged you out of the saloon and shoved your considerably-sized rear end up into your saddle.

Thankfully, your horse is smarter than you are; he led the way to your house. After I dumped you onto the floor, I shut Nickel in the stable and then came back inside and had myself a nice sleep in your comfy bed."

Jake crawled to his frying pan and hurled until his eyeballs ached.

Rob chuckled. "You did that last night too. Except Emily wasn't as understanding as I am—probably because you redecorated the toes of her favorite dancing shoes."

Jake groaned and wiped his lips with his sleeve. "Emily was there?"

"So was Kate."

Jake turned around so fast his stomach lurched in protest. "Kate was at the saloon last night?"

"You don't handle your liquor well." Rob clucked his tongue like an old woman scolding a child. "Don't you remember? Kate came in saying how she needed to talk to you about something, but Emily got to you first. If you ask me, Kate was none too pleased about the way Emily was lounging all over you, or how Emily's best parts kept brushing up against your hands."

Jake swung his legs out from under himself and scrambled to his feet. Once he was upright, he staggered across the room and hit his head against the wall. He felt nothing in his rush to get to Kate.

"Where's Kate now?" he demanded, struggling to slide his uncooperative arms into his coat sleeves.

"Don't know, but she's a quick one. I hauled you out about five minutes after she left and didn't see any trace of her."

Jake grabbed his cup from Rob's hand. He took a swig of coffee, swished it around his mouth, spit into the frying pan, and then headed out the door, rifle in hand. He retrieved Nickel from his stable, grateful Rob hadn't pulled off his saddle, then mounted up and rode out.

The ride took less than two minutes, but it felt like forever.

He stopped Nickel at the front of her house, grimacing to see the splintered door latch and her door hanging by only one hinge.

Someone had kicked in her door.

"Kate!" he shouted, dismounting and pulling his rifle from the scabbard.

"Jake?" Her pale face peeked out the doorway, half hidden. "What are you doing here?"

"I came to see what you needed." He stepped onto the porch, falling to his knee as one of the rotten boards gave way under his foot. "Are you going to let me in?"

She didn't move, and neither did the door.

"I needed you." Her tone was flat, emotionless. "I needed to tell you I was wrong. But last night at the saloon I learned I was wrong about so much more than I realized."

Jake righted himself, wincing as pain shot through his leg. "I don't know exactly what you saw—"

"I saw what I needed to see." Her expression was bland and unreadable, to his growing frustration. "I don't blame you, either, because I'm the one who pushed you away. I'm the one who didn't believe you, who didn't heed all the warnings you tried to give. It's no wonder you've taken up with that harlot again."

"Kate, that's not what happened last night. Or any other night for that matter." Her eyes narrowed but she said nothing, so he stumbled on. "I went to the saloon for a reason, but it wasn't to be with Emily." Just saying her name left a vile taste in his mouth. "Rob clued me in on what happened last night with her, and I can assure you that her actions were done solely to make trouble, not because of desire on my part. Rob and I left less than five minutes after you did."

She disappeared from the doorway.

"Kate?" He waited for nearly a minute, then pushed the

door aside and stepped into her house. She was standing at the fireplace, her back to him, staring at the cold ashes.

"What happened to the door?"

"It's broken."

"I see that. How did it happen?"

She turned, revealing a long, purple bruise across her cheek.

"What happened to your face?" he asked, tossing his hat onto the table and leaning his rifle against the wall. "Did you fall?"

Kate blinked back the tears filling her eyes. "No."

A horrible feeling planted itself firmly in his gut and wouldn't let go. "Did someone hit you?"

"No." She lowered her head to her chest and looked so forlorn and small he couldn't bear it. He wanted to do something, anything, for her.

"How about you sit while I build a fire?"

She went to a kitchen chair without a fight. He looked around for a blanket to wrap her in until he got the fire going strong, but saw none. Come to think of it, he saw no dishware, food, or bedding either.

He took another look around the house and found it strangely bare. Even the maroon dress he'd bought her was gone from its hook on the wall. The only thing he saw was the same green cloak he'd watched Theo retrieve for her after church, and he'd build the fire sky high before warming her with it.

So he did.

Once the fire roared he looked for a place to sit, but found none. "Where's your other chair?"

"Broken."

Goosebumps ran along his arms and up the back of his neck. "Is what happened here why you came to see me at the saloon?"

She nodded. "What was the reason?"

Jake stared at her, confused at the question.

"You said you went to the saloon for a reason," she said. "What was it?"

"To try to forget about you." He stared at her in chagrin. "With liquor, not Emily."

She was silent for a time, letting his last statement sink in. Finally, she spoke. "I don't know how to begin."

Jake hated his next words even before they left his mouth. "I hear congratulations are in order. I see you're already packing up, getting ready to go live with Theo."

Kate recoiled, wrinkling her nose in disgust. "What makes you think that?"

"From what I heard all over town yesterday, I assumed you two were on your way to the preacher." He'd heard plenty of chatter from men in the saloon on the subject.

Kate shook her head so hard her hair flailed against her shoulders. "That couldn't be further from the truth."

"I saw you at the church together and thought..." He trailed off, his hopes soaring.

"Theodore gave me a gift; a cloak. I wouldn't have accepted it, but he told me it was from Clara. I went to the Christmas Eve service with him because he said Clara would be there, and she wanted to see me." She rose to stand before the fire, and spoke to the flames. "He lied."

Jake took a step to go to her, to comfort her, but she tensed and he froze.

"He insisted on seeing me to my house, and then he followed me inside and asked me again to marry him." Kate shuddered and wrapped her arms around herself. "I told him no. I told him to leave and take the cloak with him."

Jake waited for her next words with growing apprehension.

"That's when he got rough. He grabbed my hair and told me I could either marry him or go to jail for fraudulently claiming my land. I fell to the floor, crying, and he left."

She whirled to face him, and he saw her fear had turned to fury.

"Look at my house." She spat the words from her mouth in undeniable anger. "Theodore is responsible! I heard Murray tell Cyrus they were being paid to destroy everything I owned." She motioned to Theo's gift hanging on the wall. "Except the cloak."

She waved her arm over the room. "They tossed my dishes in the fire, scattered my food, and they took knives to my clothes and bedding. They even broke my mother's teapot and sliced up her portrait."

Shocked, he stared at her. "Where were you during all this?"

"Hiding under the bed like a cornered animal." She pointed to her cheek. "That's how I got this. My face was pressed against the chamber pot and I couldn't move." Her voice caught and her chin wavered. "Because I was scared they would hear me."

"Oh, Katie," he murmured, cursing his own stupidity. How could he be the man she needed when at the first sign of trouble he'd tucked tail and run, to the saloon no less?

"I had my father's rifle with me, but I was too scared to use it." She sank to the hearth and lowered her head in her hands. "If I hadn't been such a coward, I could have protected my property. My home."

Jake knelt before her and pulled her against his chest, cradling her in the protective circle of his arms. While he was grateful she'd done nothing and kept out of sight, he knew the regret she felt would stick with her for a while. Perhaps, like himself, forever.

Twenty-one years ago, when he'd been ten, he'd hidden while his mother, father, and two younger brothers had been shot and killed by two ruthless men bent on revenge. He'd stayed hidden while the murderers had ransacked his home and stolen everything worth anything, including his father's horses. He'd lived every day since wishing he'd done something to stop them instead of merely watching them disappear over the hillside beyond his house.

Knowing nothing he said would convince Kate she'd done the right thing in hiding instead of challenging two brutal men like Cyrus and Murray, he settled for holding her tighter.

"I'm glad you're safe," he whispered.

"I'm glad you're here," she whispered in return.

A sudden rush of emotion washed over him. He'd felt horrible about what he'd said to her outside the livery, but too many words and weeks had passed since then, leaving him with a feeling of hopelessness. Until now.

"I'm sorry, Kate."

He felt her back arch against his arm and looked down to see her staring at him with obvious bewilderment. "For what?"

"For everything I've said and done that caused you pain."

"I'm sorry too." She splayed her fingers and rested them on his chest. "I ignored you, and my own intuition, and because of that I nearly lost the one thing I care about most in this world."

Jake didn't have the courage to ask if she meant her claim, or him.

CHAPTER FIFTY-EIGHT
Confrontation

KATE RODE INTO TOWN WITH JAKE by her side and a fury burning within. They headed for the mercantile first; they'd already decided on the need to buy more food supplies, and reasoned they wouldn't want to make the stop after confronting Theodore with his actions.

As they walked the aisles and gave Albert the long list of replenishments, Jake looked as tense as she felt. Neither said a word as they loaded up Old Dan and Nickel. When Jake finished, he dug into his saddlebag and brought out his leather holster.

It wasn't empty.

Kate tightened the final strap on her saddlebags, then looked up to see Murray ambling by as if he didn't have a care in the world. As if he hadn't stomped, slit, or shattered almost every possession she held dear.

Kate stepped into the street. "Murray!" she shouted, pointing her finger at the man when he turned in startled surprise. "I'd like a word with you."

The man's lips stretched into a sneer. "I'd like more than

that with you, but we can start with talkin'."

Jake appeared beside her and she took comfort in seeing he'd tied down his holster.

"I heard you came into some money," Jake said, coolly removing his hat and hooking the brim over his saddle horn.

"I hired out for a few odd jobs. What's it to you?"

Though Kate wanted to save her anger and energy for the coming argument with Theodore, there was no way she was going to let this man terrorize her ever again. "You aren't a thorough worker. Otherwise, you would have taken two extra seconds and checked under the bed before you broke up my house."

Murray's bravado faded fast. "I don't want any trouble. From either of you."

"Too late," Jake said. "You're nothing more than a woman-groping lackey who does Theo's dirty work for him. Others in this town might think you deserved a second chance, but I don't."

Murray opened his mouth as if to protest, but the rage on Jake's face kept him quiet.

"You or Cyrus ever set foot on my land again, I'll use my rifle." Kate cocked her head and flashed a cold smile. "And I don't miss."

"Neither do I," Jake added, shifting his stance so his palm draped over the handle of his pistol.

Murray swiped at sudden sweat dotting his forehead and upper lip.

"How about you run a little errand for us?" Jake's tone revealed it was more an order than suggestion. "Go find Theo and tell him we're aiming to have some words with him."

"Tell him yourself," Murray said, pointing over Jake's shoulder before scurrying into the shadows like a cur dog hiding from his master.

Kate spun to see Theodore headed their way with George LeBreton and another impeccably dressed man she didn't recognize walking on either side of him.

"Good afternoon, Kate." Theodore eyed Jake, then the bags of flour and sugar strapped behind Old Dan's saddle. "I see you're in town for supplies. I do hope you'll pay me a visit before you leave." His bright smile betrayed none of his recent actions.

Kate's jaw tightened at his audacity. She hadn't crossed thousands of desolate miles—losing her family along the way—only to be oppressed by a sadistic hotel baron who didn't know when to quit. After giving a genteel nod to George and the other man, Kate settled her gaze on Theodore.

"You've got some nerve, smiling at me after threatening me with jail to try to influence marriage, and then laying your hands on me."

Kate felt Jake's hand settle on her back and was reassured by his presence.

"Well now." Theodore's voice boomed across the street and two passing men stopped walking. "That's quite an imagination—and some wild accusations—you've got there, young lady."

"I say the lady speaks the truth," Jake said firmly, leaving no room for argument.

Theodore sneered at Jake "Your word means nothing."

George stepped forward, frowning. "Jake Fitzpatrick is a lot of things, but I've never known him to be a liar."

Theodore shook his head. "He's a liar and this woman is nothing but a squatter speaking lies about me, one of the most respected businessmen in the entire Oregon Territory."

Kate rolled up her sleeve and held out her forearm to George and the well-dressed stranger, and then Travers, who'd joined the gathering. "Would a respected businessman grab a woman so hard that three days later I still have the bruise to show for it?"

"More lies," Theodore responded smoothly. "I don't know what you think happened that night, but that was definitely not what occurred."

Kate looked around; their loud arguing had drawn quite a crowd of curious onlookers, which did nothing to dissuade her from making her final point. "And when I told you I didn't want to marry you, instead of taking no for an answer, you hired those two ruffians to break up my house. How dare you!"

"This is preposterous." Theodore puffed out his chest, his face an expression of indignant astonishment. "I'll thank you to take your unproven accusations elsewhere."

"She's got proof," Jake said quietly.

Murmurs and gasps rippled through the surrounding crowd.

"She's got nothing." Theodore flicked his hand in the air as if dismissing an errant servant.

"Next time you convince others to do your dirty work," Kate said, "remind them to first check if anyone is hiding under the bed. Murray and Cyrus ran their mouths about why they were hired, and I heard it all."

Guffaws and hoots erupted from the men and George took a wide step sideways, distancing himself from Theodore.

Theodore's cheeks and lips whitened, but instead of acknowledging his actions, he dug in further. "She's an outlandish woman bent on revenge, and you all should know better than to believe her allegations."

"Gentlemen," Jake said, spinning to address the crowd, which was now three men thick. "You've been told the truth here today. Theodore Martin cannot be trusted, and now that you know what he's capable of, you can decide whether to do business with him."

"Enough!" Theodore roared, his eyes wide with panic and rage. "I'll not stand here and be insulted by the likes of a saddle tramp and a brazen hussy who travels unescorted in town and beyond with no concern for her reputation."

Kate gasped and Travers clasped his hand on Jake's

shoulder, convincing him to stay put even as Theodore took several quick steps backward, stopping just out of Jake's reach.

"Hey now!" shouted a man from the edge of the gathered circle. "I don't much care if she's a brazen hussy or not, but is that true what he says about her being a squatter?"

Kate turned to the direction of the voice, inhaled a long, shaky breath, and then did her best to speak with confidence.

"I'm not a squatter. My father contracted the deed from a man in Virginia and he intended to make the claim our home, but he and my brother died on the trail, leaving me as the sole owner of the deed. Jim from the Champoeg land office and Claude from this town's land office have both confirmed my deed as valid, and Article One of the Land Claims law allows me to legally make the claim my own. Which is what I intend to do, like the rest of you, by proving it up in six months' time."

"All right men, she's had her say." Kate recognized the voice of Albert Wilson, owner of the mercantile. "Let's move it along now."

While the crowd slowly dispersed, their chatter amongst themselves guaranteeing the rest of the town would hear of the Theodore's exploits, Theodore charged forward and slammed his fist into the side of Jake's jaw.

Jake stumbled, then fell to the ground.

CHAPTER FIFTY-NINE
Two Competing Barrels

JAKE ROLLED ONTO HIS BACK, SAT up, and stared at Theo while he wiped the corner of his mouth with the back of his hand. Sighting blood, he grinned.

"Let's get to it then," he said, shrugging out of his coat and rising to his feet in anticipation of a lengthy battle he'd waited years to fight.

Theo's raised fists shook wildly and he stared at Jake with panicked, bulging eyes. A childlike scream of terror filled the air as Theo spun around, clawed his way through the crowd, and ran down the empty street.

"The mark of a true coward," Jake muttered, shaking his head in disgust. "He retreats." Retrieving his coat from the dirt, he looked to Kate, who bore a similar expression of revulsion at Theo's antics. "Ready to go home?" he asked, bending his elbow at a jaunty angle that beckoned her close.

She obliged by sliding her arm through his, and together they returned to their waiting horses, mounted up, and rode out of town. About half a mile later, Kate broke the silence.

"What's going to happen to Theodore?"

314

"I'd say he's about to get what's coming to him. Men out west might be wild, but there's still things they won't tolerate, and laying a hand on a woman is top on the list. After the rest of the townspeople hear of that—and everything else he's done—he'll have a tough time maintaining the reputation he's created for himself. I doubt he'll be too welcome at the next meeting of the Provisional Government. Influential men of the territory won't appreciate how he tried to manipulate others for his own benefit."

Kate grimaced. "What about the men who will think I manipulated the land office and claims law for my own benefit?"

"After the outstanding speech you gave to nearly half the town, I'd say your troubles with keeping your claim are over."

Kate lurched forward in her saddle as Old Dan stumbled and nearly went down on one knee.

"Whoa," she said, giving him his head as he recovered his balance.

"He all right?" Jake questioned.

"I think so," Kate replied. "He probably stepped in a hole or twisted his hoof on a stick. He's walking without any trouble now, so I think we should keep going."

Five minutes later, Old Dan began limping. Kate dismounted, then squatted to run her nimble fingers over the horse's front fetlocks.

"He's fine," Kate declared, breathing an obvious sigh of relief. "He's just thrown a shoe. I heard something land in a shrub about twenty yards ago; that must have been where he lost it. I'll fetch it and be right back."

She was gone around a bend in their back trail before he could open his mouth to protest. Jake chuckled as he leaned to his right and took Old Dan's reins in hand to prevent the horse from following his spirited, impulsive owner.

A rustle in the bushes on his left made Jake turn. To his disbelief, Theo stood at the edge of the trail, holding a pistol leveled squarely at the center of Jake's chest.

He slowly slid Old Dan's reins into his left palm and then inched his right hand toward the holster still tied to his leg.

"Keep your hands where I can see them," Theo said, his calm voice at odds with his mottled cheeks and the veins protruding from his neck. His gaze settled on Old Dan and the empty saddle on his back. "Where's Kate?"

"Not here," Jake answered, glad she knew well enough to hide and stay out of harm's way.

"Where is she?" Theo shouted. "That's her horse so I know she's close!"

"She stayed in town to shop for more supplies." Jake shifted his weight in the saddle, subtly preparing to jump should the opportunity arise. Long ago his father had taught him when it came to fights—be it with guns or fists—timing was the key to winning.

"Put down the gun, Theo. You've already lost your reputation. Kill me, and you'll lose your freedom too."

Theo pressed his left palm against his eye that had begun twitching. To Jake's dismay, his right hand never wavered in its aim.

"Why'd you tell Kate the secret to making a claim?" Jake asked, hoping to anger Theo into distraction. "If you'd have kept your mouth shut, she'd never have known it was possible, and she'd probably still be in your hotel."

Jake thought he heard soft footsteps approaching on his right side, then stop. It was all he could do not to turn.

"I told her so she'd respect the knowledge and power I wield." Theo snorted, then brought his left hand to join his right in gripping the gun's handle. "I never thought she'd actually follow through with wanting to live alone in squalor."

Recalling the times he'd seen Theo hiding papers in his desk drawer within seconds of anyone entering the hotel lobby, Jake took an intuitive risk. "And the land deed fraud?"

Theo's jaw went slack. "How did you know?"

Jake deftly dodged the question. "It's a brilliant scheme, except for the one problem you're too stupid to have foreseen."

"What?" Theo snarled.

"All the people you've defrauded are going to start pouring into Oregon Territory. Others are bound to figure out your role in the rush of forged deeds." Jake raised his brows. "When that happens, the law will be the least of your worries."

"Tough talk for a man on the wrong side of a gun."

Jake was convinced he'd heard scuffling in the shadowed woods to his right, but Theo was too consumed with boasting to notice.

"No one will know what I've done, because nothing can be traced back to me." Theo eyed him with contempt. "With power and money you can hire others to do your bidding—something you'll never experience."

"How'd you get the deeds back east?" Jake asked, noting how bragging brought a wobble to Theo's aim.

"Tom Baker was a rich man looking for adventure, so he came out here for a few years. When he was ready to go back east I simply convinced him to buy all the deeds I'd spent a year creating. After he carried them across the trail, he was free to recoup his investment by selling them to unsuspecting buyers at double what he'd paid me."

Finally Jake understood. He'd always wondered why only one of Elijah's deeds had been forged. Baker had sold him a fake along with his own real claim.

Theo's grin turned bitter. "It seems I've finally found a good use for my painstaking attention to detail. Another batch will head east next spring once I find an investor rich enough to purchase them from me."

"It's over, Theo. I figured it out. Others soon will too."

"Your death will buy me the time I need to cover my tracks." Theo closed one eye and stared down the barrel of his pistol.

Jake gave up on subtlety and whisked his pistol from the holster.

"Now we're even," he declared, lining up the end of the barrel with the center of Theo's forehead. "Even a gambler like you knows when he's licked, and we both know I've got a whole lot more experience at pulling a trigger. Drop your gun and step away."

Crack!

Old Dan—always fearful of sudden, sharp noises—shied backward, pulling his reins from Jake's grip.

Theo's gasp of horror made Jake twist in his saddle, then groan at what he saw.

CHAPTER SIXTY
Again

KATE FELT A STICK SNAP IN half beneath her foot and cringed as Old Dan skittered off, revealing her hiding position. Knife clenched in her right hand, she froze.

Theodore did not.

Keeping both his gun and his gaze on Jake, still perched in his saddle, he walked a wide path around Nickel's head, stopping less than a foot in front of her.

"I heard it all," she declared, jutting her chin in the air in defiance of the man responsible for deceiving her father. "I'm telling everyone."

"I think not," Theodore said, then snatched her arm and yanked her against his side. Fighting his strength earned her a slap across the cheek with the gun barrel that made her see stars.

"See this, Jake?" Theodore taunted, positioning her between himself and the barrel of Jake's gun. "What are you going to do, shoot her?"

"No," Jake said. "Just you."

Her bruised cheek burned from Theodore's strike, but

she ground her boot heel into his toes anyway, furious at what she'd suffered at the hands of this man.

"Hold still!" Theodore shouted, panting with exertion as he pulled her closer and dug the end of his gun deep into her neck.

Jake cursed as she cried out.

"Perfect!" Theodore let out a burst of maniacal laughter. "I'll shoot her first, and then after you watch her die I'll kill you."

Kate winked at Jake, then went limp.

Theodore dropped her, kicking her in the ribs as she landed. She screamed, then lay motionless and silent as even shallow breaths brought on a blinding rush of pain.

Swinging his boots free from his stirrups, Jake leaped through the air and landed on Theodore's back. Jake's gun flew into the bushes as they both tumbled to the dirt in a rolling ball of rage. Theodore landed several punches to Jake's jaw and one to his stomach before Jake got the upper hand. He flipped Theodore onto his back, then heaved himself upright and straddled the man between his legs.

Gripping Theodore's neck with his left hand, Jake pummeled his nose with his right.

A sickening noise filled the air—the crackling of bone and cartilage shattering beneath Jake's fist. Amidst Theodore's primal howls of pain, Jake struggled to his feet and staggered to the edge of the trail, searching for his gun.

Ignoring the agony shooting through her side, Kate got to her knees. Gripping her ribs with one hand, she inched toward where she'd seen Jake's the gun land.

Rhythmic gurgling behind her caused her to turn.

Theodore stood in the center of the path, laboring to breathe through his twisted nose and mouth awash with blood.

Gun in hand, he raised his arm, aimed at Jake, and fired twice. The thundering roar of the gunshots muffled the sounds of his retreating footsteps.

Jake collapsed to the ground.

CHAPTER SIXTY-ONE
Awake

Saturday, December 30, 1843

JAKE WOKE INTO BLACKNESS, GROANING AS waves of excruciating pain washed over him. Gingerly he brought his fingertips up to explore his eyes and the top of his head.

Bandages. Why would there be bandages?

Suddenly, everything came flooding back. Theo standing with a pistol in his hand, confessing to everything, their fight, and then gunshots.

Kate!

Panic overwhelmed him. Ignoring the dizziness and pain pulsing through his temples, he tore off the bandages covering his face. Doing so revealed both the early morning light, and a sight so beautiful it made his breath catch in his throat.

Kate was asleep, curled on an overstuffed chair next to his bed, her arms outstretched and her fingers twined protectively through his own. He smiled, thinking his hand sandwiched between hers was the reason his left arm wouldn't move until he saw the heavy cloths wrapped around his left shoulder. He looked again at Kate, noting her disheveled hair and bloodstained dress, and wondered what day it was.

The realization he'd been shot was just starting to sweep over him when Kate stirred in the chair. She stared sleepily over at him and he gave her a weak smile.

"Hello, beautiful." His tongue felt thick.

"You're awake!" She gasped and stood up in a rush, rubbing her eyes as if incredulous at what she was seeing.

"Hello, beautiful," he repeated, stronger this time.

She blushed and placed a cool palm against his forehead. He reached up and caught her hand.

"What happened?"

She bit her lip and glanced at the closed door. "I better get the doctor."

"Don't go," he said, tightening his grip. "Come stand on the right side of the bed, so I can hold your hand easier."

She obliged.

"What happened?" he repeated.

"Theodore shot you. Twice," she said, blinking back tears. "Once in the head, and once in the shoulder. The doctor determined the one to your head was a surface wound. It grazed your temple, but you bled so much..." Her voice broke and she trailed off, unable to continue.

"That was a brave risk you took," he said. "Going limp in his arms."

"You remember?" She stared at him in surprise. "The doctor wasn't sure if you'd recover any memories of that day."

"I remember fighting with Theodore and hearing gunshots, but nothing after." He ran his thumb gently over her knuckles and asked the question even as he dreaded hearing the answer. "Did he hurt you?"

She shook her head. "No, he took off running before you hit the ground."

"Where am I?" he asked, looking around at the unfamiliar surroundings.

"The doctor's house. He said you wouldn't be able to be moved for at least a few days, and for a while he wasn't sure if you would recover at all."

"How long have I been out?"

"It's Saturday morning." She ticked off the days on her fingers. "Three days."

He looked at her bloodied dress again in disbelief. "You've been here the whole time?"

"I couldn't bear to leave you," she whispered.

Jake shifted in the bed, wincing as pain pulsed through his head and shoulder and prevented him from pulling her close.

"I'm going to get the doctor," she said firmly.

She returned about five minutes later, trailed by a balding man wearing rumpled clothing, wire-rimmed glasses, and a brilliant smile.

"We were beginning to wonder if you'd ever wake up." The doctor unwound the strips of cloth covering Jake's shoulder, inspected the wound, and replaced the bandage with a fresh one. "You've got this little lady here to thank for being alive."

"How did I get here?" Jake asked, recalling he'd been shot half a mile from town, yet now he lay in a comfortable bed.

Kate spoke so quietly he had to strain to hear. "I got you onto Nickel and brought you here."

"You lifted me?"

She shrugged. "You helped some."

As Jake stared at her amazement she blushed and looked away, much to the doctor's amusement.

"Yes sir, she brought you in on the back of that horse more dead than alive from all the blood you lost. It took three men to get you out of the saddle and into this room. She's the talk of the entire town, being such a little thing and saving a big lad like you. She's been here the entire time, too, nursing you back to health."

Kate's cheeks flushed crimson, but she said nothing.

"I have some news about Theodore that might be of interest to the both of you," the doctor said as he wound a new strip of cloth around the top of Jake's head. "Thanks to Kate's testimony about the shooting, Theodore was escorted to the jail about an hour ago." He took scissors from his pocket and snipped the end of the bandage before continuing. "Folks in this town—and the entire territory, for that matter—took note of what he'd done and viewed it as an opportunity to show them fellers back east how this here is a lawful place deserving acceptance into the United States of America.

"The trial didn't take long, and afterwards there was quite the crowd gathered to see Theodore off. He didn't go quietly, either; it sure was something to see a grown man dragged away kicking, screaming, and ultimately sobbing." He slid the scissors back into his pocket and then patted Kate on the shoulder. "He'll never hurt you again, miss."

He shifted to focus his attention on Jake. "Now, as for you. Stay in this bed and don't tear off your bandages again. I'll be back in a few hours to check on you."

When they were alone again, Jake reached for Kate's hand. "Sounds like I missed out on the good times," he said, stunned at all that had transpired while he'd been out. "Where are Nickel and Old Dan?"

"Travers took them back to my barn, and I had your friend Rob go to your stable and bring Plug over to my barn too. They've both been out each day to feed and water all six of the horses."

"What about you?" he asked quietly. "Who's been taking care of you?"

"I'm fine," she replied. "You're awake and that's all I need."

She slid her hand free and bustled around the room, giving him a few sips of cool water, wiping his neck with a damp cloth, and then lifting his head to switch out his pillow with a fresh one.

"There now," she said, giving his blankets a final pat. "I'm going to let you rest, but I'll be back soon."

"Katie?"

"Yes?"

He hesitated, unable to find the right words.

"What is it?" She rushed to his side. "Should I get the doctor?"

"It's not that so much as…" He lowered his gaze. "I'm so sorry I wasn't able to protect you."

"I don't *always* need you to come to my rescue." Her eyes sparkled as she gave him a chiding smile. "Sometimes I do fine on my own."

"Stay with me?" he whispered, hating himself for the fear in his voice, and that he'd resorted to begging.

"Of course," she murmured in return.

As Jake's eyes drifted closed and he submitted to sudden, overwhelming exhaustion, he was dimly aware of Kate climbing into the bed and snuggling in beside him.

CHAPTER SIXTY-TWO
Healing

HOURS LATER, KATE STOOD BESIDE JAKE'S bed and watched him sleep.

The past three days had been horrific. Jake's collapse to the ground and the subsequent brutal struggle to get him onto Nickel and back into town had only been the beginning of her journey into despair.

After she'd ridden up and down the streets, screaming of her desperate need for the doctor, he'd finally appeared in the doorway of the restaurant where he'd been dining with Clara. The doctor had taken one look at Jake—unconscious, blood-soaked, and slumped across Nickel's neck, and his expression had gone grim. Immediately he'd summoned Clara and told her to take Kate to the hotel, where she could await updates.

Kate had refused. Adamantly.

At the doctor's office, she'd helped position Jake on the examination table, then cut apart his shirt while the doctor readied his equipment. The sight of the jagged scar across his chest was a sobering reminder of the bravery he'd displayed while trying to save her father's life. And he'd gotten hurt again saving hers.

With practiced efficiency, the doctor had removed the bullet from Jake's shoulder, bandaged the wound, and established the second bullet had actually just grazed Jake's skull instead of piercing it like he'd first suspected. Then he'd crushed Kate's glimmer of hope by stating that due to all the blood Jake had lost, there was only a slim chance he'd survive the night.

Stubborn as always, Jake had proved the doctor wrong. Then a fever had taken hold. For two days he'd sweated profusely while hovering between shouting in delirium to incoherent babbling to thrashing about in a glossy-eyed, unfocused daze. For two days Kate had vigilantly watched him suffer, terrified with memories of how her dear brother had fought a fever for days, then quietly slipped into death.

The doctor had come by to check on Jake's improvements—and setbacks—every few hours, but Kate refused to leave the room except once. Even then, she'd only strayed as far as the hallway when she'd given her sworn statement about the details of the shooting to a representative of the law. Clara had taken charge of making sure Kate ate at least a few bites of food a day, and provided updates to the steady stream of Jake's friends inquiring of his progress.

When Kate had finally collapsed from sheer exhaustion early that morning, she'd nearly lost hope that he'd ever recover. Then, when she'd woken and seen his brilliant blue eyes open and alert, she'd nearly cried with joy.

She laid a testing palm across Jake's forehead and breathed a sigh of relief to again confirm his temperature remained normal and his skin was dry to the touch. After tucking in the blankets around him, she blew out the candles and settled into the nearby chair for the night.

****

Thursday, January 4, 1844

Kate entered the room, lunch tray in hand.

"Clara made this meal special for you—ham, carrots sprinkled with brown sugar, and two slices of freshly baked bread." Kate set the meal tray across Jake's legs. "Perhaps once your stomach is full you'll quit being so cranky."

"I mean it, Kate. I've been cooped up in this room for the past four days, and I've had enough."

Kate held back a grin as she watched him devour his food with the gusto and wariness of a caged bear. Unbeknownst to him, he was eating the last meal of his captivity. The doctor had already agreed to let him leave, with the implicit understanding he would accompany Kate straight to her house, where he should stay in bed for at least another week.

The day before, she'd sent Rob to gather all Jake's belongings from his dugout, then worked with Clara to prepare her house and unpack the long-forgotten supplies she'd purchased at the mercantile minutes before the shooting. As they'd finished making up the freshly sewn and stuffed straw tick, Rob had returned with Jake's bedroll, clothes, saddlebags, and meager food stash. After piling everything on the kitchen table, he muttered something about how he'd left Jake's frying pan behind and Jake would know why, and then headed back to town.

Everything was ready for Jake's arrival, including Nickel and Old Dan currently saddled and waiting outside at the hitching post.

"We'll see what the doctor thinks," she said, glancing at the clock on the wall. "He's due any minute."

"I don't care what he thinks." Jake popped the last bit of bread crust in his mouth and then pushed the tray onto the nearby table. "I'm leaving."

A knock at the door signaled the arrival of the doctor.

"How's our patient doing?" he asked, stepping into the room. "I hear he's being a bit *impatient* today."

Jake crossed his arms over his chest, not amused at the joke. "I want out of here, doc."

"Let's take another look at how you're doing," he replied, then lifted Jake's shoulder bandage and examined the wound. "It's healing well, but you have to take it easy for the next few weeks. The body needs time to heal after losing a large amount of blood."

He stepped away from the bed and waggled his finger in warning. "You can go, only if you agree to do what this young lady tells you. You'll be weak for the next few days—or longer—and you'll need her help."

The doctor winked at Kate before leaving the room and closing the door behind him.

"Let's get your boots on," Kate said, kneeling down at Jake's feet and pulling his boots to her side. "Here, give me your foot."

Jake shook his head. "I'm not a child that needs help getting dressed, and that doctor doesn't know what he's talking about. I'm not weak." He swung his legs off the bed, planted his feet on the floor, stood up, swayed mightily, and then promptly sat back down.

"You're coming with me," she said, sliding his boot over his toes and then pulling it into place, "and I'll have no arguments on the subject."

CHAPTER SIXTY-THREE
Recuperation

To Jake's disgust, it took him three tries to pull himself into his saddle. By the time he had Nickel's reins clenched in his fist, he was sweating from exertion and shaking from exhaustion.

To her credit, Kate didn't comment on his struggles; she just passed over a fresh handkerchief and waited silently while he mopped the dampness from his forehead and neck. She was similarly silent when retrieving his gun from the bushes as they traveled to her claim.

When they arrived at her house, it took all his strength to dismount and walk inside, where he shamefully threw up into her chamber pot seconds after toppling onto her bed.

His last thought before falling into a dreamless sleep was of how his body had betrayed him.

****

Friday, January 5, 1844
Jake woke ten hours later feeling better than he had in

days, until he saw Kate asleep on the floor in front of the fire. He vowed this would be the last time he'd let her sleep on a bedroll while he lounged in her bed. Injured or not, he'd be on the floor tomorrow night.

Judging by the light filtering in through the oilskin-covered window, it was just past dawn. Intent on visiting the barn to check on the horses, and perhaps chop a few days' worth of wood on the way back, Jake sat up.

Or rather, he tried to sit up—until his left arm buckled beneath his weight.

Muttering a string of curses, he flailed about beneath the blanket until he recognized the wisdom of rolling onto his right side and heaving himself upright in stages.

Giggles erupted from the floor in front of the fireplace.

"What are you laughing at over there?" he asked.

More giggles, then a burst of laughter. "The most stubborn man alive."

Jake chuckled at his own ridiculous antics. Less than a minute ago he'd had the loftiest of goals. Maybe the doctor had been right.

As she sat up and smiled at him, the soft glow of the firelight highlighted the red in her hair, the porcelain of her skin, and the fullness of her lips. Kate was a beautiful woman—inside and out. A woman who possessed powerful strength and courage when facing tragedies. The woman he loved.

"What are you thinking about?" she asked.

"Us, together again. First the trail, then the hotel, and now here."

"You can't stay away from me," she teased.

"You're right," he answered, his smile waning as he wished he wasn't so frail, or that she wasn't so far away.

He considered the white box still buried deep in his saddlebag—a saddlebag he'd noticed was now sitting on the floor next to the kitchen table—but knew now was not the time.

****

Thursday, January 18, 1844

Kate sat on her newly repaired porch and gazed over her land. It had been a good day—the skies were clear, her coffee was hot and fragrant, and the recuperating man inside her home was already asleep for the night.

As the bottom of her cup came into sight, she heard a loud noise followed by a curse. Kate went inside, sighing as she found Jake bent over the hearth, a log near his foot.

"What are you doing out of bed?" she asked for the fifth time that day.

"Getting the fire going again," he answered, then straightened and gave her such an impish smile that she had to laugh.

She crossed her arms and tapped her foot while eyeing him with what had become an all-too-familiar scolding expression. "You're supposed to be resting."

With an exaggerated, though good-natured groan, Jake trudged to his bedroll he'd set up on the floor at the end of her bed the day after he'd arrived. As he stretched out and laced his fingers behind his head, a series of thoughts occurred.

It felt *right* to have him share her table.

It felt *right* to have him checking on the horses in the barn.

It felt *right* to have him bringing in wood.

Most of all, it felt *right* to have him in her life.

Kate turned away, yet again hiding her sorrow. She'd spent the past week wavering between jubilation to see his strength returning and misery that since he'd arrived under protest, he'd have no reason to stay once he was well.

CHAPTER SIXTY-FOUR
Certainty

Friday, January 19, 1844

JAKE LEANED AGAINST KATE'S DOORWAY, WATCHING her walk toward the barn, her face tipped to the sky as she enjoyed the unseasonable warmth of the day. In the three weeks it had taken for him to heal, his love for her had grown stronger with each passing day.

After he made certain Kate was out of sight, he pulled the white box from his pocket. Using his left hand, he tossed it into the air and then caught it, marveling at how his strength and dexterity had returned.

Toss, catch.

The night on the trail they'd spent in a cave lying together before the fire as a thunderstorm had raged outside, he'd been wholly unprepared for the feelings holding her in his arms had evoked in him.

Now he knew without a doubt how much he loved the headstrong woman, and he wanted to make her his wife. Not to spite Theo, not out of obligation to her father, but because he truly did love her. He wanted nothing more than to spend the rest of his life loving her, caring for her, and building a life together with her.

Toss, catch.

Though he'd had the best of intentions, he'd made a mess of things with his first pathetic proposal. This time there would be no stammered words, no sentences bungled. This time he would make her understand he wasn't asking because she was in trouble, because he thought he could save her, or because of a promise to her father. This time he'd convince her he wanted to spend the rest of his life trying to become the man she needed. The man she deserved.

Toss, catch.

Sighting Kate returning from the barn, Jake slid the white box into his pocket and stepped off the porch.

It was time.

CHAPTER SIXTY-FIVE
A Long-Awaited Second Try

KATE PULLED THE BARN DOOR SHUT and headed toward her home, smiling to see Jake waiting for her beside the porch. As she neared he held out his hands, palms up. She went to him without hesitation, curling her hands around his when his fingers beckoned them close.

He cleared his throat and shifted his stance. "Kate, I need to do something."

Dread settled in deep. He was leaving.

"I can do anything you need done," she said, hating the pleading in her voice but continuing on in the hopes she'd find the right words to convince him to stay longer. "You're still favoring your shoulder, and the doctor's orders were for you to get plenty of rest, and we both know you've been pushing yourself too hard this week."

Jake kissed her gently on her forehead, then pulled back to look at her, a hint of a smile playing across his lips.

"The night we spent in the cave gave me a glimpse of what it would be like to have you in my life, and I've longed for you ever since. You've given me a second chance on life, and I can't imagine one more day without you by my side."

He squeezed her hands before letting go and lowering himself to one bended knee. She gasped and her hands flew to her chest as he pulled a small white box from his pocket.

"Katie," he said, opening the box to show her a gold ring resting atop a blue velvet cushion, "will you marry me?"

"Yes," she said breathlessly. "Yes!"

Elation coursed through her as Jake stood and slid the ring over her finger, then subsided into a delicious anticipation of the bliss to come when he lifted her into his arms and carried her through the doorway and into their home.

EPILOGUE
The Good Life

Sunday, September 8, 1844

KATE SMILED AS JAKE APPEARED ON their porch, carrying two steaming cups of coffee. He leaned to kiss her, then straightened.

"I'm thinking about going into town for a few hours. Two more wagon trains are expected to roll in today and the men want to greet them." He knelt beside her, pressed a hand against her gently rounded stomach, and looked at her in concern. "Of course, I won't go if you need me here."

"I'll be fine."

As she watched Jake ride over the rise toward town, she thought of how he had proven to be a wonderful and caring husband, and now in only a few months she would undoubtedly see him do the same with their child.

They'd married earlier that year, on Saturday, February 24th. Since theirs had been one of the first weddings Oregon City had ever witnessed, the townspeople had worked together to host a fantastic reception. Clara had come with the doctor at her side, and William and Margaret had even managed one of their rare trips into town for the occasion, bringing along their beautiful, healthy daughter.

Theodore was still in jail, and would stay for years to come. He'd initially been put away only for the unsuccessful attempt on Jake's life, but after proof of his deeds scheme had been uncovered when Clara had cleaned out the contents of his desk drawer, more time had been added to his sentence for fraud.

Kate hadn't recovered her father's money, but her appeal to the Provincial Government had been a success. She'd been granted her father's claim, where she and Jake had decided to make their home. Albert at mercantile had agreed to buy all the contents of all the wagons her father had arranged to have sent out, and she and Jake had already invested in two more mares for their fledgling horse ranch.

Kate dozed in the rocking chair Jake had made her for a wedding gift, happy to feel a gentle breeze that would keep all but the most persistent mosquitoes away. She woke to see the sky, the clouds, and the trees dotting the hillside had turned fiery orange as the sun was just beginning its descent over the home, their crops, and the horses still out grazing. Winter was coming and they still had much to do—chop wood, gather and shock the hay for the horses, harvest and sell their crops, and buy supplies—but she smiled at the thought of doing everything with Jake by her side.

Hearing a far-off whinny, Kate turned her attention to the rise at the end of their claim and watched her husband, the love of her life, and the father of their unborn child ride toward their home and her waiting arms.

ABOUT THE AUTHOR

CHRISTI CORBETT lives in a small town in Oregon with her husband and their twin children. The home's location holds a special place in her writing life; the view from her back door is a hill travelers looked upon years ago as they explored the Oregon Territory and beyond.

www.cleanreads.com

Made in the USA
Charleston, SC
20 July 2015